THE BLACK

Paul E Cooley

Dedication:

To Justin Macumber and Terry Mixon:
For bringing me into the fold. For beta-reading. For brain-storming.
For friendship.

Part One: The Deep

Chapter One

The waves rocked against the support ship. Thomas Calhoun stood at the aft lookout and watched the slate colored water. The occasional fin appeared and then turned over. Porpoises or sharks, didn't matter to him. He was more interested in the huge storm-front they had left in their wake.

Breaking through the pounding rain and ten-foot swells had left him exhausted and weak kneed. If he'd stayed in his cabin for the entire trip, it would have been filled with vomit. As it was, he'd only managed to miss the toilet once. After that, however, he'd decided to lose his lunch topside. Better to feed the fish than stink up his cabin.

If he'd known the support ship was going to bounce around so much, he would have tried to find another way to the rig. A helicopter couldn't make it out in a single trip; the aircraft had to refuel at sea. That would have cost PPE a lot of coin. He should have forced them to pay for it anyway.

So now he was only half a day away from the rig, the storm was behind them, and the air was fresh, except for the smell of diesel. Calhoun was used to it, but that didn't mean he liked it. He was about to spend months on a rig that was going to smell a lot worse.

The constant grinding of the engines was nearly soothing. The captain, a horrid little Portuguese man all of five foot four, had expressed displeasure at his being on the deck. Calhoun had argued with the man's broken English over and over again. They finally came to an agreement that he'd stay aft and away from the damned pilothouse.

At least he didn't have to worry about Standlee's gear; the prototype AUVs and ROVs had been delivered last week. According to the last email the tech had sent, he'd already broken them in and checked their programming. That was at least something.

When Petro-Pem Exploration hired his team, they'd been more than willing to pony up the cash to use Standlee's new designs as well as Calhoun's new drilling equipment. That had been part of the deal. Calhoun's team kept the patents and IP, and PPE got a jump on the rest of the industry. A fair deal as far as Calhoun was concerned.

Craig "Catfish" Standlee was his partner in the design and programming of the robots. While other companies were catching up, he and Catfish's designs, control systems, and sensors were the best in the world. Catfish was a whiz kid. Between Calhoun's engineering expertise and the robot technology, the company bought their services at a premium.

PPE was trying something new with Leaguer. Instead of bringing in contracting firms to handle mud logging, tool-pushing, and the actual drilling, they'd decided to purchase specialists and all the technology they could. The idea was for PPE to become the world's foremost offshore exploration company. If Leaguer was successful, then PPE could sell their services to all the major oil companies. Less expense, less personnel turnover, and a single integrated safety regimen could theoretically save production companies billions in finding oil.

Calhoun wasn't sure their strategy would work. He knew the rest of the offshore industry was watching Leaguer and PPE with great interest. If M2 turned out to be the largest offshore find in history, PPE would be set for decades to come.

In less than a few hours, the ship would cross over the undersea field. The best guess from the seismic team was that it was larger than Saudi Arabia in terms of oil. If, of course, you sank the Arab country in thirty-thousand feet of water.

The trench, known as M2 to the PPE project, hadn't been mapped and had barely been discovered. In two years, PPE hadn't managed to do shit as far as exploration. They'd wasted two years getting their shit together with a possible goldmine sitting in their licensed area. Just based on the possible reserves, their share prices had skyrocketed. But not a single drop of oil had been drilled. Not even for analysis.

Catfish's original seismic/magnetic equipment had found the area quite by accident. While Calhoun and his team had been in Nigeria handling a heavy oil recovery project, Catfish had signed up with NOAA for a less than well-funded effort to explore M2. Calhoun had allowed him to join the mission because of the tax incentives. Well, that and the chance to try out some new drones.

But Catfish's gear did more than simply perform a survey. His autonomous underwater vehicles (AUVs) had scoured the area performing their tasks. When they surfaced to burp back information via satellite, Catfish had seen something more important than the shelf topography. The magnetic sensors picked up something he hadn't counted on—oil sitting beneath the trench's surface.

Since NOAA wasn't interested in the possible oil find, he hadn't bothered to tell them about it. He had, however, sent Calhoun a PGP encrypted message with the reports. In a sweltering hotel in Abuja, Calhoun had received the email and checked Standlee's figures. After a little study, he'd been ready to leave Nigeria and never come back.

Calhoun pulled a cigar from his shirt pocket, clipped the end, and lit it with a gold-plated torch. His long-sleeved tropical shirt flapped in the breeze as smoke curled from his nostrils. He brushed a sheen of sweat from his forehead and went over the day's plan in his head.

First order? Making sure the idiots who loaded the gear didn't fracture any of the new drill bits. Second? Get the rig staff to perform a full inventory before the support ship left. Once it did, it would be impossible for them to resupply for several days, if not weeks.

Lightning forked across the billowing black cloud bank. Calhoun shivered. He hoped the storm wouldn't follow them to the site. If so, this was going to be one hell of a start to the week.

"Thomas?" a voice said from behind.

He turned and blinked at the short, wiry, pale woman dressed in Bermuda shorts and a white t-shirt. Thomas smiled and blew a plume of smoke into the air. "Shawna. What's up?"

She looked up at him and nodded. "Just got off the radio with Catfish. Sounds like they're going to be ready for us. He's chomping at the bit to get the rest of the gear down."

Thomas nodded. "You've been over the survey maps and they parked the rig where you told 'em," he drawled. "I think we're all ready to find out what's down there."

The geologist rubbed her hands together. "If this damned tub will get us there already."

"Ain't that the truth," Calhoun said. He stared back out at the ocean. Another fin turned over in the distance. "Hope you brought your fishing tackle."

"Oh, hell yes," she said. Her voice struggled to be heard against the wind and the pounding waves. "I talked to JP too. He brought his spear-fishing gear."

Calhoun rolled his eyes. "Vraebel is going to freak," he chuckled. "That asshole already hates us. And you guys are going to drive him nuts."

She tapped her foot. The little woman swayed easily as the ship lurched. "Not our fault he's a killjoy. Besides, JP has been there as long as Catfish has. And Vraebel hasn't thrown them overboard. Yet."

Calhoun grimaced. Vraebel, the rig chief, may not have tossed Catfish or JP into the water, but he'd certainly sent Calhoun plenty of emails threatening to do just that. The humorless redneck was in touch with the PPE VP of Operations nearly every day. Complaints about unprofessional behavior, unsafe work practices, and etc. had streamed forth in a projectile vomit of displeasure. And what had Calhoun done? Defend his people. As per usual.

He glared at Shawna. "When we get to the rig, I want a full inventory of our gear. The drill tech, your tech, Catfish's stuff, everything." He ashed the cigar. "And this time, it would be nice if you didn't leave your laptop aboard the support ship."

Shawna opened her mouth to say something and then closed it. Her angular ears burned red. "Yes, boss. I'll make sure I get all my gear this time."

Calhoun nodded. "Good. Otherwise," he said and pointed the cigar at the geologist, "I'll make you swim for it."

The short woman looked thoughtful. "So long as I have a wet-suit and fins, I should be fine."

Thomas smiled. Shawna had been with him for nearly a decade. Despite her annoying personality traits, she was reliable. "Uh-huh," he said. "You planning on going fishing with JP?"

"Of course," Shawna said. "Assuming you give us some time off."

Calhoun shrugged. "There's always time for time off. Tomorrow we're going to have to check the fittings and get the drill string set up. Once all that is done, y'all can fuck off as much as you like while Vraebel's people connect all the equipment. But two days from now," he grinned, "I want mud coming through the sluice."

"I think we can make that happen," Shawna said. "It's going to be just like last time."

Calhoun laughed and clenched the cigar between his teeth. "Let's hope not."

#

Even with his hair in pony tail, Catfish's mane swung in the wind. He stood on the observation tower, high above the rig's equipment and the scurrying roustabouts. Vraebel had made it clear that smoking was only allowed up top on *his* rig. What a prick.

He puffed on his cigarette, inhaled deeply, and then blew the smoke into the breeze. The overcast sky had turned the ocean into a gun-metal gray, shifting, and rippling creature. Fish turned over in the water. He smiled. JP was already in his cabin, sharpening his spears. The diver and undersea tech specialist had been grinning maniacally for days. Every time he came back from retrieving one of the AUVs, JP babbled at length about the fish in this area of the ocean. The diver's deep-sea gear was aboard the support ship. Catfish hoped JP wouldn't need it.

There'd been a couple of hiccups with the new AUVs he and Calhoun had designed. Especially number 5. It passed all the diagnostic tests he could throw at it, but the damned thing kept missing its surface targets. The radio bursts hadn't exactly been free of static either. It wasn't enough to keep the computers from translating the information, but number 5 was definitely making things difficult.

Catfish hoped Calhoun could figure out the problem, because after focusing on the issues for a week, he had no clue what else to try. He and the engineer had spent more than a year designing the goddamned torpedoes and stuffing all the electronic gear and sensors they possibly could into their three-meter long bodies. Even after nine months of testing in the Gulf of Mexico, they were still having problems.

He sighed, crushed out the cigarette on the railing, and tossed it into the heavy waste barrel. Its bottom was already covered in butts. Vraebel may hate smoking, but plenty of his crew were smokers. Among the rough-necks, cigarettes, booze, and fast women (usually topless dancers) were the stereotypical pleasures. And the stereotypes were spot on.

Catfish took one last look at the ocean and then walked down the stairs and into the crew quarters. He walked through the narrow hallway past rooms with steel bunks. The rig had a precious amount of space. Most of the roughnecks were two to a room and in some cases, four. Calhoun's team, on the other hand, had been given three staterooms. Catfish and JP bunked together while Calhoun and Shawna each had their own. He peeked in on Calhoun's empty room. Without Thomas' gear, the room looked barren and too damned big. Catfish grinned. It wouldn't be that way for long.

The last time they'd been on a deep sea exploration rig, Calhoun's stateroom had been covered wall to wall with maps and diagrams. The man couldn't help but draw on everything he could get his hands on. And he never stopped thinking. No wonder he'd been divorced twice. Who could put up with someone who'd give you the high hard one and then go right back to thinking about chemistry, mechanical designs, and the ever-present quest for the purest black?

He sighed and continued toward his room. A thin Hispanic man walked past him, face set in a scowl. Catfish smiled at him and tipped an imaginary hat. The roughneck sneered and moved past him without saying a word.

Typical. Whenever Calhoun's team descended on a rig, they were treated like royalty. In other words, like shit. The grunts hated them because they got all the privileges and broke all the rules. Also, as far as the roughnecks were concerned, they didn't do any real work.

He could tell them what it was like soldering circuit boards together or debugging assembly code until four in the morning before a demo. He could also tell them about putting a two million dollar prototype in the ocean and having it implode at two-thousand feet below the ocean surface. Talk about pressure—fucking roughnecks had no idea what it was like.

Nor would they. Their jobs were dangerous. They were paid well, no doubt, but not enough to risk their lives on a daily basis. He understood why they hated the so-called "white-collar" folk. But they needed to get the fuck over it. He and JP had been on the rig for over a week now, running checks, and breaking in the equipment. They got just as hot and sweaty as everyone else in the stifling compartments.

For the next several weeks, the only time Catfish would see natural light or feel the breeze on his face would be the six hours of off time. Once they started drilling, it was going to be hell. And he would be just as miserable as the rest of the fuckers on the rig. He may not get oil on his face or the rest of his body, but he would be covered in grease, grime, and salt. Every time one of the AUVs or ROVs came in, he'd have to work on them, maintain them, and repair them. All that without a lab or any kind of convenient work area. Fuck the roughnecks—they didn't know what stress was.

He shook out his pony-tail as he neared the stateroom he shared with JP. He took a deep breath, and then knocked on the closed hatch. "Yo, JP? You jacking it in there?"

Muted laughter erupted behind the door. "Get in here, Catfish."

He smiled and opened the door. JP, all five-foot-eight of him, stood near the porthole. The floor was covered with gear. Boots, fins, rebreathers, masks... JP had more or less dumped three sea-bags worth of crap all over the floor.

"The fuck, JP?"

The man ran a hand through his graying high-and-tight. "I, um, needed to do a check."

Catfish shook his head. "What? You couldn't do that on the deck?"

A sheepish grin appeared on the older man's face. "Um, well, I figured since you were out..."

"Dude, there's out and then there's *out*." Catfish stared down at the mess. "Well, you got everything?"

JP reached his hands to the lower bunk and brought up two long guns. The spears weren't attached, but Catfish knew from experience that JP had at least five for each gun lying around somewhere.

"I think so," he said and tossed one of them to Catfish.

The tech caught the weapon with one hand. He stared down at it. "So... we going spear-fishing?"

JP's weathered face split into a wide smile. "That's the plan. Although Thomas told me we had to behave ourselves until he got here."

Catfish rolled his eyes. "Let me guess, Vraebel's bitching?"

"Of course he is," JP said. "He may be management, so to speak, but he's a roughneck. He hates us as much as anyone."

"Fuck that guy," Catfish said.

JP held out a fist and they bumped. "Right. But we need to behave for the rest of the afternoon." He carefully placed the spear gun on the top bunk. "That said, we really should go for a swim."

"Yeah," Catfish said, "because Vraebel won't bitch about that."

JP shrugged. "Well, we do need to take number five out for a spin, don't we?"

Catfish smiled. "As a matter of fact, we kind of do."

"Then what are we waiting for?" JP said and tossed a pair of flippers to his friend.

#

The platform was hot as hell. Metal stairs and railings led down to the corrugated steel sheet. It was the safest place for divers to enter the water. It was also the loading/unloading dock for the AUVs and ROVs. The robots hung suspended over the grate connected by thick, steel cables.

JP wiped a sheen of sweat from his brow. He waited for Standlee to come down the gangway in his wet suit. As usual, the man known as Catfish was taking his sweet time. The long-haired computer and engineering tech had never been in the military and apparently had never learned to tell time. JP stared at his diver's watch and sighed. Well, he thought, might as well get the boat in the water.

AUV number 5, nicknamed "bitch" because of all its problems, was still in the ocean. Catfish had sent it an order to surface and return. To the bitch, "return" meant surface and sit on the waves several hundred yards from the rig.

JP lowered the Zodiac into the water and secured the tow ropes. The three meter long torpedo would force them to go slow on the way back, but that was okay; he and Catfish were going to take a swim. Vraebel be damned.

"You guys just don't know how to follow procedure," a voice yelled from the stairs.

JP looked over his shoulder. Speaking of Vraebel, he thought. The barrel-chested, sun-tanned man leaned against the railing. Like his cheeks, his close-cropped red hair seemed to be on fire. His white teeth were set in an angry grimace.

"What procedure would that be?"

"Filing a dive plan, for one," Vraebel said. "And making sure the emergency divers know you're going out. And number three, who told you to get in the water anyway?"

JP pointed to the AUVs hanging above him. "See those? There's only four there. Number five is out in the water. Didn't you get Standlee's report?"

Vraebel opened his mouth and then closed it. JP could see the wheels turning in the man's head. "Yeah, I read it."

"Then you know we have to go retrieve it."

The rig chief tapped his heavy work boots against the steps. "Well, that's still no excuse for not filing a damned dive plan. Much less keeping our divers out of the loop."

JP sighed. "Sorry, Mr. Vraebel. I guess we forgot about that."

"Damned right you did. When Calhoun gets here, we're going to have a little talk about the slip-shod bullshit you guys have been pulling."

"Yes, sir," JP said with a salute. Vraebel's cheeks turned crimson. The man nodded in JP's direction and clomped back up the steps.

JP shook his head as he watched the rig chief head up to the main deck. Vraebel was an asshole. Complete and total asshole. JP stared down at the Zodiac. But Vraebel was right—they should have filed a dive plan. JP sighed again and wrapped up the tow ropes in neat coils. Next, he grabbed two of the SCUBA tanks and placed them in the boat's holders. He unzipped his green, water-proofed sea bag and pulled out the two spear guns.

He placed them inside the boat's lock box along with four spears. Cork covered their razor sharp tips. JP always made sure they were ready for action. You never knew when you'd have a chance to spear something "special."

JP went over his mental check list. Masks were in and he'd rubbed them with an anti-fogger. Next? Tanks full? Check. Strapping and webbing for two? Check. Tow ropes? Check. He opened the small lockbox fastened to the boat and peered in. A small radio and two signal lights lay at the bottom. He smiled. That was it, all the gear they needed. Provided Catfish ever got dressed.

The two of them had been on the rig for more than a week. Running Catfish's robots through their paces had been stressful. Especially with the bitch acting up. Since ROVs were attached via cables, they weren't nearly as much of a problem. The AUVs? They went wherever they were told to go. Provided Catfish's code was resilient enough to compensate for any obstacles, they should be fine. But that didn't mean there hadn't been problems.

For one thing, the propellers on all five had become fouled when the AUVs stumbled into a kelp bed on the ocean floor.

Cursing and damned near throwing a tantrum, Catfish had waited for them to surface. All five had, but JP had to make three trips to bring them in. It made for a long day.

In addition to his dive duties, part of JP's job was to help Catfish maintain his equipment. That included the robots. Repairing the screws on the AUVs had required a damned long night. But all five had been back in the water the next afternoon. Catfish had stayed up all night writing new routines to keep them from hitting the kelp bed again. Eyes red-rimmed, voice a gravel growl, the tech had put in a thirty hour shift getting everything repaired and back to work.

He only slept after the AUVs were back in the ocean and diving back down to the sea-floor. Diving 30,000 feet took hours unless the machines were red-lined. JP had promised to sit by the console and monitor the robots, but Catfish had refused. In typical Catfish manner, he'd sucked on his E-Cig until it ran out of fluid and fell asleep in his chair at the monitoring station.

It wasn't the first time that had happened. The man was very serious about his creations and took it as a personal affront if one of them failed. JP understood Catfish's penchant for responsibility all too well. But every once in a while, the guy needed to chill the fuck out. JP hoped a little dip would make that happen. If not, then Calhoun was going to have to deal with one stressed out tech.

"We ready?"

JP turned back to the stairs. Catfish walked down the steps. His long hair was braided into a tail that danced behind his head with each step.

JP grinned. "Nice dress. You need me to zip it for you?"

Catfish flipped him off. His black wetsuit matched JPs, but the front was open at the waist. The extra material flopped as he moved. When Craig reached the bottom of the stairs, he made his way to the boat.

"You see Vraebel?" JP asked.

Catfish rolled his eyes. "Yeah, I saw him. He was pissed as usual. I filed a goddamned dive plan and let the divers know."

"Good," JP said. "We have to get better about that. Calhoun would have our balls if we did that to him."

"Whatever," Catfish said. He pulled up his wetsuit top and zipped it. "Got all the gear stowed?"

"We're ready," JP said.

Catfish smiled and stepped into the boat. The Zodiac hardly moved as he shifted his weight into the middle. "Let's do this."

"Do you know where the bitch is?"

"Of course," Catfish said and pulled a bright yellow rectangle from his belt. He clicked it and it began to ping. "350 yards away. South, southeast," he read from the display. He looked at JP and smiled. "That far enough away to get a little fishing done?"

"Hell yes," JP said. He started the engine and they left the dive deck.

#

The bridge was spotless. Vraebel sipped from an aluminum mug of black coffee. PPE's logo was branded on its side. He sighed with pleasure as the strong coffee slid down his throat. Through the clean windows, he watched the Zodiac head out into the ocean. JP Harvey was gunning the engine too fast and Standlee was standing on the bow like he was in some damned action movie.

Maybe the tech would fall out of the boat. Would certainly serve the smug son of a bitch right. God, but Vraebel hated those two. A little over a week and they'd managed to turn his crew's routines into a mess. Unannounced trips into the ocean. No dive plans, no warning they were going to drop those damned fish into the ocean.

Hell, the only warning Vraebel got was when they absolutely needed something from his crew. *His* crew. Not Calhoun's. Not PPE's. Vraebel's crew. Every worker on the rig had been hand-picked by him. Except, of course, for Calhoun's rejects.

VP Simpson had told Vraebel he was to do everything to help Calhoun's team. Without them, the rig might as well be hunting for oil in a desert. Or so the VP thought. Vraebel knew that was bullshit. He may not be a geologist, but he'd been working the oil fields and oceans for more than twenty years. He'd put his crew up against any other rig any day of the year.

But Calhoun had the toys. The new drill bit tech. Standlee's new robots. And that Sigler geologist was supposed to be a whiz kid. Didn't matter. They were all a bunch of undisciplined, entitled assholes. As far as he was concerned, Calhoun's team could go fuck themselves.

He'd sent several private emails to Simpson, begging for the right to throw Standlee and Harvey off the rig. Simpson had responded with a tersely worded email that tried to put Vraebel in his place. Fucking suit. When the executives of a major oil exploration consortium had no experience with life on a rig, the goddamned world was doomed.

So he'd have to make Calhoun happy. Or at least stay out of the man's way. So long, of course, as the old engineer stayed out of his. Vraebel didn't care if Calhoun was going to make everyone rich or not; this was Vraebel's rig and he took orders from no one.

He'd personally overseen the rig's construction. Spent every day with the crew putting the monster together piece by piece. Tons and tons of steel. Pressure vessels. Miles of pipe, generators, cabling, and hydraulics. He'd gone over every detail, knew every nook and cranny of the huge machine.

He took another sip of the coffee. He hated exploration rigs. They were built out in the middle of nowhere with no guarantee of production yield. On top of that, the rigs were usually untested and the engineers were always tweaking the design. In other words—it was a guaranteed clusterfuck.

But Leaguer was his rig. And it would work. Steve Gomez, the tool pusher, and his team would do their jobs. Provided there was some goddamned black gold beneath the soil, and provided Calhoun's team found the sweet spot to drill, it would all work.

The Zodiac had become a black dot on the horizon. If he hadn't been looking for it, he wouldn't have noticed it. Standlee and Harvey were no doubt swimming with the fish instead of doing their jobs. Typical. When Calhoun arrived, Vraebel was going to have a long talk with the man.

The rest of the crew hated Harvey and Standlee. They knew the two men were getting paid a tremendous amount of money and so far all they'd done was fuck off. They hadn't been in the crew assignments for maintenance, waste disposal, or cleaning. In other words—they only did what they wanted to. And the rest of the crew had taken notice.

Vraebel smiled to himself. Of course he'd made sure the rest of the crew knew all of that. There wouldn't be any poker games including those guys. If Vraebel had his way, their lives on Leaguer would be as miserable as he could make them. Unless they struck gold. In that case, those assholes would be heroes…at least to PPE.

Didn't matter. Leaguer was an exploration rig, not a production rig. Employees of PPE didn't get a cut of the profits, other than their 401(k)'s, stock options, and bonuses. With the exception of the bonuses and enhancing their reps, the crew couldn't care less about striking it rich. And that's why they'd work hard for Vraebel. The workers that impressed him could get jobs anywhere in the industry. Fuck up? He'd make sure you had difficulty finding a job cleaning a latrine.

But PPE was providing Vraebel one hell of a bonus if the rig did its job and found the black. So he'd play nice. To a point. Calhoun and his boys would get what they needed.

He stared out at the cloud covered sky. White puffs of cotton obscured the sun. There was no rain in the forecast, but the storm from the mainland was heading their way. It might take a couple of days, but the system could sneak up on top of them. Vraebel made a mental note to keep an eye on the radar. PPE's meteorologists would let them know if the nasty was approaching, but that didn't guarantee the landlubbers would spot it before it was on top of them.

Footsteps on the stairs. Someone was headed up to the bridge. Vraebel took a long draught from his coffee and closed his eyes. The steps were timid. He smiled to himself. The sounds reached the top of the stairs and the bridge hatch opened.

"Hello, Steve," Vraebel said without turning around.

"Martin," Steve Gomez said. "Got a minute?"

Vraebel turned in his chair and took another sip of coffee. The tool pusher stood in the doorway, his filthy black ball cap in his hands. The man's heavy denim coveralls were covered in dark stains. Steve ran a hand through his thick black hair and waited patiently. "What's up?" Martin asked.

"We went ahead and prepped the drill string," Steve said. "And according to Standlee, the ROVs are ready to drop the sinks."

Gomez cleared his throat. "I think we're pretty much ready once Calhoun gets here."

Vraebel nodded. "Good job, Steve. Is there anything left outstanding?"

"Nope. I think we got it all."

"Okay," Martin said and placed his empty mug on the console. "Tell your people they're on an extended break. We've got nothing to do until the supply ship gets here."

Steve smiled. "They'll like that."

"I'm sure you will too," Martin chuckled. "So either take a nap, or get out your lines and catch us some dinner."

Gomez bowed. "We can definitely catch some fish." He turned and walked back down the stairs.

Martin's mouth watered. Gomez and the other Mexicans were damned good at fishing. They'd stand on the lower platforms and dangle lines down in the water near the pilings. Fish treated the substructure like a reef. Once or twice, Gomez had even snagged himself a shark.

He looked at the black diving watch on his wrist. The supply ship was due in four hours. If the storm hadn't knocked them off schedule, they'd arrive before dinner. He hoped his people had a chance to eat before the load out. It was going to be a long night.

#

The Zodiac's engine died. Catfish turned around and glanced at JP. The diver was smiling. The pontoon boat slowed and then bumped gently in the waves. The clouds were thick, but there was still no sign of rain in them.

Catfish unclipped the yellow radio from his belt and stared at its display. "Dammit."

"What's the problem?" JP called from the back.

"It should be right here. We're on top of it," Catfish said.

JP leaned over the side and stared into the water. "Uh, I don't see it. You sure it surfaced?"

"Yeah," Catfish said. He walked forward to the bow and leaned over. The light made it tricky to see further than a few feet down. He held a hand above his eyes and let them relax. Finding a bright yellow torpedo in the water shouldn't be this difficult. The sensor box was getting a signal from the bitch. "We have to be sitting on top of it."

JP shook his head. "Bullshit. It's longer than the damned boat. We'd be able to see it fore or aft."

The box in Standlee's hand pinged. He stared at it and groaned. "Okay. It's here and we *are* on top of it."

"Well where the hell is it?"

He turned to JP and growled. "Fifteen meters below us. Something's wrong with the ballast."

JP rolled his eyes. "Guess I know what I'm doing." He uncoiled one of the tow cables and threw it into the water. The heavy cable dropped out of sight immediately. Catfish sighed, grabbed a SCUBA tank, and began putting it on JP.

"I love it when a man dresses me," JP said in an effeminate voice.

"I'll be sure and tell someone that gives a shit," Catfish said. He tightened the straps and clapped JP on the shoulder. "You want me down with you?"

JP shook his head. "Nope. You stay with the boat. I may need the other tow rope. Besides, one diver down at a time right?"

Catfish grinned. "Unless we're fishing?" He grabbed the orange buoy and threw it over the side. There were no other boats for miles and the support ship was still hours away, but putting the diver buoy in the water was habit.

"Unless we're fishing," JP said. He put on his mask and attached the fins to his dive boots. Once they were connected, he gave Catfish a thumbs up and dropped backwards into the ocean.

#

The moment he entered the water, he felt at home. SEAL training aside, he'd always loved the ocean. It didn't matter if he was swimming a few miles to a beachhead, placing mines beneath a ship, inspecting a rig's substructure, or spear-fishing; the water was where he belonged.

Growing up in the Keys meant there wasn't much to do that didn't involve the ocean. Reef diving, spiny-tailed lobster hunting, and spear-fishing were the distractions he loved as a kid. When he joined the Navy at eighteen, he was lean and slight, but in great shape. By the time he was twenty, he was well-muscled and a natural for the SEALs.

He floated beneath the Zodiac. The water was clear, but without steady light from the sun, the depths rapidly became dark as pitch. JP looked down and saw the tell-tale yellow of the bitch.

JP stopped and reached for the tow rope. The bright orange cable was easy to see in the water. He grabbed it with his gloved hand, pulled it through the loop on his webbing, and flipped over. He kicked hard and easily made it down to the torpedo shaped AUV.

He unhooked the cable from his belt and slid it through the steel grommets on the AUV's nose. When Catfish had designed the new gear, he'd made sure they could be towed relatively easily.

JP slid beneath the torpedo-shaped robot and felt for the bottom clasp. He found it and turned it clockwise. Green LEDs created wan light around him. He stared at the controls. A red light blinked in the corner. JP frowned around his rebreather. Catfish had been right; the ballast control was stuck.

He pushed back until he was an arm's length away from the AUV and touched the control panel's red light. Bubbles shot up as the robot emptied the rest of the water that kept it below the surface.

The AUV quickly rose next to the Zodiac. Something bumped against JP's leg and he turned quickly. A small hammer-head shark swam past him. He looked down.

A school of redfish was high-tailing it through the water. Two more sharks were chasing the group of fish. These were larger than the small hammer-head. Once the blood started flowing from one of those fish, more sharks would show up. Shaking his head, he kicked for topside. Within a few seconds, his head popped up on the other side of the Zodiac.

Catfish was already tightening up the cable that held the AUV. JP scrambled up the rope ladder and into the boat. He pulled off his mask and killed the oxygen supply on the tank.

The tech turned toward him, a grim smile on his face. "Ballast?"

JP nodded as he stripped out of the SCUBA gear. "Had to hit the control panel. Guessing you should close that."

Catfish growled and punched a button on the control box. It lit up green. "How come you're taking off the tank? Aren't we spear-fishing?"

The former SEAL shook his head. "No fishing today. Not down there, anyway. We got sharks. And more coming."

"Dammit," Catfish said. He tied the cable through the cleats and used a traction tool to tighten everything. Once the AUV was only a few feet behind the boat, he sat on the side of the pontoon and stared down into the water. "So much for time off."

JP shrugged. "Well, maybe we can figure out what's wrong with the bitch."

"Maybe," Catfish said. "Let's get back to the rig. Maybe we'll have better luck later."

#

After parking the Zodiac in the bay, JP hooked up the lift cables and hoisted the AUV out of the water. The mechanized lift made short work of raising the 1400 lbs. of steel and instrumentation.

Before JP finished putting the AUV up for maintenance, Catfish was running up the stairs to the stateroom to get his laptop and cords. The AUVs all had wireless interface points so he could communicate with them without hooking up directly, but he didn't want to chance it with Number 5.

After shrugging his way through the narrow halls and running back down the steps, he was tired and out of breath. JP just grinned at him.

"What?" Catfish asked as he hooked up the cords from the laptop to the control panel.

"If you stopped smoking," JP said, "maybe you wouldn't be out of breath after a little jog."

Catfish flipped him off, put the laptop on the deck's mechanical control box, and opened the lid. The display lit up with green text on a black background. He typed in the commands to open a connection to the AUVs on-board computer.

JP moved behind him and stared over his shoulder as Catfish ran diagnostics. "Any ideas?" he asked.

The long-haired tech sucked his teeth. "Ballast control failure." He shook his head. "We're going to have to open her up and replace the controller. Goddammit."

"Well," JP said, "so much for the fishing."

"You got that right," Catfish said. "We need the bitch online tomorrow." He turned to the former SEAL. "Calhoun wants full coverage of the drill string and the well-head. If we don't have it," he licked his lips, "it's going to be my ass."

"Well, you could always send down an ROV to check most of the drill string."

Catfish shook his head. "No. The ROVs aren't pressurized for that depth." He gritted his teeth. "Thirty-thousand feet's a bit over their design params. One of them might make it down there, but I can't guarantee it won't implode."

"And then we lose another two million dollars?"

Catfish rubbed his chin. "Right. PPE already freaked out about the lease of the equipment. Not to mention our hourly costs. I can't afford to lose any of them."

JP walked over to the row of toolboxes. When he and Catfish had arrived, the first thing they'd done, after stowing the AUVs, was unload boxes of parts and tools for the electronics. He'd hoped they wouldn't have to use them, but that had been yet another pipe-dream.

He pulled out a cordless drill, set the bit, and held it up. "Let's get into surgery," he said. Catfish groaned and moved to help.

\#

The support ship arrived early. The rig crew was on break and hadn't even eaten yet.

By the time he reached the lower decks, the ship's crane was already raised in the air. Vraebel announced over the loud speaker that all personnel were to immediately hit the chow line. Instead of joining them, he headed to the support ship's catwalk.

Calhoun and his geologist were walking off the ship and on to the rig. Calhoun eyeing the empty deck. He offered Vraebel his large hand. The rig chief shook it, but didn't smile.

"Welcome back aboard Leaguer," he said.

Calhoun looked around. "Where's the crew? We got to get this stuff offloaded."

Vraebel shook his head. "You're over an hour early. They haven't eaten. Soon as they get done with their dinner break—"

"Dinner break?" Calhoun interrupted. "The support ship has to do a turn around ASAP. The captain busted his ass getting us here early."

The rig chief clamped down on the urge to tell this asshole to go to hell; Simpson would have his balls if he was that rude to their drilling brain. "After they get some chow, they'll be down here. I promise. We'll get it unloaded."

Calhoun sighed. "Okay, fair enough. Sorry, Martin. Been a damned long day and that storm kicked our ass."

Sigler stood behind her boss. The short, thin woman stepped out from behind him and smiled at Vraebel. She offered her hand. Vraebel shook it. "Ms. Sigler," he said.

The woman's strong grip brought a smile to his face. He'd met her twice before, but every time he shook hands with her, he was surprised how strong she was.

"Martin," she said. "And Shawna, please."

"Right," he said. "Shawna." He pointed to the stairs. "If y'all are hungry, you're welcome to hit the chow line."

Calhoun glanced at his geologist. "Shawna? Go ahead and get up there. Going to be a long night. And Martin and I need to discuss a few things."

She raised her eyebrows and then nodded. She swept a lock of raven hair out of her eyes. "Guess I'll do that. Where are Catfish and JP?"

Vraebel rolled his eyes. "They're on the lower deck. Doing some maintenance on one of the robots."

She smiled. "I'll go say hello before I get some food." She started walking to the metal staircase.

"Make sure they eat too!" Calhoun called after her.

Sigler didn't turn, but raised a hand to show she'd heard him.

"Martin?" Calhoun said, "Got time for a little walk?"

Vraebel gritted his teeth, but nodded. He pointed toward the back of the loading deck. As they walked in silence toward the generators, the roar drowned out the sound of the waves and the crew. When they reached the furthest point, he slowed and turned to Calhoun.

"Well, Thomas, what do you need to babble about? I'm sure it has to do with—"

"First off," Calhoun said, "I want to apologize for Standlee and Harvey."

Vraebel blinked. "Apologize?"

The older man nodded. "Yes. I'll make sure they behave themselves. No one wants this operation to go more smoothly than I do. I'd rather we focus on getting to the black than have everyone pissed at everyone else."

"Well," Vraebel smiled, "that's good to hear."

"But," Calhoun said and pulled a cigar from his shirt pocket, "I need a little something from you too."

"And that would be?" Martin said, dreading Calhoun's response.

The engineer smiled. "We need this crew to work together, Martin. I can't have my guys treated like outsiders anymore than you can afford my team walking all over you and your rig. There has to be some mutual respect."

Vraebel nodded. He'd hated both Harvey and Standlee on sight. The rest of the crew had picked up on that, not to mention his constant bitching about them. He had expected some kind of blowout with Calhoun, some epic showdown including calls and emails to Simpson. But Calhoun had caught him off guard.

"Okay," he said. "Agreed."

The older man offered his hand. "I hope we can put this unpleasant shit behind us and focus on getting the job done."

Vraebel shook it. "All right, Thomas. I'll do my best to get along."

"And I'll do my best to rein in those two assholes," he smiled.

"Okay. I still don't like them," Martin said.

Calhoun chuckled. "You don't have to. Just know they're damned good at their jobs." He leaned in close enough for Martin to smell the ghost of old tobacco. "Otherwise, I would have fired them both a long time ago."

Vraebel laughed. "Glad to hear that." He pointed at the cigar. "You can light that down here or up on the top deck if you like. Just, um, be careful about the cherry."

Thomas pulled the wet-ended cigar from his mouth. "Sorry, nervous habit of mine," he said. "I promise not to smoke until the lamp is lit, so to speak." He tapped his foot. "You eaten yet?" Vraebel shook his head. "Then let's get some chow."

#

The lower deck was damned hot. The sun was quickly disappearing over the horizon, but between the day's humidity and the heat from the generators, the air was stifling. Her brow was beaded with sweat.

She walked down the metal stairs, work boots clanging against the steel. Above the din of the generators, she heard cursing and power tools. Catfish was throwing a tantrum. She sighed. It was time to play mommy again.

When she reached the bottom, she saw what she'd feared. An AUV hung low from the ceiling, buoyed by steel cables. The top of the machine lay on the deck. Catfish typed furiously on his laptop while JP watched a voltage meter.

"Is it clicking?" Catfish asked.

"How the fuck should I know?" JP yelled back. "I can't hear a damned thing!"

"Well, it should at least be moving!"

"BOYS!" Shawna yelled.

JP and Catfish swung their heads toward her. Catfish's patented glare turned into a wide smile. JP just groaned. It was his usual greeting to her. "Look out," JP said, "the worrier has arrived."

Shawna stepped forward and shook JP's hand. Catfish walked from the control box and hugged her.

"Good to see you, girl. Guess you guys arrived early?"

She nodded. "Good to see you too," she said. She pointed to the AUV. "Having problems?"

Catfish's easy grin disappeared into a snarl. "You could say that. Damned thing just won't get its shit together."

"Gremlins," she frowned. "What's the problem?"

JP laughed. "Ballast control. Today, that is. Yesterday? Propeller. Day before? Radio signal."

She shook her head. "Faulty actuator?"

"Think so," Catfish said and pointed at JP. "I'd know for sure if that deaf guy over there could hear it clicking."

She walked to the AUV. The leads were connected to a tiny clear box with a visible switch. She leaned down and studied it. "Try it now?"

Catfish walked back to the laptop and hit a few keystrokes. A tiny arc of light, barely visible, spread between the metal contacts in the clear box. "Stop," she said and turned to the engineer. "You realize it's fried, right?"

"What?" JP asked. "What are you talking about?"

She pointed to a black smudge on the outer case. "It shorted out. JP? Grab me a new one from the case."

The former SEAL opened his mouth to protest and then closed it. He walked to one of the black equipment cases and rummaged until he put his hands on a new actuator.

"Gimme," Shawna said and put out her hand. He put the plastic in her palm. With her other hand, she loosened the connections and pulled the actuator from the AUVs innards. Craig yelped as she tossed it to the deck.

"Hey! I only have so many of those!"

She glanced at him with a grin. "And that one is toast." She wriggled the new box in until the connections clicked. She didn't hear the contacts slide in, but she felt the sharp snap of the female/male plugs lining up. "There. Try it now."

Shaking his head, Craig typed a few keys. The tiny actuator arm flipped and the light went green on the control board.

"I'll be damned," JP said.

Catfish whooped. "Dammit, girl, where you been all my life?"

Shawna smiled. "Sometimes it takes a woman's touch."

"Or a clue," JP said.

Fingers flying across the keyboard, Catfish stared at the laptop as the commands went through. After a moment, he grinned. "I think we might be in business."

"Good," Shawna said. "Now let's get this damned thing back together again so we can get some food."

"Food," JP growled. "Hungry hungry diver."

Shawna reached over and petted the AUV's side. "Calhoun told me to make sure you kids ate."

"Kids," JP said. "We're both older than you."

She glared at him. "And yet you still need a mother to make sure you behave."

Catfish chuckled. "True dat." He closed the laptop. "Before we get up there, is Thomas in a bad mood?"

She shrugged. JP put the top fitting back on the AUV. "He's not happy about all the screaming and bitching Vraebel's been doing."

"Great," Catfish said. "That man is a fucking killjoy."

"Language," she said and shook a finger at him. Catfish blushed beneath his scraggly beard. "And yeah, he's a serious fucktard. But we have to work with him."

JP fitted torque screws into the holes. "We know," he said and guided the power tool's bit onto the head. "He's just such an officious prick."

He thumbed the trigger and deck filled with noise. The bit whirred and tightened the screw. When it reached the torque limit, the bit slipped and clicked. JP turned it off, and slotted the next one.

"I know," she said. "But we're going to be living with these folks for at least six weeks. Might be good for you two to make amends before we kill each other."

Catfish rolled his eyes. "Yes, mom."

She nodded. "Now let's get this sucker put to bed so we can eat. I'm freakin' starved."

Chapter Two

Calhoun awoke to a purple sky. He smiled at the porthole in his stateroom. The horizon wore a heavy suit of clouds, but the rising sun colored them in dark pastels. It was the kind of morning he lived for.

The rig stank of diesel, grease, and metal. In other words, like every other rig on the planet. The breeze added the ocean's saltwater perfume to the mix. Once the purples faded to orange, Calhoun dressed and headed to the top deck after securing a cup of coffee.

He stared out at the ocean. Below the grind and hum of the rig's engines, he could hear the rig crew working on the drill string. In an hour or so, they'd begin feeding the string down to the well head.

Even before JP and Standlee had boarded the rig over a week ago, Vraebel and crew had started the process of prepping the site. They sunk the lines, an emergency cap, and other gear. All of it was sitting in over 30,000 feet of water. The trench didn't even have a name besides M2, but from the early seismic and magnetic surveys, they should be able to drill anywhere along its spine and find the black.

Catfish had sent his AUVs down to film the bottom and ensure the equipment was where it was supposed to be. Simpson, the PPE vice president over the project, had told Calhoun Vraebel's crew was the best in the industry. Without any help from electronic surveillance, they'd managed to place the gear perfectly. He hated to admit it, but he was impressed. Vraebel might be an uptight asshole, but he knew what he was doing.

It had taken the crew over four hours to perform the load out from the supply ship. The cranes ran fast and efficiently. PPE had paid a lot of money to ensure they had the best personnel covering every aspect of the venture. Just getting the equipment on the rig should have taken at least seven hours. But Vraebel's people had gotten it done in no time.

Then they'd sacked out for a total of six hours before having breakfast and getting back to work. JP, Catfish, and Shawna had all turned in as soon as the crew was done. Calhoun had stayed up another two hours going over the AUV/ROV reports and footage. Four hours of sleep? Perfectly fine for the first day. If he was lucky, he'd get a hell of a nap once the drilling was up and running. At least after the first couple of hours.

When a team drilled a test well, Thomas wanted to be awake and apprised of every little detail. If anything went wrong, he wanted to know as soon as possible. The difference between hitting the sweet spot or drilling into a pocket of dangerous gas was pretty thin. Geologists and mud loggers constantly watched the readouts to ensure that didn't happen, but it was hardly real-time. Some of the engineering companies had spent millions and millions of dollars on creating real-time tools, sensors, and software to assist in decision making, but it wasn't foolproof. Shawna had learned to trust her instincts more than any software or technology and Thomas trusted her. Between the two of them, they'd never made a mistake during drilling. At least not a fatal one.

Bits break. Machines malfunction. Parts fracture. That was the reality. When it happened, you fixed them and moved on. As long as you had a good design and a good plan, you could encounter anything and succeed. Unless, of course, the oil wasn't there.

The seismic and magnetic surveys showed it was there. The only question was how much water sat below the surface and how sweet the crude was. But the surveys showed no echo from water. And that was strange to say the least. It was that little detail that had excited PPE and Calhoun. If the trench was truly free from underground water, much less salt water, then it would be a unique offshore find; processing the crude would be simple and inexpensive.

He took a deep drag from the cigar and let the smoke sit in his mouth. Besides a good single malt, cigars were his only vice. When you spent most of your time drilling, smoking was a privilege. Long ago he'd learned there was always at least one spot on the rig for the smokers.

Larger rigs had more space. Something as small as Leaguer only had the top deck. It would suck if there was a storm, but it was workable. He'd have to ration out his habit. It was going to be a long month. Longer if they didn't find a strike and had to hunt for the sweet spot.

But Shawna had a feeling. He had it too. This was going to be the big one. The big strike that he could retire on. He and Catfish could spend the rest of their lives designing better AUVs and ROVs. Shawna could go do…well, whatever she wanted. And JP? That bastard would probably move back to the Keys or maybe Hawaii and spend the rest of his days beneath the ocean.

Calhoun heard a shout below decks and grinned. The roughnecks were doing their jobs. The drill string would be ready by late morning. And then, the fun would begin.

#

Even high up on the bridge, he heard the pandemonium from the deck. Large men walked with wrenches the size of a baseball bat. Others dragged lines and cables. The machinery was getting going and it wouldn't be long before the rig was in action.

Vraebel sipped a cup of coffee. Dinner with Calhoun had been…well, interesting. They traded the usual war stories, but Calhoun had more than he did. The older engineer had been all over the world including Algeria, Nigeria, and South Africa. Vraebel was thankful he'd never been to those hell-holes.

"Thomas," Vraebel had said, "how the hell did a guy like you end up with Harvey and Standlee?"

Calhoun had laughed. "Harvey's the easy one. Met him while he was doing a demonstration on underwater demolition to put out well fires. Plus, he did some work with Boots and Coots. So I'd heard of him. Didn't take long for him to decide to join up with me." The older man had paused and then tapped the table with his fingers. "Standlee?" He shook his head. "That bastard came to me."

Vraebel raised his eyebrows. "Came to you?"

"Yeah," Calhoun said. "About fifteen years ago, I was giving a seminar on AUV technology and how it was the future. Some long-haired punk of a kid kept asking questions about artificial intelligence and automated sensor tech." He grinned. "He was basically interviewing for a job. Or so he thought."

"He wasn't with anyone?" Vraebel asked and sipped his coffee.

Calhoun shook his head. "Standlee bought a ticket to the conference representing his own company—Catfish Technologies. He had a degree in Engineering from Houston and thought he was hot shit." Thomas' Cheshire grin returned. "And he was. I had no idea how to do what I was proposing. I mean, I knew how to put the AUVs together. That's pretty damned simple. But the programming?" He tented his hands and rested his chin on them. "That's mostly Standlee."

"That's pretty standard stuff now," Vraebel said. "I've had ROVs on my rigs for years."

Calhoun nodded. "And a lot of the patents used in them came from the work that long-haired punk did." Thomas sipped from his half-empty glass of iced tea. "The other half? Those are mine." Calhoun smiled. "Besides, whatever AUVs or ROVs you've worked with before are nothing like the ones we brought." Calhoun stabbed his index finger on the table. "Our stuff is like nothing you've ever seen before. And tomorrow, you'll understand why."

"Bullshit" was what Vraebel had wanted to say. Instead, he'd just nodded and let the engineer talk. Simpson had told Vraebel over and over again that Calhoun's tech was the best in the industry. "Come hell or high water," the executive had said in his thick Texas drawl, "he'll find the oil. And we're all going to make a lot of money."

Vraebel finished his coffee and placed the cup on the console. The crew was working fast. Instead of fighting with the drill bit, Calhoun's new design coupled easily. Maybe the old man wasn't so full of shit after all.

"Deck to Chief," the radio squawked.

He glared at the speaker. The voice was most definitely Standlee's. He reached out and took the silver mic off the stand. "Vraebel here. That you, Standlee?"

"Yes, sir." He sounded respectful, but Vraebel could sense that snot-nosed attitude just below it. "Wanted to get permission from you to take out the AUVs. We want to get them diving."

Vraebel smiled. For once the little shit was asking for permission. *Guess Calhoun made good on his promise.* "Aye. You're a go to take out the Zodiac for tow. Any idea how long?"

There was a pause. "We'll need to get each AUV about 500 yards out from the rig. And we'll need to do it one at a time. So it's going to take a couple of hours."

"Understood. You're a go. Let me know when you're done."

"Aye aye," Standlee said.

Vraebel put the mic back in its clip. At least Harvey and Standlee were finally going to get some work done. More importantly, they would be off the rig.

He stood up and stared down at the deck. The drill string was dropping through the slot. A fifty foot section of steel was slowly lowered into the hole before another section was attached. Vraebel had never seen a drill string put together with pipe sections this large. They were usually 46 feet long or less. But these were a new design—Calhoun's.

Vraebel had been uneasy when he'd first been told they were going to use new gear, new tech, new everything. There were many horror stories of new designs being tried out on exploratory rigs with disastrous results. Drilling was dangerous enough without taking components out of the lab and trying to apply them directly to the real world.

But Calhoun's reputation was golden. The man's tech had never been blamed for an accident. Whatever new invention he applied to a new well, it just plain worked. Or so the stories went.

Vraebel believed in mitigating risk. After you see a man lose his hand while trying to do the most simple task on a rig, you realize just how dangerous drilling is. You learned diligence. He'd worked rigs where the chiefs pushed the crew too hard. When a crew felt rushed, they made mistakes. Mistakes meant injuries or deaths.

Regardless of how hard Simpson or Calhoun wanted to hit the well-site, no matter how much oil might be beneath the surface, Vraebel wasn't going to push his people. He and Gomez had worked together for over five years. The tool pusher knew to take his time. If there was a delay, so be it. As a rig-chief, Vraebel had never lost a crew-member and he wasn't planning on putting that track record in danger.

The crew worked in 12 hour shifts for weeks at a time. This far out from land, it wasn't the normal two weeks on, two weeks off schedule. It was three weeks on, three weeks off. Some of his people wouldn't even bother going home. They'd just head to the mainland, stay in one of the company's bungalows, and hit the streets. The family men would spend nearly 36 hours getting home and after two and a half weeks, spend another 36 hours getting back to the rig. It was a rough life, but they were paid well for it.

Vraebel picked up his coffee cup and headed to the back wall. He'd plastered topographical maps constructed from the AUV surveys to the west wall. Several safety and procedure signs covered the south and east walls. The north wall? That was the coffee station.

He slotted a pod in the machine, pressed the brew button, and waited for the black coffee to drop into the cup. By lunch time, the crew would probably have most of the drill string assembled. After that? They would spend the afternoon readying for a core sample.

Vraebel had half a mind to postpone that until tomorrow. He'd worked the crew hard the last 24 hours. Between offloading the supply ship and getting the drill string ready, they'd not had enough rest. The machine burped a cloud of steam as it finished brewing the coffee. He picked up the cup and sipped. Perfect. As always.

He turned to the bridge windows and stopped in mid-sip. Down on the deck, Calhoun stood off to the side of the drill crew. He watched as the crew put together the drill string, a strange smile on his face. Vraebel groaned. The rumors were true.

Vraebel had heard Calhoun wasn't the typical engineer. Instead of sitting in the bowels of the rig watching TV and waiting for someone to tell him there was a problem, the man supposedly walked the deck before drilling started and during. He liked to be down with the crew in case there was a problem.

"One more fucking thing I have to worry about," Vraebel said aloud. If PPE's star engineer was injured at all during this trip, Vraebel would no doubt lose his job.

But Thomas was far enough away from the crew. He was near the steel shelter in case something bad happened. If there was an accident powerful enough to take him out, the entire crew would be gone anyway. Vraebel shook off a chill and took another sip of his coffee.

Yup, that was that. As soon as the drill string was ready, he was sending the crew on break. A long one. He'd talk to Gomez at lunch and have him choose a skeleton crew to monitor for problems. Calhoun could wait. PPE could wait. He had a bad feeling. And until it went away, he wanted to take every precaution possible.

#

Catfish sat at his console. Two energy bar wrappers and three empty cans of Monster sat on the desk next to the screen. Bright, blue-white light illuminated the nearby workstations. When Catfish had first seen his work area lit up like a cube farm, he'd retrieved a stepladder and unscrewed all the bulbs directly above him. It didn't completely diminish the brightness, but it left his workstation in a pool of twilight.

Any idiot knew that fluorescents were bad for long-term computer work. They glared off the screens (even if they were matted) and made for tired, strained eyes. Catfish preferred to work in the dark. All his console backgrounds were black with green text. The custom software he'd created for AUV/ROV control and monitoring was fully color customizable. He'd created this theme, however, for himself.

The four 27" screens created a panorama of alert and tracking data. The first two screens were lit with AUV/ROV readings while the third and fourth were for mission commands and navigation programming.

The five AUVs were still diving. He'd lose communication with them very soon. When he and JP first arrived, the ex-SEAL dove beneath the rig and installed the remote radio/WiFi sensors. For a time, the extra bandwidth and radio reception would help Catfish correct the dive characteristics. But once the AUVs went below 15,000 feet, the reception would be spotty at best. After 20,000, he'd be lucky if he managed to get a status ping.

The ROVs were different. They were attached to the rig via specialized tethers that allowed for near real-time control and communication. The increase in bandwidth meant the ROV cameras could send actual video, albeit only ten frames per second, at ridiculous depths. The only problem? The tethers had to be watched and constantly massaged. You had to spend a lot of time controlling an ROV to make sure it didn't get wrapped around the drill string or the tether didn't get fouled by subsea fauna and flora.

Catfish loved driving the ROVs. It was like a video game where you had to incorporate the sensor data to decide which move to make. The yaw, pitch, and throttle controls were affixed to a metal plate next to his workstation. Another of Calhoun's inventions, it allowed Catfish to control the ROV the same way he played actual video games. It was slick and every other ROV driver in the industry would no doubt salivate in envy. If, that is, they ever saw it.

Prototypes. Everything on this mission was new gear. It had been tested in the lab, field tested in the Gulf of Mexico, and then finally brought out here. The difference? He'd never pushed the AUVs or the ROVs below ten-thousand feet of water. Thus, the week long break-in.

Catfish had tested each of the robots by sending them down to the trench floor. The AUVs had to travel roughly thirty-thousand feet before they neared bottom. He'd played with the ROV controls to get a feel for how sluggish they were at the maximum depth of 20k . Because of the delay between the electronic impulses that traveled down the wires and the return signal from the ROV, you had to think a second or two ahead of what you did. Otherwise, you'd have to over-compensate. Over-compensating could lead to a damaged ROV or worse.

R3, his favorite of the ROVs, was diving steadily and without issue. The video feed displayed a vampire squid jetting through the water. The strange looking creature had no doubt been attracted by the ROVs headlamp. It kept circling the machine, unsure if any part of the robot was edible. Catfish smiled. The ROV was already eighteen thousand feet below the ocean surface. At that depth, all was darkness with a near-freezing temperature. The only creatures that plumbed those depths were ancient evolutionary marvels.

He'd never seen a vampire squid at this depth. They usually stayed out of the lower midnight region of the ocean, but here it was. Catfish made a mental note. NOAA would want to know any biological specimens he found during the dive and exploration. He always made sure to send them reports out of courtesy. After all, their research money is what had uncovered this find.

An alert window popped up on the left screen. He glanced over at it without turning his head. AUV 1 was out of contact range. A second later, the other AUVs followed suit. They'd descended into deep midnight and wouldn't be heard from again until their return to the surface. When "the bitch" lost contact, Catfish sighed deeply and then turned back to the ROV feed.

He was nearing its design threshold for pressure. If he went another three thousand feet down, he'd be risking the robot. Ever since Mass had lost an AUV due to a decompression incident years ago, Catfish had worried he'd make the same mistake. All it took was one minuscule air bubble to be in the wrong place and all the design in the world couldn't save you; your two-million dollar toy would turn into a storm of undersea shrapnel.

Catfish stopped the ROV's descent and set it to hover. According to the coordinates, it would be well out of the way of the drill string when it dropped. But that fucktard Vraebel had postponed finishing up drill string construction until tomorrow's morning shift. Apparently Vraebel was worried about fatigue. Catfish harrumphed. "Sleep when you're dead, fuckers," he said aloud.

He took another sip of his third energy drink and realized his foot was tapping. *Too much caffeine,* he thought. *Maybe I should get some sleep too.* He'd programmed the AUVs to start taking video and sensor readings near the well-head. They would carry out their missions even though the drill string hadn't yet been fully deployed. He'd have to wait until they surfaced or came in radio range to send them back on the same programmed routes.

He'd no idea what "the bitch" would do. Number 5 had given him so much trouble with navigation, it would be a miracle if he'd finished working out the bugs. Catfish checked his watch. It was after five in the afternoon. Vraebel had announced over the radio that everyone was to get rack time and they would resume building the string at 0600. That would let the night shift do light duty around the rig and go to sleep just as the morning crew came on.

Standlee's stomach grumbled. It had been too long since he'd eaten. Period. When he and JP had taken the AUVs out into the ocean, they'd just had breakfast. After three hours of towing them offshore and setting the robots in motion, Catfish felt exhausted and starved. But instead of taking a break, he'd wanted to jump in on the monitoring as soon as they'd stowed the Zodiac.

Number 5 hadn't given them any trouble when they put her in the water. She started her dive immediately as programmed, but diving had never been the problem with that one.

Catfish rubbed his eyes and his stomach grumbled again. The ROV was stationary in the water. He thought about putting it on auto-pilot so it would stay in its position, but instead he chose to bring it back up. He could check the sections of the drill string that had been deployed. If nothing else, he'd be able to update Calhoun and Vraebel if he found a problem.

He took his hands from the controls, reached in a drawer, and pulled another protein bar out of the box. The wrapper said "chocolate peanut butter" but it still tasted like ass. Oh, well. It would have to do until the ROV was put away for the night.

#

The deepest parts of the ocean are known as lower midnight. No sunlight from the surface reaches these depths. Born in darkness and near freezing temperatures, the sea life is an evolutionary marvel that may very well be older than the dinosaurs.

Some fish survive the incredible pressures of the deep only to rise to the surface. No one knows why these strange creatures choose to leave their birthplace and struggle against the pressure to taste the sunlight.

Their bodies have molded themselves to not only survive the unfathomable pressure, but somehow reorganize their internal ballast bladders and float to the warm ocean surface. Evolutionary marvel or prehistoric cast-off, these creatures are remarkable in their abilities and design.

Like the creatures it encountered at the extreme ocean depths, AUV 5 had been designed much the same way. As it dove from the surface to reach lower midnight, it expelled every last remnant of air. If a single air bubble was trapped inside the machine's body, the incredible atmospheric pressure of lower midnight would result in catastrophic decompression.

Its twin ballasts, looking like steel remora fish attached to its undercarriage, were filled with seawater to accelerate its dive to the ocean floor. When it was time to surface, the AUV would open a control valve and expel the contents. The sudden buoyancy of the tanks would aid its ascent.

Number 5's programming led it into slow lazy circles around the area where the drill string should have been. The other AUVs were further off, their cameras pointed straight at a target that wasn't there. Number 5's thermal imaging and blue-light cameras snapped the programmed 10 frame per second video and stored them on an internal SSD array. It would continue doing this until it ran out of space or it was time to surface.

The yellow-painted robot, invisible in the pitch-black depths, continued its descent until it reached the well bore. It studied the spud site. Number 5 pinged the area, analyzed the data, and ensured to the best of its ability that the readings were as expected. The drill string hadn't yet been dropped, so it found no sign of the metal pipe or the blowout preventer.

Normally, if it found a problem, its subroutine to ascend until it was in radio range would kick in, but Standlee had programmed the robots to ignore a missing drill string. Number 5 was as content as a machine could be. None of its warning or emergency routines were running. As long as that was the case, it would wait and monitor. As the SSD filled with video, the AUV fired off another sonar burst at the rock and sand surrounding the spud site. The return was…strange. AUV 5 marked the reading, but analyzing the data was far above its pay grade.

The robot continued pinging the area as it looked for other anomalies. Perhaps the strange echo was a glitch in its system. Or maybe something below the rock moved. Either way, it continued its pinging, gathering as much data as possible. Provided nothing of import occurred, it wouldn't begin its trip to the surface until 0400. It continued checking its internal clock, counting off the seconds until the ascent program began.

Chapter Three

Catfish sucked on his e-cig and blew a cloud of vapor above the workstation. Shawna rolled her eyes. The long-haired tech had been using the vape non-stop since the drill string had fallen into place.

When the AUVs had reached a depth of 18,000 feet, they started sending radio signals. Catfish had awakened for breakfast at 0500. He'd scarfed down a world-class omelette, three cups of coffee (which he hated), and headed to his consoles to check on his babies.

They were there, waiting for him to send instructions. Rather than bring them to the surface, he put them in a holding pattern while he sent down the ROV. Because the human controlled vehicle was tethered, it was capable of capturing large amounts of data and sending them back up the lines. Once it reached a depth just above the five AUVs, he cycled through the robotic probes one at a time and had them dump their data to the ROV.

Raw telemetry, sensor reports, and thousands of small videos began uploading to the ROV and in turn to his consoles thousands of feet above. As each AUV finished its dump, Catfish's RAID arrays captured the raw data. His programs filtered and sorted them by depth and time.

From an analytical point of view, the videos and stills were the least useful. He'd deal with them last. His computer crunched the readings and began their statistical analysis.

As his consoles lit up with reports, he gave them a cursory glance before shunting them to the shared server. He was sure Shawna would want to look at them before the rig crew started drilling the core. He had, of course, been right.

But it was Number 5's sensor data that made him call her. It had marked a group of readings as anomalies from its sonar and thermal arrays. Catfish had no idea what he was looking at, but it was something the geologist would.

"See here?" Catfish said and pointed to the furthest monitor on the right.

Shawna stared at the peaks and jumps in the graph. When Catfish's programs unpacked the binary data, it came across the byte indices for annotations made by the sensors. They were confusing to say the least.

She cleared her throat. "If I didn't know better, I'd say Number 5 came across a large fish. Something moving down there."

He shook his head. "We can check the video and still footage, but I don't think that's the case. Something else happened."

Something else. Bullshit. Catfish was having another of his hinky moments. The man frequently blamed gremlins for bugs in his code, or some unknown person for messing with his workstation and designs. She was used to hearing him go off at length about paranoid conspiracies. He was a genius, but he was hardly well-adjusted.

She sighed. "You compiled Number 5's footage yet?"

"Yes, and no. They're split into folders just like the others. But I haven't run the program to splice them. They're on the fileserver."

"Okay," she said. She took the well-lit console next to him and sat in the expensive chair. She logged in and her fingers danced over the command line interface until she brought up the folder for Number 5.

The pictures and videos were named by depth/timestamp. The ten frame- per-second videos were stored in five second segments. It was going to be a pain in the ass, but she knew analyzing the videos was the only way she'd get Catfish back on track. Once the man found a hiccup in his systems, he'd eschew all other tasks until he solved the problem. It was one of his many personal traits that drove her batshit.

She searched for the max well-depth and then found the corresponding videos. Number 5 had taken nearly forty minutes of video at 30,162 feet. She opened another window, brought up the strange readings, and looked at the time slice. Shawna nodded to herself and opened the relevant video.

Instead of seeing the glare of bright lights from the well-head's surface, the images were clothed in a strange ghostly blue. The new camera technology for subsea depths didn't use thermal imaging or traditional methods to capture pictures. Instead, they used a special range of light that allowed them to "see" even in the pitch-black.

Unlike black and white photography, the blue-light afforded many more shades of contrast and it was less possible for details to be lost in the continual shift of colors. The sand and rock around the well-head was clearly visible. It looked undisturbed as the video played and then there was a skip.

She frowned. With a touch of her finger, the video started over again, but at one frame per second speed. Number 5 was relatively stationary in the water, but that didn't mean there wasn't a bit of change between the images. Even at that depth, the constant push and pull of the water was enough to jar its position. The cameras were affixed to motion-compensating mounts, but they weren't perfect.

Frame 23 displayed and she saw the jump. She hit the space bar and froze the image. Number 5's position hadn't changed, but the image had jumped up in the air as if a sudden burst of water had disturbed it. In the next frame, it was back to where it had been.

Her eyebrows knit together. "Catfish?"

"Yeah?" he asked as his fingers continued typing.

"Can we check Number 5's camera? Something's strange."

He glanced at her. "What do you mean 'strange'?"

"Well," she said, "I checked the footage from that timeframe. Looks like the camera image jumped although the AUV stayed stationary."

Catfish blinked. "What?"

"Seriously," she said. "Come here."

Except for the hum of the computer fans, the room went quiet. Catfish slowly rolled his chair next to hers. "Okay. Show me something I haven't seen before."

She rewound the video and started it again at normal speed. Catfish watched. When the shift in the frames came up, he glared at the monitor. "Run it again. Slow-mo."

Shawna reset the video and once more ran it at one frame per second. When the image jumped, he sucked his teeth. She paused it and turned to him. "Well? What do you think?"

He shrugged. "That's fucking strange." The words came out in a hushed whisper, but a smile crept across his face. "I've never seen a camera do that."

"Interference from the sensors?"

He shook his head. "If it was, we'd have seen it before. Plus, the rest of the videos and stills would have the same problem."

"Who says they don't?" she asked. "I think I need to view the rest of these and see if I can find another. How many anomalies did Number 5 mark?"

"Seven," he said.

She sighed. "Good thing the drill string is still a few hours from getting all the way down there. Once the mud starts coming up, I'll be trapped in my chair."

"Whah," Catfish said.

She punched him in the arm and he cursed. "Right, Mr. Computer, because you don't have to analyze a 100 meter core once they pull the damned thing up."

"Well," he said, "that's your job, ain't it?"

"Ain't ain't a word," she said. He rolled his eyes. "Yeah, Catfish, it's my f'ing job."

He laughed. "Why can't you just say 'fuck' and get it over with?"

She turned in her chair to face him. "Because, I am a lady."

He raised his hands and flashed a grin. "I'd never say otherwise."

"Better not," she said. Her look of consternation slowly melted into a soft smile. "Otherwise I'll kick your fucking ass."

#

The crew had finished assembling the drill string for the core sample. Over 600 sections of pipe had been spliced together to reach the ocean floor. Now they were at the spud-in site. All the drilling team had to do was start the fluid, turn on the drill, and wait.

Much like the center of a record player, the end of the drill string sat in the middle of a large circular steel mechanism. The visible leader pipe was connected to tanks of fluid. When drilling started, fluid would flow down the drill string to lubricate the drill bit and force a return of sediment and other particles known as mud. The giant record player would begin to spin. The centrifugal force would grind the drill bit into the ocean floor. The diamond studded core bit would cut a 100 meter long cylinder through the rock and the shelf. As it drilled, the mud would rise back up the pipe to a return trough. The crew would strain and filter the mud so Shawna and Harobin, the mud-logger, could analyze the results.

Once the drill reached its target depth and the core was salvaged, the crew would raise the 100 meter long cylinder of rock and soil through the string. At that point, it would have to be extracted so Shawna could analyze it and report as to whether or not the prospect was black gold, or just shit.

Calhoun stared out toward the open ocean. The choppy waves frothed beneath puffy, white clouds. The massive storm that had chased them into the ocean was still out there, but it was no longer heading toward Leaguer. And that was a good thing.

He reached into his shirt pocket and pulled out a cheap cigar. Its end was dark and moist where he'd had it clenched for most of the morning. He'd smoked one of the good ones at daybreak while the sun slowly crawled over the horizon. The cheapie in his hand wasn't something he'd ever smoke—it was for chewing on.

Once between his lips, his teeth clamped down on it. He rolled it from cheek to cheek in nervous anticipation. Any time a crew started drilling, a billion things could go wrong. Connections on the pipe sections might fail, or fluid wouldn't reach the drill bit, or the drill bit would break. The worst? They could hit a gas pocket.

He'd seen pictures of rigs that had hit massive natural gas or CO_2 reservoirs. The gas would travel up the pipe or possibly explode causing a massive shockwave. Worst of all? A bubble might form.

One rig had been destroyed by a bubble. When its crew realized they'd hit a gas pocket, they'd dumped all the concrete casing they had down the pipe. While it had contained the gas and kept it from blowing the well-head, the gas had instead ruptured part of the sea floor. A massive gas bubble roared out of the damaged trench and floated toward the ocean surface. It hit the semi-submersible rig at an angle. The force was enough to rock the rig and make it list. Once that happened, the rig was doomed.

The ballast keeping the rig afloat took on more water on one side than the other. Unable to right itself, it kept listing. By the time the support ships managed to evacuate the rig, it was at a 25° angle. An hour later? The rig was gone. Just plain gone with nothing but wooden debris and trash to mark where it had disappeared.

From start to finish? The event had taken five hours. In that short timespan, an 800 million dollar investment ended up on the bottom of the ocean. And that incident had occurred near land and in only 2,000 feet of water.

If such a thing occurred out here in the middle of nowhere, it would be a race for the crew to get off the rig and into their lifeboats. Auto distress beacons would send out signals and the choppers and support ships would rally to their aid. But that was only if there was time to get off the rig.

Calhoun wasn't worried about an explosion. They weren't fucking BP—they knew how to build a goddamned well-head with a proper blowback preventer. Those idiots shouldn't even be allowed to cook with oil, let alone drill or refine it.

PPE wanted the black, but they were savvy enough to know the difference between delays due to caution versus the risk of acting with reckless abandon. Before Calhoun had signed up with them, he'd looked at the track record of those involved. This was PPE's first real venture in the deep ocean. They weren't willing to risk losing their new toy under any circumstances. If they had, he would never have agreed to join the project regardless of how much money had been on the table. You couldn't spend money if you were dead.

The loudspeaker sprang to life. "Steve Gomez. Please call the bridge."

The short Hispanic man in the bright red hardhat walked away from the turntable and headed to a phone attached to the wall. He picked it up, spoke a few words, and then turned to the men on the deck. He gave them a thumbs up and cradled the phone.

Calhoun pulled up his ear pieces and put them on as the pumps roared to life. Fluid started its long descent to the drill bit. He longed for the roar of the turntable as it turned and drilled, but it would be a while before that happened. Everything had to be nice and lubricated first.

The crew was spread between the pumps and the turntable, everyone watching gauges and looking for warning lights. Up on the bridge, Vraebel and his XO, Terrel, would be doing the same. Catfish's AUVs would be swarming down near the spud site, taking pictures, and monitoring the systems. If something went wrong, at least they'd get good film.

Nothing is going to go wrong, he told himself. *Just black gold waiting to be brought up.*

#

At lower midnight, there is hardly any sound. The waves 30,000 feet above the ocean floor have little to no effect this far below. The fauna lived in near silence broken only by the sounds of their fins moving against the water or their teeth upon a meal.

AUV 5 couldn't hear—it hadn't been given sensors for that. What it could do was detect the rush of fluid through the drill string. Its thermal sensors spotted the pipe's temperature change and began tracking it. Motionless in the pitch black, AUV 5 started sweeping the spud site with sonar pings. Its cameras sprang to life and began recording video and photos.

Its thermal sensor detected a strange reading near the spud site. The AUV focused the video on the area, marked the data as anomalous, and continued its inspection job. The fluid was circulating through the drill string. As it traveled down to the bit, it was recycled upwards through another part of the pipes.

Hovering a few feet above the ocean floor, the robot turned on its magnetic sensors as a subroutine kicked on. It would scan for fractures or disturbances once the bit began rotating into the rock and sand. If something went wrong, the rig crew could analyze the data and determine if it was due to mechanical failure or damage to the spud site.

If AUV 5 had been given the power to hear, it would have been startled as 30,000 feet of piping began to move. The long pipe rotated in a barely perceptible clock-wise motion. The fantastic weight of the drill string kept the bit flush with the rock and soil. As the turntable spun, the pipe and bit followed suit. AUV 5 would have heard the sound of diamonds pulverizing rock into dust.

A few meters away, a large field of tube worms began to sway in the calm ocean depths. The tentacle-like creatures turned toward the source of the vibration. Whether they did this out of reflex or some inbred knowledge of danger, we'll never know.

AUV 2 was stationed above the bed of worms. It slowly tilted downward to snap pictures and video of the fauna. Its primary mission was to keep an eye on the drill site, but its secondary routines had started the moment the worms began responding to the drilling. Even in the dark of lower midnight, its motion sensors had picked up their movements.

It pinged the creatures with sonar and they responded by reaching toward the AUV although it was safely out of reach. Its video feed would show the behavior later if anyone cared to watch. AUV 2 marked in its logs when and where the creatures started to react to the drilling.

Far above the ocean floor, the turntable continued to rotate. Fluid was recycled from the trough and sent back down the drill string to lubricate the bit and seal the well as a thin cylinder was cut out of the ocean floor. It would take hours for the core drilling to finish. The AUVs continued their missions of sensor sweeps and filming. They didn't hear the groan of something below the ocean floor, but their sensors did. The giant tube worms shook as if with ague.

#

The rig rumbled beneath the sounds of the computer fans, the air conditioner, and conversation. Its pumps were on. The turntable was rotating. The crew watched their stations. Vraebel, his seventh cup of coffee loosely gripped in his left hand, wore a thin smile.

Gomez had reported in twice to give the all clear and ensure no warnings had been issued. Vraebel was happy to tell the man *all is well and keep drilling.* His people were good. So was Calhoun's bit. They'd already had to add two more sections of pipe to the drill string. The core was being drilled in record time, but not because they were rushing it. It was all about the bit.

At some point he would have to ask Calhoun what was so special about it. But for the moment, he was too focused on his screens to do more than give it a thought. The drilling console displays were lit up above the bridge windows. They showed a diagram of the drill string boring into the ocean floor. Mud readings scrolled by on another screen. The drill string was already 20 feet below the ocean surface and quickly plummeting. In another 300 feet or so, they'd be done taking the core sample and the crew would start the long task of bringing up the core.

Calhoun and his crew were all in the drilling office. He'd no doubt the engineer and his people were studying the displays and raw data coming back up the pipe. Digital gauges showed pump pressure, fluid consumption, and approximated the bit's descent. This was Vraebel's favorite part of his job—watching the drill string slowly work its way into a find.

Even at the speed the bit was traveling, it would still be several hours before it finished. When he'd first seen the results of the seismic and magnetic surveys, he'd noticed that Sigler had marked several areas of the trench as "optimal prospects for coring." The geologist obviously knew her shit because he'd never seen drilling this easy.

He looked down at the computer screen and the messaging windows. In the drilling office, Harobin and Sigler were sending instructions to the drill operators. Years ago it would have been impossible, but with the new sensors, the geologist and mud-logger could determine the characteristics of the well-bore in near real-time. Harobin was studying the mud while Sigler quickly analyzed the geology to make sure they weren't about to hit something that could snap the bit.

Vraebel sipped his coffee. He sat straight up in the black captain's chair. He wouldn't lean back and relax until the core was finished. By the end of his watch, his back would ache and his joints would feel like he'd been encased in steel.

#

Quiet conversation filled the drilling office. Shawna was riveted to her screen as she kept an eye on the particulate matter coming up in the recycle as well as the mud-log Harobin kept marking. Mud-readings scrolled across one of her four displays. Topographic maps based on the magnetic and seismic readings taken months ago filled the other three.

A drill reading popped onto the screen. She shook her head. The topography had...changed. The initial readings they'd taken during the surveys didn't match up with what she read now. She cursed herself for not studying more of the AUV film. If there was magma down there, they were screwed. And magma displacement was the only thing that explained why the ocean floor differed from the survey taken several months ago.

"Unless someone screwed up the survey," she said to herself.

"What?" Harobin asked. He pushed his horn-rimmed glasses up on his round face. The wispy blond beard gracing his chin waggled as he ground his teeth.

"Nothing," she said. "Just talking to myself."

Harobin nodded. "I don't see any problems with the fluid. And we're getting good flow." His short index finger dug into his left nostril.

Shawna shook her head. The mud-logger was good at his job, but he'd obviously been out on the water and surrounded by men for far too long. He wasn't the only one. Most of the rig crew were barely above the level of savages when it came to talk about women or their manners.

When her father had found out she'd signed up with Calhoun seven years ago, and what she'd be doing, he'd sucked his teeth and ran a calloused hand across his five o'clock shadow. "Shawna, you don't want to consort with those kind of people," he'd said.

Shawna was the first in her family to graduate from college. She was the first not to join the military. Her family had been mining coal in West Virginia for so many generations, she wasn't sure they knew how to do anything else. Men with dirty faces walked out of the mine while men with dirty fingernails walked in. It was the same procession that had graced the mine for over a hundred years.

"Paw, it'll be fine," she'd said.

He'd lifted a cigarette to his lips and blown out a cloud of blue smoke against the dying afternoon light. "Trucking with those boys out there on the ocean? Or in some country in Africa? Don't sound very lady like."

"It's where the work is, Paw. It'll be fine."

"Work," he said in a low voice. "Plenty of jobs in labs and such, aren't there?"

She nodded. "But I don't want to be a lab rat, Paw. There's more to life than just sitting in a lab analyzing boring samples."

"Boring job is still a job. Better than being out on a drill site, or whatever it's called."

Shawna had sighed. "Paw, I'll be fine. Mr. Calhoun takes good care of his employees."

He blew smoke out of his nose. "And how many of them are women?"

"What does that matter?" she asked.

Her father took another drag of his cigarette. "Just worry about you, Shawna. You're a good looking woman. Young. And old men can get all sorts of bad ideas."

She laughed. "You haven't met Mr. Calhoun. He's not some kind of lech."

Tim Sigler harrumphed. "We're all lecherous, girl. Can't believe you ain't figured that out."

The conversation had continued, but ultimately she'd convinced her father to just be happy for her. He'd died a year later in a mining accident. She knew he'd been proud of her, but he'd never really understood what she did for a living. Her other sisters, three of them, were still in her home town and more than likely would never leave.

Shawna frowned at the screen. "Andy? Do you see anything odd in the mud?"

Harobin glanced at her. "No, ma'am. I surely don't. What I see is..." His voice trailed off. He rapped a knuckle on the workstation. "Okay, I see what you're talking about." His gnarled fingers tapped a few keys. "Some of the particulates don't look like sand to me. Or rock."

"Same here," she said. Shawna left her station and stood over Harobin's shoulder. His screens were lit up like hers, but the programs he had open scrolled with depth/time data and rough chemical approximations. "Yeah," he said, "something really strange coming up. Wonder if we hit a pocket of algae or something like that."

She shook her head. "No algae below the ground, Andy. Could be the underside of a bed of tube worms, but I don't think they plant themselves that far underground."

"Is it something we need to worry about?" Harobin asked.

Shawna chewed the corner of her mouth. *Something to worry about*, she said to herself. "No. But we definitely need to point it out in the reports."

"I mean, it's not enough to foul the samples."

She pointed at the data scrolling across the screen. "Make sure you mark that."

"I will," Harobin said. He pulled open a report file and began scrolling backwards through the data to find the strange particulates. He typed one handed, the index finger of his other hand digging for nostril gold.

Shawna wrinkled her nose and headed back to her workstation. As she sat, she looked down the row. In a pool of shadows, Calhoun was hunched over Standlee's chair as the two looked at readings. Her mentor and boss had a concerned look on his face. He said something and Catfish began typing into a console.

Another AUV fuck up? She wondered.

Calhoun turned to her and he waggled his eyebrows. She laughed and stared back at her screen. The topography was still very wrong. It made no sense for the ocean floor to have changed so much. She'd have to talk to Calhoun about that once the coring was complete. Regardless of the changes in the areas surrounding the drilling, the drill had no problem cutting through the test site.

She felt a hand on her shoulder and twitched.

"And how is it going?" Calhoun asked in his gravelly voice.

Shawna shrugged. "Don't tell Catfish I said so, but I think the seismic survey is wrong."

He frowned. "What do you mean 'wrong?'"

She pointed a finger at the reports filed by the AUVs earlier that morning. "See this? There should be a gentle rise off the spud site leading to the edge of the trench."

"Yeah," he said. "What part of the ocean floor are you looking at?"

With a sigh, she pulled up the original survey map and placed it on the left screen. After a few mouse clicks, the right screen filled with another map. "The left is the original survey."

Calhoun chewed the side of his cheek as he flipped his eyes from one side to the other. "Can you superimpose the recent one atop the old?"

She nodded and dragged from the right screen to the left. She clicked a few icons and the newest map line became a thick blue. She changed the transparency level until the blue lines sat atop the original map's black ones.

"Shit," Calhoun said. The area surrounding the well-site was no longer a gentle slope. Instead, the spud site sat in a divot. The ocean floor surrounding it was rutted and irregular as if it had become a wash-boarded road. "The hell is that?"

Shawna clucked her tongue. "Like I said. I think the original survey was wrong."

"Not possible," Calhoun said. "Not *that* wrong anyway. The AUV sensors are top notch, Shawna."

She nodded. "I know. But how the hell else do you explain it?"

"I—" He looked over his shoulder at Standlee. The man was frowning at his console as he went over the earlier data-sets from the AUVs. "I think we need to ask Catfish."

"He's not going to take that well," she said.

Calhoun grinned. "It'll be fine, Shawna. It'll be fine."

She let out a sigh. "Boss? When we get that core up, it might be a bit messier than we expected."

He laughed. "At the rate its going, we'll be able to drill two more and still be on schedule."

"Whoa!" Harobin yelled from workstation and clapped his hands. "We have oil." Shawna looked up at her screen. Alerts popped up on her screens. They'd hit a pressurized pocket and something was coming back up the drill string.

"You don't know it's oil," Shawna said with hesitation in her voice.

Harobin stared at her. "You're such a spoil sport."

Calhoun pointed at the readouts on her monitor. "How much pressure?"

She clicked a button and another window popped up. "A lot."

Her boss growled low in his throat. "What does that mean?"

Shawna wrinkled her nose. "Three atmospheres relative to the pressure at the ocean floor."

"Holy shit," Calhoun said. "That's a fuckton." He turned to Harobin. "Any danger of blowout?"

The mud logger shook his head. "No, Thomas. Nothing like that. We're still in the green."

"For how long is the question," Shawna said. "Andy? Let me know when the mud comes back up."

"Should be soon," Harobin said. "Muds been moving pretty fast. If we hit a pocket of liquid, it should stream up at a good clip."

Calhoun nodded. That was one thing they hadn't counted on—pockets of pressure. The original surveys showed moderate to light rock formations beyond thirty meters. But this was odd. Damned odd. If the mud showed nothing but liquid, their original surveys were way off. He wondered what else could be wrong.

Calhoun turned to the tech. "Catfish?". The man ran a hand through his long hair and slowly looked up from his keyboard. "Can we plan on having an AUV perform another magnetic survey tomorrow morning?"

The tech-head squinted at Calhoun. "Why the fuck would we do that?"

Calhoun took a deep breath. "Because something is off. And I want to know if our original sweeps were wrong. We need to check the area around the well-head in about a 200 meter circle."

Catfish groaned. "Okay. After JP retrieves them, I'll have to do some work to get that done. You sure you need it tomorrow morning?"

"If possible," Calhoun said. "But don't stay up all goddamned night doing it. I need you in good shape for the next well."

Shawna cleared her throat and he looked at her. "I wouldn't plan on drilling another one until we figure out what's going on down there."

The engineer nodded. "Right. So let's get that mud up here and see what the hell is going on."

#

When the drill string stopped turning, AUV 5's thermal sensors triggered an event. A listener marked the time and temperature change. Another event launched into the main program. AUV 5 responded by tilting its nose toward the ocean surface. The ballast subroutine sent an electrical impulse to the switch-box. Water jettisoned from the tanks and AUV 5 began to rise.

In the black of lower midnight, a giant lantern fish sped after it. The bio-luminescent leader protruding from its head danced with a blue glow—it was the only light that could be seen for over a mile. The fish thought it had spotted a morsel to feed upon. As it raced after the ascending robot, the dim light from its head shined off the AUV's yellow painted skin.

The fish, in an orgy of excitement, flew through the water toward its target with reckless abandon. AUV 5's screws started up and it began to pick up speed. The lantern fish felt the vibrations of the screws and realized something was wrong. It slowed itself by waving its fins and changing its trajectory. Before it managed to strike the metallic robot, the fish ducked beneath the AUV. Jets of moving water from the screws knocked it aside as the AUV flew toward the surface.

The fish, angry that it had missed its chance, headed back toward the ocean floor. The water buzzed with the vibrations of the other robots as they emptied their ballasts and headed toward the surface. The lantern fish rested a few feet above the ocean floor. It turned and stared at the well-head and drill string. Uninteresting except for the way the metal reflected back the light.

Another vibration slammed through lower midnight. The fish swam away from the well as fast it could. The drill string slowly ascended out of the well in a smooth motion. When a full section of the string was exposed, the movement paused. After a few moments, it rose again and then stopped. The process continued for hours.

The lantern fish lost its fear once it was certain the vibrations were harmless and it hadn't become the thing's prey. The fish watched and waited. Its instincts told it to wait, to observe. Perhaps the strange metal creature would deliver food, or finally show its true form.

After another hour of waiting, hunger pangs drove it to search for a meal. It headed toward the bed of giant tube worms. The waving tentacles always attracted morsels. The lantern fish hovered a few feet away from the tentacles ensuring it was safe from the gluttonous creatures.

As it searched for food, its fins flapping to keep it from getting sucked down, it didn't see one of the worms reaching for it. It also didn't see a new crevice open in the middle of the bed. In its tiny brain, an alarm bred from hundreds of millions of years of evolution buzzed. It canted to look down, swim bladder ready to release a jet of water so it could rise out of harm's way.

The lantern fish's dim bio-luminescent light flashed off a large eye. Before its fight or flight response could trigger a panicked ascent, a tentacle reached for it with dizzying speed. Long protrusions morphed from its ends and snatched the fish.

The lantern fish emptied its swim bladder. It squirted feces and urine into the water and wriggled against the alien touch. It tried to swim backwards and somehow release itself from the thing's grip. Flesh parted and a hole appeared in the tentacle. The fish had no choice but to swim into it. When it reached the bottom, it found teeth. It was the last thing the fish would ever find.

#

The crew had stowed the drill string and carried the core sections to the small lab off the personnel cabins. Calhoun had watched them raise the sections of pipe from the ocean floor out of curiosity.

As much as he hated being trapped on the rig, he loved watching this part of exploration. It never ceased to amaze him that a small group of people could get so much work done in so little time. The meticulous attention the crew paid to the drill string was impressive.

Calhoun had seen it done more times than he could count, but the Leaguer crew was better than most, and quite possibly the best he'd seen. Vraebel might be a humorless prick, but he definitely knew how to put together a good crew.

Those who weren't sleeping were probably lounging in their rooms or making use of the commissary. Calhoun stood on the top deck, a Rocky Patel stuck between his lips. He puffed out a large cloud into the night air as the waves crashed against the submersible rigging.

Even from this high up, he could hear the water as the crests broke against the metal. It was a sound he loved and loathed. It made him sleepy. Tonight, that was a good thing.

Drilling the core had been too easy. As Shawna had said, the floor's topography had shifted. Calhoun took another puff and chewed on the end of the cigar. A gentle breeze wafted smoke away from his eyes.

"What the fuck would make that happen?" he asked the darkness. It didn't make any sense. Tomorrow morning, he'd have to get on the internet and research that. Although he was certain Shawna was already doing it, she had to focus on the core tomorrow. After fourteen hours of mud-logging and compiling drill reports, she had been completely exhausted. She'd practically fallen asleep at dinner.

Calhoun smiled to himself. Catfish's resolve had finally broken an hour ago and he'd headed off to bed with a belly full of green chili and heartburn. The tech was merciless in his work ethic, but even he had to sleep. Eventually.

While the crew had brought up the string, JP had headed out in the Zodiac with another diver to retrieve the AUVs. All five had risen to the surface long before the drill string was up. This time, "the bitch" had returned without a problem. The heavy steel robots were now in their berths charging up for another run.

Since they were done drilling the first exploratory site, there would be little work for the AUVs for the next few days. But he was sure Catfish would run "the bitch" through its paces again and take another topographic survey. And tomorrow, while Shawna studied the core sample, he and Catfish would have to dig through the AUV videos, sensor reports, and run diagnostics. It was going to be a damned long day.

He puffed out another cloud of smoke. The breeze shifted and his eyes burned. His thick, strong fingers removed the cigar while he brushed away a tear. Never failed. Damned ocean.

Calhoun spat a piece of leaf and it fluttered in the wind before flying over the side and into the ocean. It would degrade in no time in the salt water. At least he could count on that.

Vraebel hadn't been at dinner. Calhoun assumed the rig chief had either sacked out once the drill string was raised, or was still sitting on the bridge. If the unpleasant man was still at his post, then he'd be damned tired tomorrow morning.

Thomas wasn't sure he could sleep. The core would prove the test well was either a boom or a bust. If it was the latter, they'd keep drilling throughout the possible reservoir until they struck oil or the powers that be called it. PPE had paid a fuckton of money for the best exploration crew and the execs would not be happy if they didn't hit it big. Especially after Calhoun and Shawna assured them the oil was there.

Finds like this were rare and the surveys showed something below the surface. Since reservoirs were almost exactly like water aquifers, peering below the rock using seismic and magnetic sensors showed hollowed out sections. But those surveys could only go so deep into the earth.

The core drilling had gone easy. A little too easy. And the pressurized pocket they'd hit? It damned near flooded the drill string with liquid. According to the mud log readings, the liquid was indeed oil, but Harobin kept going on about strange particulates. They'd collected more than enough for Sigler to analyze. Her sample barrel to send back to the Houston lab was ready to ship out. Assuming, of course, there was a point.

Shawna had shown Calhoun the mud log readings, but the engineer hadn't really known what he was looking at. He agreed it was more than likely anomalous. But the anomalies were adding up and something about that made his balls shrink.

Tomorrow would tell the tale. The real tale. They knew what was likely in the first 30 meters of core, but until Sigler looked at it? Anyone's guess. He blew a smoke ring into the breeze. It quickly disintegrated as the wind ripped it apart.

The complete darkness was punctured only by the slowly blinking rig lights and the bright moon. A halo of moisture glowed around the pale yellow of the far away satellite. The cigar was nearly finished. He took it out of his mouth, exhaled a large cloud of smoke through his nose, and tossed the butt into the air.

The remains tumbled in the wind before he lost sight of it. He wondered if it sizzled as the water drowned the cherry. Maybe a fish would mistake it for food and devour it. Or maybe, it would disintegrate into loose flakes of tobacco that settled on the ocean floor. Didn't matter.

He sighed and headed to the stairs leading back down into the cabins. The weather forecast was good, but that damned storm off the coast was still swirling around. In a few days, it might completely evaporate. Or maybe it would come visit. Either way, they had a lot of work to do in the next two days. And then, it would be time to drill another well.

Chapter Four

The large lab table was packed with cores. Nine 35-foot cylinders. Each core had been carefully raised from the drill string via wire-line and brought to her for analysis. And the analysis was terrifying.

The rock in the first 25 meters was as expected. The usual granite, igneous, and sedimentary layers were stacked atop each other in a gentle gradient of colors. But the last five? They were the oddest damned thing she'd ever seen.

It looked like rock. But it was…well, spongy. She hadn't yet identified what it was and without more powerful equipment, it would be nearly impossible to tell. If they hadn't struck the pressurized pocket of liquid, she would have been going over the entire core for the next two days. As it was, she needed to focus on the actual liquid. That's what Calhoun and PPE wanted to hear about.

Calhoun visited twice and both times she told him to get the hell out. She didn't like people hovering over her while she worked. That went double for Thomas. She knew he was excited to see what they'd brought up from the well, but he could wait until she had some definitive answers.

With that in mind, a beaker of black liquid sat atop the steel table. She'd already taken a few drops and run them through a gas chromatograph. When she'd looked through the readings, her breath had stopped and her white teeth flashed in a large grin.

She fought the urge to call in Calhoun; he was going to freak out when he saw what she had. But until she finished studying the oil beneath the microscope, she wasn't going to get his hopes up.

The chromatograph was simply the first step in the process. The mud log report had indicated the liquid was oil, but it was impossible to simply look at the mud and know you had anything more than that. She needed to determine the sweetness of the crude.

Rigs didn't have large labs; they didn't need them. Exploration rigs tended to have better facilities, but they were still too small to do precise analysis. Exploratory wells were just that. If the samples from a core looked good, then the drill would drop the bit through the drill string back down to the spud and bring up enough oil to fill a small barrel. Four gallons was all that was needed. Because of the anomalous geology of the drill site, Leaguer had more than enough oil to ship out to Houston for in-depth study.

Proper petrochemical labs usually take a week or two to complete any kind of serious analysis, but PPE had already paid for expedited service. When the barrel arrived at its destination, the lab would drop everything and analyze the molecular structure and provide a chemical breakdown. Their report would be forwarded to PPE and Calhoun's team.

Before email, it could take up to a month for a finished report to reach the field. By then, an exploratory rig would have punched at least three more test wells and shipped their contents to the same lab.

Since the rig had satellite communications, the moment the chemists in Houston did their jobs, the results would be transmitted to Leaguer. But that was still at least a few days away—the sample had to be taken off the rig by helicopter or ship and then flown all the way to the lab. Technology might have made information gathering near instantaneous, but it had yet to create a teleporter.

That meant her analysis was all they'd have to go on. She checked the digital timer on the desk and then stared up at the oil. Particles floated on top of the thick dark liquid. Looking at the black wasn't going to be enough; she needed to figure out what those particles were.

Shawna rose from her chair and stretched. Between taking apart the cores and setting up the equipment, she hadn't left the lab in nearly seven hours. Her stomach was a growling, starved carnivore. Unlike Standlee, she didn't have a cache of snacks. When you were working with chemicals, having food or drink around was a bad idea.

She grabbed the thermometer lead and placed it in the beaker. The digital readout immediately jumped to 75°. She smiled and removed the lead. *Time for the fun,* she thought.

A gleaming gravity stand composed of a series of funnels and filters sat on one of the large tables. She used a pair of large forceps to pick up the beaker. As carefully as she could, she walked to the gravity stand and slowly poured the liquid into the first funnel.

Shawna might not have a degree in chemistry, but part of her focus had been on Petrosciences. That meant studying chemistry and a lot of it. Calhoun had no doubt hired her all those years ago for more than just geology. Like this, for instance. She could separate the oil, measure its gravity, and analyze enough of it to determine if the crude was acceptable for the refining operations their employer had in mind. All oil was "commercial" so to speak, but heavy oil or reserves that had a high concentration of water were more difficult to refine. With the continual rise in the price of oil, however, more and more companies were interested in the heavier and nastier stuff. Refining heavy oil was more expensive, but if the price was high enough, it was worth it.

She stepped away from the stand and pulled off her gloves. They were heat-resistant and protected her from any kind of chemical residues left by the mud. If that stuff got on your skin, it was bad news. A rash was the best case scenario. Third degree chemical burns were common when the chemicals were mishandled.

The liquid burbled from one stage of filters to another. She watched the dark liquid as it flowed through the clear glass tubes. Its color was changing. After the second filter, it was no longer jet black, but a sweet mocha brown. Shawna grinned. A few more minutes passed and the liquid poured into the return beaker. Her smile widened. After passing through the filters to remove the mud fluid, the oil was a healthy amber instead of midnight black.

Shawna stifled a yawn as she waited for the dripping to stop. With a sigh, she pulled on the heavy gloves and took the beaker she'd originally had the oil in and placed it beneath the gravity stand's spigot. Any remaining oil in the system would drip harmlessly into the already contaminated beaker. She took the beaker with the filtered oil to a clear table against the wall.

First, let's take a picture, she thought. She moved a small box in front of the glassware. Her fingers adjusted knobs on the box as she peered through a viewfinder. When the beaker was completely in view, she pressed a button. The box clicked. She smiled at it, pulled an SD card from its side, and slid it into her pocket. Once that was done, she returned the box to its spot on the table.

A hydrometer and several other measuring tools were in an organized tray with labels. She fought the urge to roll her eyes. Evidently PPE wanted to make sure its personnel knew what each instrument was. Although why any of the drilling crew would be using a hydrometer was beyond her.

She picked up the tool and ran her gloved fingers over the heavy glass instrument. It was bulbous at the end and relatively thin up top. A digital screen stared at her from the end in her hands. She slowly lowered the bulbous end into the liquid and waited.

The hydrometer's digital readout blinked as it measured the sample's water content. She didn't manage to choke off the next yawn and the sound echoed in the relatively small lab. After a moment, the digital readout went blank. She cocked an eyebrow at it and then a series of numbers replaced the empty space. "No fucking way," she said aloud.

Water content was commonly found in samples. Very common. Therefore, a bit of guesswork was involved in interpreting the results of any tests. But this made no sense. "10 ppm," she said aloud. That just couldn't be.

Oil always had water in it. Period. That was the rule. Oil was viscous and lighter than water. It floated atop any moisture that seeped out of the rock or sand. But this was…impossible. She removed the instrument and quickly cleaned it using the chemical bath sitting in the nearby sink. She set it aside to dry and stared at the beaker. She wasn't sure she wanted to tell Calhoun about this; he wouldn't believe it.

The black liquid defied the rules of geology and of oil itself. Where the fuck was the water? There had to be more to this.

As she watched the beaker, she noticed a tiny air bubble pop to the surface. Her mouth opened and then closed. *Air bubbles? In oil?* Her heart beat fast in her chest. She didn't know why she was suddenly so afraid of what was in the beaker, but she was. The reptilian part of her brain was telling her to leave the room and leave NOW. In the past, Shawna had obeyed that ancient holdover from evolution. But not this time. Instead, she walked to the stand next to the specimen table and grabbed a filtration mask off a hook.

With her hair tied back, she was able to put the mask on and tighten the straps without too much pinching. She kept her eyes on the beaker as her fingers felt for the tabs on the straps. Once it was secure, she felt better. But not as good as she felt when she put on the safety glasses.

She should have put them on in the very beginning. It was, after all, procedure. But she was always careful. Now she was scared and wanted a bio-hazard suit.

Hands shaking as she approached the beaker, she forced herself to calm down. *It's just oil*, she told herself. *Maybe a little odd, but it's just a fucking collection of hydrocarbons. Get over it!* But that reptile part of the brain wouldn't stop screaming at her.

Once her hands steadied, she picked up the beaker using forceps and carried it to the small centrifuge-in the corner. It was filled with test tubes. She grabbed a small glass funnel and placed it inside the mouth of the closest tube. Using the forceps, she lifted the beaker inch by inch until the amber liquid poured out. When the tube was little more than half full, she righted the beaker and placed it back on the table.

Her deft fingers arranged the other tubes to counterbalance the sample's weight. If you didn't do that, the centrifuge would wobble and possibly break the glassware. She put a top on the tube and then pushed the hood down over the apparatus.

She swiveled the knobs to 2k revolutions per minute, set the timer for 2 minutes, and started the machine. It whirred and spun. The noise wasn't uncomfortable, but it was loud enough to obscure quieter sounds. She didn't hear the burbling and bubbling inside the gravity stand. Nor did she see more air bubbles pop inside the beaker.

Shawna waited while the centrifuge did its work. Her stomach continued its insistent grumble and she continued to ignore it. She could feed herself once the centrifuge was done. *Just a couple of more tests,* she told it. Her stomach didn't care.

While the seconds ticked down, she stared over at the LCD display hanging from the east wall. The screen was split into four equal sections. In the upper right, a camera view of the rig deck showed the men inspecting the pipe stands. Next to it was a view of the ocean waves. They were a little choppy today. The lower screens had a satellite view of the ocean weather report.

She didn't like the look of that storm to the south. When they'd barreled through it on the supply ship, it had been a severe annoyance, but not hazardous. 48 hours later, it seemed to have grown. No mention of tropical storm winds. Yet.

The centrifuge engine ceased its growling and the whir slowly dissipated as it spun back down. The digital timer beeped twice. She turned back to look at the machine and sighed.

As she reached the centrifuge, the loud hum of the air conditioner stopped. She guessed the thermostat was happy with the temp. She put her gloved fingers on the edge of the centrifuge hood and then stopped. It was barely audible, but something was crackling.

She looked around the room for the source, but only saw the test equipment. It sounded like acid chewing through something. She stared at the decanters on the back wall. The liquids were still in their beakers, deathly silent, and inert. The noise stopped. Shawna took one last look around and then focused her attention on the centrifuge.

Stifling another yawn, she lifted the hood and stared down at the test tube. She carefully unlocked it from the compartment and squeezed on the removal tool. The metal forks slid past one another and created a gap larger than the cylindrical Pyrex specimen. She released the pressure and the grips locked around the glass. She lifted it up into the light.

The oil was an even deeper shade of amber than before. She stared at the bottom. There were no particulates. There was no stratification. The oil was absolutely free of sediment.

That wasn't right. At all. Oil always had water. Oil always had sediment. Crude was never just crude. A bubble popped inside the test tube. She jumped, the tool still in her hands. The liquid tried to slosh out of the glass, but didn't. Her heart thumped in her chest and blood pounded in her ears.

Treating the test tube like an explosive, she walked to the west wall and placed it in a test stand. She squeezed the tool and the tube slipped into an open slot. She stepped away from it. Searing halogen light blazed down from lamps above the tube stand. Another bubble popped from the tube. Then another. And another.

The oil sizzled as though carbonated. She walked backwards, eyes riveted on the sight. *What is this shit?*

She was afraid to go near it. Shawna looked around the lab. A metal tray hung from the wall. It was too big, but it would have to do. She pulled it from the wall and placed it atop the tube stand.

The metal covered it fine, but looked as though it might slide off the stand. Shawna walked to the lab's hatch. She stripped out of her safety gear and threw it to the floor. She wasn't coming back to the lab. Ever. Her fingers found the hatch handle and she opened it. Eyes still fixed on the metal tray, she stepped backward into the hall and slammed the hatch behind her.

#

The crew had stowed the pipes. The crew was cleaning out the mud traps. The crew, *his* crew, was kicking ass. Vraebel was happy.

Once the drill string had been brought up, he'd handed over the bridge. He'd been awake for 20 hours and it was time to sleep. Although he was the rig chief, he was supposed to work the same 12 hour shifts as his crew. That was company policy.

For the first few days of drilling, Vraebel found it impossible to rest. The bridge was where he wanted to be to handle any emergencies. His former boss had told him that he had to learn to let go and trust those he hired. Which is why he spent so much time finding the best people possible. But as far as letting it go? That was still a work in progress.

Down in the lab, Sigler would be examining the drill core and analyzing the liquids they'd pulled up. Gomez was going over inventory reports and inspecting the equipment. His men, those that were on duty, would be doing the same. Any anomaly, no matter how small, was to be reported immediately. Vraebel had made that clear to the men over and over again.

All it took was one drill string section with a crack or metal fatigue to destroy an entire drilling operation. Pressure, mud, the actual rotation of the drill bit, all those different variables put a lot of stress on the steel pipe sections. Each of the 600 plus tubes had to be inspected and reinspected after every drilling event.

Production rigs carried a large number of spares. Sections on the drill string would eventually weaken and have to be replaced. A small exploratory rig like Leaguer? Not as many spares as he'd like. But they could always get more from the supply ship. And if they had to wait a week or two to get them, tough shit. PPE would wait. The operation could wait.

Companies like BP didn't perform their due diligence and people died as a result. Vraebel wasn't ever going to let that happen, regardless of the deregulation Congress constantly pushed through. The lobbyists could go fuck themselves—this wasn't just a business; people's lives were at stake.

He blew steam off his coffee. The sun was high in the sky, but obscured by fluffy clouds. He'd checked the weather from his stateroom the moment he'd regained consciousness. The storm that had been cycling near the coast was still there. It was pounding the outer islands, but was no threat to them. Yet.

Every hour the storm existed was another hour for it to shift and drift toward them. If the waves rose high enough, the relatively small rig would start moving around. Rigs were built to survive that kind of turmoil, but undersea volcanic activity or hurricanes had a habit of damaging them. Leaguer, built with the latest safety and semi-submersible technology, was capable of surviving fifty foot waves. Beyond that? Who could say?

He tapped the keyboard on his console and pulled up reports. Gomez and his men were reading the RFID tags on the pipe inspection apps and putting in data. Vraebel remembered when all this was done with paper and pen and damn, but that was messy. Thankfully, technology had made the process a lot easier. But every report had to be checked; the human capacity for mistakes would always exist.

Gomez had marked a pipe section as suspect and put it aside. According to the inventory, he'd already had a replacement pulled and reinspected. They had ninety-nine spares now. Vraebel wondered how many they'd have by day's end.

He sipped his coffee. An email alert popped up on his screen. He read the summary and sighed. It was from Executive VP Simpson. He clicked the mouse and the email filled the screen. He read it and sipped more coffee. Simpson had gotten his message regarding the first test well and wanted Sigler's report as soon as she was done. "Micro-manage-itis," he said to the empty bridge.

Of course he'd send the goddamned reports when they were done. What did the asshole think Vraebel would do? Sit on them? The exec also wanted to know when they were going to send the samples to Houston.

"As soon as fucking possible," he said aloud and drank the rest of his coffee. Fighting the urge to send a flame-mail to the big boss, he clicked "reply" and started crafting something more diplomatic. "It'll be done when it's fucking done" was not an appropriate response, no matter how badly he wanted to write it.

When he finished the email and clicked "send," he leaned back in his chair and tried to calm himself. Between Calhoun's team and Simpson breathing down his neck, he was going to get an ulcer.

"Gomez to chief," the radio growled.

Glad for the distraction, *any* distraction, he pulled the mic from the clip. "Chief here. Over."

There was a slight pause. "The team has finished the reports on the mud trap and recycle. We have another two-hundred pipes to inspect. Over."

Vraebel nodded to himself. "I'll check out the reports on the mud. Take your time on the pipes and be sure. Over."

"Understood. Over and out."

He put the mic back on the clip. Gomez was a good man. Vraebel was damned glad he'd found him. It had required a hell of a job offer from PPE to get him off contract, but Gomez had agreed to come work as an actual employee.

The oil biz was a mess. Job-jumping was a constant threat even with lower-paid workers. For the best people in the industry? It was more dire. PPE knew that. That's why they made sure their people were highly paid and well taken care of. That included benefits, stock options, bonuses, paid vacation, you name it. Although they were hourly employees, they might as well be on salary.

Vraebel stood from his chair and headed back to the coffee machine. He slotted a pod, put the mug beneath the machine, and pressed the button. The machine hummed as it turned water into steam and spewed it through the grounds. The smell was glorious. His doctor had told him drinking so much coffee was hell on his kidneys, but Vraebel had never had a problem. And without coffee? Man, he'd just cease to function.

There was a knock on the closed hatch. Vraebel looked toward the door and cocked an eyebrow. "Come in," he drawled.

The hatch opened and Calhoun walked in. The older man was dressed in a pair of heavy khakis and a dark blue PPE work-shirt. Sweat had already blossomed beneath his armpits. The rig might be air-conditioned, but that didn't seem to assuage the heat. Not for Calhoun, anyway.

"Morning, Martin," Calhoun said.

Vraebel smiled and looked at the dive watch on his wrist. "Morning? I think it's afternoon."

The engineer grinned. "Well, it's always morning somewhere."

Vraebel rolled his eyes. "Right." He nodded to the coffee machine. "Want an espresso or something?"

Calhoun shook his head. "Already had my fill of coffee this morning. Going to head to the commissary and get some iced tea. Much better for the afternoons."

"Right," Vraebel said. "What can I do for you?"

The engineer's grin faded into a thin line. Vraebel could tell the man was about to say something unpleasant. Or something he *thought* Martin might object to.

"With your permission," he said, "Standlee would like to send another AUV out. We need to see if we can clear up some topographic anomalies."

Martin's stomach filled with acid. He'd known this was going to come up, or hoped it would. Now it was time to lower the boom. "Considering an AUV was launched this morning, without my knowledge, I assume you're talking about another one?"

Calhoun blinked. A sheepish grin filled his face. "You were sleeping. Catfish and JP decided not to wait."

The coffee machine burped one last gout of steam and Vraebel pulled out the mug. His eyes bore into Calhoun's. "I'd thought we had this conversation and that you agreed there wouldn't be anymore cowboy shit."

"We had, we did, we do," Calhoun said. "But this is important."

Vraebel sipped the black liquid. His tongue burned, but he didn't care. "I'm sure it is. But we have procedures for a reason, Thomas. And your boys have to follow it."

"Agreed," Calhoun said after a pause. He rubbed a hand through his thinning hair. "And I'll make sure—"

"I'm getting tired of you saying you'll make sure and then not doing it, Calhoun." Vraebel's easy grin disappeared. "So do me a favor. Stop talking, start doing. I don't want anyone injured on this rig. Not my people," he said pointing to himself, "and not yours." His index finger stabbed in Calhoun's direction. "And I will go to Simpson if this shit continues."

Thomas chewed his lower lip and sighed. "Understood."

"Bullshit," Vraebel said. "Stop grin-fucking me and make it happen."

The engineer's face flushed. Vraebel knew he'd just tweaked the man, and that wasn't a good idea, but fuck it. The asshole needed to know where he stood.

"Just stay out of my team's way, Martin. I'll do my best to 'make it happen.'"

Vraebel smiled. "Anything else?"

"No," Calhoun said in a clipped voice. "I think we understand one another."

Vraebel nodded to the man. "Then if you don't mind, I have reports to read."

Calhoun turned on his heel and lumbered out the hatch. Vraebel let out a deep breath. His body tingled with stress. Since Simpson thought he was a god, fucking around with Calhoun could be bad. He could have been more diplomatic about the AUV bullshit, but it never seemed to end. Standlee's pet project was out of control and he was the only one that seemed to see that. *Topographic anomalies? My pimpled ass,* he thought. Standlee just wanted to play with his toys.

He walked back to the captain's chair and rested the coffee mug on the console. Reports to read. Reports to study. Reports to double check. It was going to be a damned long afternoon. He shoved thoughts of Calhoun and Standlee out of his mind and began to read.

#

Six hours. From the time he lay his head on the pillow to the time his eyes popped open, only six hours had passed. For Catfish, that was a record when he was working. And it seemed like he was always working.

He rubbed his eyes as he stared at the monitors. On the far left, he had a window filled with code. On the far right? Diagnostic reports. The two middle screens had held his attention for the past half hour. He popped the top of the aluminum can and gulped. The energy drink's signature buzz on his tongue sent a flame of heartburn into his stomach. He hated the shit, but it was the only thing that got him through the long hours.

After a fast breakfast of oatmeal and greasy bacon and eggs (had to stay regular!), he made his way to the drilling office and plopped down into the chair. His hair was a tangle of curls and knots and he just didn't give a shit. He hadn't even bothered tying it up. Vraebel would have a shit attack if he saw long hair unchecked by a cap, braids, or a hair tie. But fuck him and his stupid goddamned rules.

JP had dropped AUV 5 back in the water as soon as Catfish finished updating its mission parameters. Instead of taking Catfish along for the ride, JP had taken another diver with him. Something about rig solidarity. He was pretty sure that had been Calhoun's idea. JP and Catfish were very much alike when it came to meeting new people and trusting them—they didn't. The fact JP had volunteered to take one of Vraebel's crew along for the ride had to be the result of Calhoun. Well, whatever. Calhoun was there to engineer and keep the peace. The old man was doing his thing. Now it was time for Catfish to do his.

AUV 5 sent reports up to the drilling office until it dove below the 18k range. Once it reached lower midnight, there was little for him to do besides pore over the code, examine the diagnostics, and wait. Oh, and answer email. And that's what had him staring at the screens.

Yesterday, he'd sent pictures of the tube worm beds scattered throughout the trench to Dr. Macully. Macully, friend and occasional lover, was a marine biologist. Since he spent most of his time deep ocean drilling, she always wanted pics from his drones. His machines had captured pictures of five new species of deep sea fish in the last three years. Macully wrote them up, categorized them, and published papers on them. When he was in San Diego, she fed his stomach, and then fed his body. She was a sweet woman.

When he'd opened the email client after AUV 5 passed lower midnight, it had dinged four times. Sure it was more bullshit from Vraebel, or Calhoun requesting reports, he'd sighed and started to read. But the subject lines did more than catch his attention; they made his nerves sizzle.

Macully had analyzed the tube worm beds. All four of the new emails were from her and each was more frantic than the last. She was freaking out over the size and construction of the tube worm beds. Over and over again, she mentioned new species and possible evolutionary throwbacks. In the last email, she'd sent pictures of the oldest known tube worm species and laid it out next to the pictures AUV 5 had taken. Then, she'd superimposed the two.

Standlee wished he'd seen the emails before he sent the AUV back into lower midnight. If he had, he would have ordered it to do more than just take surveys.

The superimposed photos that Macully had put together made it pretty clear what she was so excited about. Normal tube worms congregated together in a patch. There was little to no gap between the bases of the worms. They did this for protection. If a single tube worm was found by itself, predators would quickly consume it. As with most herd species, there was safety in numbers.

But the ones AUV 5 had discovered were different. Instead of growing from a bed in a clump, the new worms were, well, laid out in a precise circle. The middle of the bed? Completely exposed.

Macully had never seen anything like that and according to the email, she'd stayed up all night trying to find an example. But no known species of tube worms acted like that. In addition, the worms seemed longer. Because of the blue-light photography, it was difficult to tell what color they were. But instead of the beige hue worms usually had, these looked, well, strange. They were multi-colored and not in any way uniform.

But the strangeness didn't end there. Instead of being near perfect cylinders, each worm's end was flattened like an eel. Catfish tapped a finger on the keyboard's edge. Macully wanted more pictures. Close-ups. And if possible, a sample.

Standlee leaned back in his chair, swallowed another gulp of the cherry-flavored heart-burn generator, and glared at the screen. *Sample? How the fuck am I going to get a sample?*

The hum of the computers in the drilling office were comforting. The ambient noise allowed his brain to race and dream. He closed his eyes and let the sound inundate him. Until Harobin or Shawna showed up, he had the place all to himself. He'd even killed the lights. He could sleep here without worrying about noise from the off-shift rig crew or the sound of clanking from the rig floor.

He tried to imagine a creature's life at the depth of 30,000 feet. Tube worms were eating machines. Nothing more than that. They lived in darkness, died in darkness, and they'd never known any kind of light until the last fifty years when humans started to explore the deeps with robotic assistance.

Did they think? Did they "see?" He didn't even know if they had nerves with which to feel. Did anyone know?

Questions for Macully. Eyes still closed, a slow grin spread across his face. "You want a sample?" he said aloud. "I'll get you a sample."

He opened his eyes and brought up the AUV design drawings. The two middle screens lit with the schematics. His grin widened into a ferocious smile.

When he and Calhoun designed the AUVs, they hadn't made them specifically for oil exploration. That was their primary goal, of course, but Calhoun insisted they think bigger. Why design a different AUV for each type of sensor? Why wouldn't you make those pluggable and extensible? Just like code?

His AUV toy box had a number of implements he could attach in order to perform specific tasks. One of them? Soil collection. A small shovel with jaws that screwed into the AUV below the ballast tanks. The AUV could sweep low over a field of sand, extend the shovel, calculate the size of the sample, and then retract the tool before rising to the surface.

All he had to do was write a new program. Instead of the AUV sweeping up sand from the ocean floor, it could ride at a good speed through the top of a tube worm clump and use the shovel as a blade. He couldn't guarantee it would manage to collect a sample, but the chances were good something would get captured. He could change the weight algorithm too. Instead of ensuring it had so many ounces of particulate matter, he could program it to require a minimum weight and density before the AUV knew its mission had been accomplished.

With all the damned problems AUV 5 had had, it was by far the worst candidate for the job. He'd have to work on using one of the other metal fish to carry it out. He had four candidates. Shouldn't be too much of a problem.

He'd have to get Calhoun's permission, of course, and probably that prick Vraebel's as well, but it wouldn't add any kind of risk. Worst case scenario? The AUV returned with nothing or burned out the retraction motor in the shovel. It could get trapped in the worm bed too, but he doubted that was a real danger.

Rather than talk to Calhoun about it, he started going over the specifications of the shovel rig. He needed to recalculate the physics and then work out how to code it. Macully might have some idea of the kind of resistance the shovel would meet.

He replied to her email and told her his plan. With any luck, she'd see it in the next couple of hours and send back word on the strength of tube worm flesh. Whatever calculation she came back with, he'd double it. Just to be sure.

#

Belmont, the other diver, was yet another humorless asshole. JP was beginning to wonder if everyone Vraebel hired was as tightly wound. Perhaps the rig chief was only interested in hiring the most insufferable shit-heads in the industry.

Ukrainian, Belmont had never been in the US military. The man's English was excellent, but his accent set JP's nerves on end. Belmont's hair wasn't much longer than Harvey's, but it actually had a "style." Grease-ball-gangster were the words that came to mind the moment he'd met the other diver.

Instead of having a nice chat comparing war stories, Belmont had hardly spoken or shown any interest in conversation. The man only replied when forced and in as few words as necessary. JP didn't think Belmont knew how to smile, much less what a joke was.

But he had to admit Belmont was a professional. Instead of having to worry about some newbie getting tangled up in the lines as they lowered the AUV, or banging their head on the ballast tanks, Belmont had treated the metal robot with care and caution.

When the AUV sped away and headed for the bottom of the ocean floor, Belmont had climbed back into the Zodiac, taken off his mask, and stared at JP. "Is anything else necessary?" he'd asked.

Harvey had forced a grin. "You handled that well. Most people—"

"I am not most people," the man had replied in a robotic voice. "Is there anything else?"

JP had shaken his head. "No. Time to get back to the rig."

Belmont had nodded and headed to the boat's bow. He stripped off his gear, stowed it, and then sat in his wetsuit on the recessed bench. With a sigh, JP had started the engine and drove the Zodiac back to the rig.

After a shower and a gear inspection, he'd headed to the commissary. Catfish hadn't woken him up soon enough to get a bite before dropping the AUV in the water. After last night's work-a-thon to recover all the AUVs and get them recharging, Harvey had been exhausted. The moment his head hit the pillow, he'd been out like a light.

Stomach rumbling, the commissary looked like a glutton's delight. It was still early enough in the morning for the omelette station, not to mention the waffle irons and pancakes. JP had been on rigs where there were eight chefs in total. Four were on duty at any one time. While two served or cooked short-order, the others were prepping or cooking the good stuff. But mornings? Mornings were for the typical American fat bastard diet. Fuck a bunch of Dennys—JP would opt for a rig commissary on any morning.

A small rig like Leaguer had a commissary crew of four, meaning only two of them were on duty. JP had thought that would lead to problems getting meals, but as with everything else, Vraebel's hires were excellent at what they did.

He stood in front of the omelette station for a total of twenty seconds before the chef appeared. Cups of crumbled fried bacon, shredded cheese, freshly diced vegetables, including jalapeños, and ham were spread out in front of the chef. Harvey ordered a four-egg omelette with everything. Unlike the rest of the rig crew, the chef not only had a personality, but smiled. It was a refreshing experience.

After devouring his breakfast and two cups coffee, he leaned back in his chair and rested. He'd probably eaten too much, but fuck it. He was going to get on the submersible crew for Vraebel and spend time inspecting the rig's under structure. Until Catfish had something else for him to do, he'd just end up pissing off the rig chief.

Harvey had been somewhat surprised when Calhoun had knocked on his door that morning. The older man was dressed in his trademark khakis and long-sleeve shirt. JP had been dreaming about some horrible creature lurking in the ocean. After all his years diving, it was a pretty common dream.

JP had scratched his nuts through his boxers and loosed a huge yawn. Calhoun had shaken his head.

"Time to wake up," the man said.

"Uh-huh," JP said in sleep-gravel voice. "Is the goddamned rig on fire?"

Calhoun grinned. "It's 0900, JP. Catfish wants AUV 5 in the water."

A groan escaped the diver's lips and the fuzz of sleep left his brain immediately. "Shit. Didn't realize it was that late."

"Not like you to oversleep," Calhoun said.

"No. No, it's not. I'll, um," he looked down at his Oscar the Grouch boxers, "get dressed. After some breakfast—"

Calhoun shook his head. "No time. We need to get the fish in the water. ASAP."

Harvey's eyebrows scrunched together. "Why? What's the—" He paused when he saw the stern look on his boss's face. "Shit. We're doing another end-run."

"Right," Thomas said. "I doubt Vraebel will have a problem with this, but I'd rather put it down to miscommunication and frantic thinking."

"Uh-huh," JP sighed. "So is Catfish waiting for me?"

Calhoun's sour visage melted into an easy grin. "Yes. But not at the platform. He's at his console."

"So, what, I'm going out by myself?"

"No. I want you to take one of Vraebel's people with you," Calhoun said.

"Shit." JP ran a hand through his close cropped hair. "Why?"

"Because it's a good idea. That's why. Also, I want you to volunteer to help inspect the rig's sub-structure."

"Ah," JP said. Calhoun was a devious bastard. "You're going to smack around his authority and use me as an olive branch."

"If it comes up," Calhoun chuckled. "I've no doubt he's going to have his panties in a twist. But he's not awake. So, he'll have to deal with it."

JP shook his head. "You sure like playing with fire."

"Get moving," Thomas said. He looked down at the boxers. "Stay Drunk and Grouch On," he read. "Definitely sounds like you." Calhoun tipped an imaginary hat and disappeared from the doorway as if he'd never been there.

JP didn't want to know how Calhoun's conversation with Vraebel went. He was sure Belmont had reported the unauthorized trip out on the water. The diver seemed enough of a "company man" to scream bloody murder over it. Which begged the question—why had he agreed to go?

JP was going to need a nap and soon. He doubted Vraebel would pass up the chance to hound and bully one of Calhoun's team. And since JP was an employee of PPE like the rest of the rig crew, Vraebel was certainly within his rights. Calhoun had made it clear that while they *were* PPE employees, Simpson had promised them a bit of freedom from the bureaucracy. Vraebel hadn't gotten that message. Or maybe Simpson had been too chicken shit to explain it. Either way, he'd have to don a wet-suit and get his ass low in the water. He wondered if any sharks were down there. If so, he'd have to inspect more than the rig's substructure.

#

The drilling office was still quiet. Catfish was checking his programming, running simulations, and more or less ignoring everything that was going on around him. Calhoun was glad for that.

He sat in a chair next to Shawna. Her screens were filled with chemical analysis and figures regarding gravity, humidity, and viscosity. When he'd searched for her in the lab, he'd found it a mess. The gravity stand was still foul with oil, beakers were unwashed, and the centrifuge hood was raised. A metal tray covered the test tube stand. Somewhat angry, but more confused than anything else, he'd walked from the lab and headed back up to the crew quarters. When he'd reached her room, he banged on the door with his huge hands. It had opened slowly. Shawna stared out through the crack.

Calhoun took a deep breath and forced himself to keep his voice barely above a whisper. "Would you like to explain to me why you're not in the lab? And why it looks like a classroom of second graders have been playing with a chemistry set?"

She opened her mouth to reply, and then swung the door wide. She stepped out of the way and motioned him in. Eyebrows raised, Calhoun had walked across the threshold. She closed the door behind him without a word.

Her room was spotlessly clean. Even her damned shoes had been pushed beneath the bed. This was the Shawna he knew. OCD about cleanliness, always looking fresh and ready to attend a dinner party or a prom, Shawna was not one to look disheveled.

The room may have been squared away, but Shawna wasn't. Her hair was a mess, eyes puffy, and she wore nothing but a long t-shirt and a pair of gym shorts. Her skin was red and raw as if she'd spent an hour beneath a hot shower head. He'd never seen her like this.

"Shawna? You okay?" he asked. When he saw the look on her face, a tremble of fear mixed with volcanic rage hit his stomach. His fists clenched. "Did one of the crew do something?"

She shook her head. "No, Thomas. Nothing like that. It's okay." She touched his shoulder and his fists unclenched at once.

"Then, what the hell is going on?" He pointed to the bed and she sat. He pulled a chair from the desk in the corner, flipped it around, and sat with his arms dangling over the chair's back. "Let's talk about it."

Shawna rolled her eyes and then chuckled. Her voice was small like a child's. "Can't explain it," she said. "I—" She stopped and then shook her head. "It's stupid," she giggled. "And you're going to fire me."

Calhoun grunted. "I don't see that happening. So why don't you tell me what's going on?"

She looked up at the ceiling and wiped at her face. Calhoun wasn't certain, but he thought she'd wiped away a tear. When her eyes drifted back to stare at him, they were red and watery. "I've never seen—" She paused. When she tried to continue, it looked as though her throat had vapor-locked.

"Take a deep breath," he smiled. "Let's start this way. What's the water content of the oil?"

"10 ppm," she said immediately.

"Gravity?"

"45 API."

Calhoun blinked. He'd planned on asking the stats to get her brain going again, but now his was stuck. "Wait. You said 10 ppm of water?"

She nodded. "I ran the tests three times. I know it's still guess-work but—"

"Bullshit," he said.

She laughed. "That's what I thought you'd say, Thomas."

"And the gravity? There's no way in fucking hell it's that."

"I know," Shawna threw up her hands. "I've got the analyses at my computer if you want to look at them."

"Is there any way you made a mistake?" he asked.

"Sure, of course." Her fingers clasped together in a giant fist. "But I ran them multiple times and followed the same procedure every time. The numbers are consistent."

"What about sulfur?"

Shawna shrugged. "Didn't get to run that test. But I can tell you this much—it doesn't have a smell."

Calhoun's mind raced. The figures she cited weren't just improbable, they were damned near impossible. Oil without the stench of aromatics? He'd never heard of crude that sweet or clean. Especially offshore. If she was right, they'd struck more than a gold mine. It might as well be an ocean floor filled with diamonds. "That's, um, that's incredible."

She nodded. "That's not all." She stood from the bed, walked to the porthole, and looked out over the ocean. "There's something in the oil, Thomas."

"Well, yeah, I expected that." He turned his head and felt like a lech. He could see her perfectly shaped ass through those shorts. "What's the ratio?"

Shawna shrugged. "Didn't finish the analysis."

Thomas raised an eyebrow. "You didn't?"

She turned to him and leaned back against the bulkhead. "No." She laughed and her voice shook. "I got a little wigged out."

"Wigged?"

"It's stupid," she said. "It's a fucking hydrocarbon and it freaked me out!"

Calhoun flinched in his chair. He'd never seen her act like this. Cursing? Yelling? What the hell was going on here? "Shawna, calm down."

"I am calm," she said. "I can't explain it. It makes no sense."

"Okay," he said and stood. "Get dressed. You need a spot of lunch followed by an old man's ear." He headed to the door and opened it. "I'll be waiting outside."

"Thomas, I'm not—"

"Yes," he said turning around, "you are. You are coming with me for some food and then we'll look at this together, okay?"

She opened her mouth to speak and then closed it. She managed a nod.

"Good," Thomas said. He walked out the door and closed it behind him.

He'd only had to wait a few minutes before Shawna appeared. Her hair was tousled, eyes clear, and she looked normal. Then he'd taken her to the commissary. She explained about the bubbles in the oil. He tried to follow and understand what had freaked her out so badly, but couldn't quite get a bead on it. The readings were odd, sure, and no oil he'd ever heard of bubbled without a heat source, but that was no reason for her to get so spooked.

Sigler was the best geologist/chemist he'd ever worked with. She rarely cracked jokes inside the lab and was a consummate professional. More than that, she had the same passion for her work he had for his. She was the perfect partner when it came to drilling for oil and predicting refinery needs. No one in the industry was better. So seeing her this bent out of shape was chilling to say the least.

He stared at the screen in front of them. They'd been talking over the numbers for the last twenty minutes and neither of them was smiling.

"We need to figure out what those bubbles are," Thomas said.

Her hand moved the mouse to a menu and clicked. A strangely colored image appeared on the screen. "That's a UV picture."

"Yes," Calhoun said with impatience. "You always take those. Just in case."

"Right," she said. The beaker of oil was solid black except for thousands of tiny red dots. "And what the hell are those?"

Calhoun frowned. "I have no idea. You think those are what's causing the, um, bubbles?"

She nodded. "No other explanation. But I checked for heat signatures. The oil was normal. No radiation. No other chemical markers."

He clucked his tongue. "Has to be a faulty sensor somewhere." Shawna said nothing, but tapped her fingers on the desk. Thomas knew what that meant. "Okay, spill it."

Her hand drifted to a lock of hair and pushed it away from her face. "We can test the sensors all we want. But this many failures? I don't see how that's possible."

"More possible than that," he said, index finger pointing at the UV image. "That makes no sense at all."

"The AUVs would have picked up any radiation," she said.

Catfish's head swiveled toward them. Calhoun fought a grin. Catfish always pretended to not pay attention to the conversations around him and frequently acted as though he had no idea what was going on. But the man's ears somehow managed to catch every word. "I've checked the sensor logs over and over. All five AUVs are operating fine on the sensor front."

"Even Number 5?" she asked.

Catfish nodded. "Yeah, even my problem child."

Thomas chuckled. "Okay, so we're kind of back to square one here. The downhole tools would have picked that up anyway."

"Exactly," Shawna said. She hissed through her teeth. "I just don't get it. None of this makes any sense."

Calhoun turned and faced the topographic maps of the trench pinned to the wall. "When are you going to have a new survey from AUV 5?"

"As soon as it gets back from lower midnight," he said. "I made sure that once it gets in range, it'll start squirting data. By the time it reaches the surface for retrieval, I should have the full picture."

Calhoun turned back to Shawna. "Okay, so let's stop trying to blame the readings. And start fresh."

"You mean just accept them?" she asked.

Calhoun rubbed his chin. "Yeah. So if the sensors aren't lying and your tests are as perfect as I trust them to be, then what are we looking at?"

Shawna shrugged. "Shit that's not just oil. And something no one has ever seen. I find that hard to believe."

"Remember," Calhoun said, "we've only had a lot of these sensors and technology for forty years. We've been drilling for oil a hell of a lot longer than that."

"True," she said. "But I can't believe this stuff is that isolated. I mean, it's probably all over the trench."

Calhoun blinked. "Why do you say that?"

She clicked the mouse a few times and brought up the original seismic scans. The ground penetrating waves showed an incongruous shape beneath the rock and sand. "Because we drilled here," she pointed to the far end of the shape. "And after thirty meters, we struck the black." Her index finger followed the shape. "It's shallower here, and deeper here. But it's the same. It's like there's a giant cavern beneath the surface."

Catfish laughed. "Biggest goddamned oil reserve in the world," he said. Calhoun and Shawna turned toward him. Neither of them were smiling. "Or, um, is that bad?"

"Don't know," Shawna said after a beat. "And that's what scares me."

#

Lower midnight was still. There was no current, no sign of movement. AUV 5 bounced radar down toward the ground. It didn't penetrate deep, but it wasn't supposed to; the AUV had been programmed to map the trench surface as opposed to what was beneath.

Catfish hadn't had time to add a differential algorithm against the original readings, so AUV 5 just floated along as it mapped the trench's rises and troughs. It had analyzed the dimple around the spud site and marked it as anomalous. It was the only area it knew from the original survey and it took hundreds of photos of the ten meter pucker. The sand and rock had surrounded the well-head until it was barely visible.

AUV 5 snapped pictures as it hovered a few meters above the ocean floor. It swam to and fro in tight parallel lines. When it found itself nearing tube worms, it released a bit of ballast and floated a little higher. It didn't notice the flattened worm ends reaching for it. Nor did it notice the circle in the center of each bed opening and then closing as it passed.

The photos caught glimpses, as did the video, but the AUV ignored the movements. It was too interested in the sand and rock formations. That was its job, after all.

When AUV 5 finished its survey, it emptied the right ballast, but not the left. It took photographs of the entire trench as it rose. The quality wouldn't be good enough to determine shallow rises or troughs, but it would be enough to get a good feel for the trench's over all shape. Once the video and photos were finished, it vacated the other ballast and began a quick ascent toward the sunlight.

As it left lower midnight, the tube worms stopped moving and hung limp. Their prey had left the area. Now they had to wait for more as they had for millennia.

#

Dinner was welcome. A dark gloom had replaced the light in the sky. The cloud bank spun off by the storm to the south had finally made its way offshore. Another day or two, and they might get the whole shebang, surge and all. During his time in the military, he'd sailed through plenty of storms. The rig might be small compared to the floating cities of production rigs, but it wouldn't be any worse than being on an aircraft carrier during a cat 3 hurricane.

He sat at the table next to Catfish. The tech's hair was tied back in a braid. He'd devoured an entire half-chicken and was sipping water. JP wasn't sure, but he thought Catfish was eyeing seconds as another tray of exquisitely spiced roasted chicken appeared.

Thomas and Shawna sat on the other side of the table. She had eaten slowly and quietly. Her easy laugh and trademark smile had rarely put in an appearance even while JP related the story of Belmont. He didn't quite understand what the rest of the team was so concerned about, but something was on their minds.

Before going out to capture AUV 5, JP had gone to the bridge to talk to Vraebel. The rig chief had listened to his request, told him he appreciated the heads up, and gave him permission to take Belmont and retrieve the robot. During the trip out, Belmont had been just as tight-lipped and assholish as before. JP couldn't stand the man. Which was unfortunate, because Vraebel had also approved his request to go on substructure inspection. He hadn't realized it before, but Belmont was also the diving team lead. It was going to be a long few days. If the storm came at them, the diving would have to wait. No one wanted to be in the water during twenty-foot swells.

"So," he said. All three of his team looked up from their plates to him. "Want to tell me what the fuck is going on?"

Shawna shrugged. "We told you. It's strange. Very strange."

Catfish took another sip of water, seemed to wince, and then put the glass back on the table. "Beyond fucking strange."

"I get that the oil is, well, unusual," JP said.

"Try the word 'unique,'" Calhoun said. "And that's the least of the problem."

"What problem?" JP asked. "We got a huge oil reserve down there. We didn't have any problems with the test well. The helo is on its way to pick up the sample. I mean, isn't this what we wanted?"

"And the ocean floor is changing," Catfish said.

JP blinked. "What?" He turned to his friend. "What do you mean 'changing'?"

"I mean," Catfish pushed away his plate, "our topographical survey is fucked. It's way wrong. Number 5 took a new survey. It's subtle, but it's different. Especially around the well-head."

The diver studied Catfish' face for any kind of tell. All of this had to be a joke. They were obviously fucking with him. JP broke into a giggle.

"Something funny?" Catfish asked. His face was stone.

JP's grin faded. "You're serious."

Catfish threw his hands up in the air. "That's what we're trying to tell you, asshole. This isn't some goddamned joke. Something's going on down there. Something," he pointed at Shawna and Calhoun, "they can't explain. And I sure as shit can't."

The diver locked eyes with Calhoun. "Thomas? Can't we send the maps to PPE? Ask them what their experts think?"

Thomas laughed and nudged Shawna. "She *is* PPE's expert," he said. "What you mean is sending these images back to shore for a vulcanologist to take a look."

JP's eyes widened. "Vulcan…You mean we have a fucking volcano down there?"

Calhoun shrugged. "I don't know. But magma is the only thing that makes sense to me."

Shawna shook her head. "If it was magma, our drill string would have been vaporized. Completely. There's no way it's something like that."

"Well," JP said, "then what the fuck, man? You telling me we should get the hell out of here?"

A grin slowly spread across Calhoun's face. "No. I'm telling you we need to be careful. But I don't think we're looking for oil anymore. I think we need to study this."

Catfish and Shawna both looked at him. She slowly shook her head. "I don't want to know." Her voice was barely audible amidst the noise of the other rig workers.

"Macully sent me the specs for the tube worms," Catfish said. "I'm going to send AUV 2 down tomorrow. If Vraebel allows it."

"He will," Calhoun said. "But he and I have to have a chat tomorrow. We need to be very careful on the next well."

"Wait a second," JP said. "We're going to drill again?"

Calhoun shrugged. "PPE calls the shots. And I doubt Vraebel's going to listen to us. He already thinks we're just talented shitbags that add nothing to his crew. So we do our job. Let's scan the new topography and see where the safest place to drill is."

"My vote is nowhere," Shawna said. "And you can have Harobin work the next sample. I'm not going near that crap again."

The engineer glared at her and then his eyes softened. "Okay. Fair enough. You can analyze the data he gathers." Calhoun nodded to Catfish. "Get your AUV prepped for tomorrow. And you better get Number 5 and its remaining brethren ready for another drill site. Simpson is having an orgasm over our data. Regardless of the anomalies."

"Never fails," Catfish muttered.

"What?" JP asked.

Catfish glanced at Calhoun with a grim smile and then turned to the diver. "Everything's about safety, slow-going, precision, all the great grin-fuck words and phrases you can imagine. Until they see the gold staring them in the face. And then it's no holds barred fucking greed."

The diver opened his mouth to respond and thought better of it. The three members of his team had lost their fucking minds. Speaking of grin-fucking, that's exactly what he was going to do. They could go crazy over fucked up sensors and Catfish' trashed out AUV designs. He was going to dive and do his job.

#

Sleep wouldn't come. The moon light barely managed to break through the clouds. She stared up at the ceiling with open eyes. She was tired, no doubt about it, but that didn't mean she could turn off her brain.

The problem was the helicopter. It would be at the rig in the morning. Roughly forty-eight hours after it took off, the samples would get to Houston. PPE had paid the big money to expedite the sample, but it would still take at least 24 hours of non-stop work by the technicians to produce a report. It might even take two days. By then, they'd be drilling another well.

She and Calhoun had been to see Vraebel after dinner. The man was on the bridge staring out into the gloom and drinking a cup of coffee. She wondered if he ever drank anything else.

"Martin?" Calhoun asked. "You have a minute?"

Vraebel blew a cloud of steam from his coffee cup and swiveled his chair to face them. His face smiled, but his eyes didn't. "Thomas. Ms. Sigler. What can I do for you?"

Calhoun glanced at Shawna and then back at Vraebel. "I assume you saw the reports?"

The rig chief nodded. "Certainly did. I forwarded them on to Simpson and he was ecstatic. Y'all did a good job. Found the mother lode. Or at least, you will have once the lab gets a hold of the sample."

Shawna gulped. "So it's going to Houston?"

"Simpson reserved a chopper the moment he heard we had brought up a sample." Vraebel pointed at her. "You should be proud. Harobin tells me you're the best he's ever worked with. And obviously the geology was dead on."

Thomas chewed his lip. "Right." He cleared his throat. "Did you actually read the entire report, or just the statistics and chemical compositions?"

Vraebel's smile disappeared. The hard look in his eyes intensified. "I read the whole report," he said in a monotone. "And I can't tell if you people are just out to sabotage me or yourselves." He leaned back in his chair. "PPE is convinced your sensors are wrong. Maybe they were damaged in transit. Or maybe there's something down there interfering with them. Bottom line?" he said. "We don't give a shit." He smiled at Shawna. "Pardon my language."

Lips in a thin line, Thomas spoke in a clipped cadence. "The sensors are not wrong. The analysis is not wrong. We need to be careful if we're going to drill a new well. Very careful."

"Wouldn't have it any other way," Vraebel said. His smile was back and his eyes had softened. "Tomorrow we'll be setting up for another well. Do you have a mark yet?"

Calhoun and Shawna exchanged a glance. "Yeah, we do. It's the layer that's deepest as far as the rock is concerned."

Vraebel cocked an eyebrow. "Why wouldn't we go where it's thinnest?"

"I'm concerned about gas pockets." She hoped the lie sounded better than she thought it had. "We may have gotten lucky with that first well. But the pressure was pretty extreme."

The rig chief sipped his coffee and looked past them toward the topographic map on the wall. "Show me."

She stared at the map. She'd studied it for months before the rig was even constructed. She knew every line, every hump, and valley in the entire trench. Or she had. She remembered the coordinates she and Calhoun had agreed on. She stabbed a finger on the map. "Right here."

"And that's the deepest surface layer?" he asked.

"According to the surveys," Calhoun said. "Even the, um, revised survey suggests it's the deepest."

"Okay," Vraebel said. "Send the location to Gomez and he'll start prepping things." He stood from his chair and placed the coffee cup on the console. "Now if you'll excuse us, Ms. Sigler, Mr. Calhoun and I need to have a private word."

She'd stepped out of the hatch and closed it behind her. After a few moments, it opened and Thomas stepped into the hallway. His face was flushed and a vein in his temple throbbed. "Fucking asshole," he said as he walked toward the staterooms.

"What'd he say?" Shawna asked as she fought to keep up.

Thomas slowed his fast walk and then stopped. He turned to her, his face a rictus of anger. "I think you need to join me for a cigar."

Shawna rolled over on the bed and tried to get comfortable. Staring at the ceiling wasn't shutting off her brain. She tried to find the sounds of the ocean below the hum of the rig's generators, but she couldn't.

Every time she closed her eyes, she saw the bubble in the oil. What about the filters in the gravity stand? The dense paper had been designed to filter out anything in the liquid. But besides a film of black, they were empty. Worst of all, the porous material looked like it had been shot with BBs.

Calhoun had helped her clean the lab and it wasn't until that moment she was certain he believed everything she had said. Not only that, but he'd looked...scared. She was glad she hadn't been the only one.

They'd handled every bit of cleaning while wearing all the safety gear they could find. The idea of the black liquid touching her skin had made her shudder while they ran chemical baths and did their best to remove any trace of the black.

The beaker and the test tube? Calhoun placed those in the sample closet after putting stoppers in both. She was glad he didn't ask her to help with that task.

When she and Calhoun had reached the top of the rig so he could smoke, she'd finally relaxed. A little. The smell of the fresh ocean air and the light breeze coming from the south helped settle her nerves. In the red flashing lights of the helipad, Calhoun had lit a fresh cigar using a torch.

"What did he say?" she asked.

Thomas blew a thick cloud of smoke into the air. The breeze quickly decimated it into a memory. "He's petitioned Simpson to take me off the rig. You as well."

She blinked. "What? Why?"

A malevolent smile crossed his lips. "Because," he took another drag on the cigar, the smoke flowing out of his nostrils like an angry dragon, "he feels the two of us are no longer essential to the mission. After the report, he feels we will only serve to hinder future exploration."

"Hinder? How the fuck would we hinder?"

He laughed and another gout of smoke filled the air before disappearing into the wind. "By spreading rumors that something odd is going on down there. He assured me that he would proceed with all caution. Fortunately for him, I believe him. He won't put his men at risk if he knows there's an issue."

"There *is* an issue," Shawna said. "Shifting floor? Oil that doesn't act like oil? New species of tube worms? I mean, what the fuck else does he want?"

Calhoun placed a hand on her shoulder and grinned. "I haven't heard you curse this much as long as I've known you. Calm down, it's okay." He removed the hand and put it back on his cigar.

She didn't take offense—she knew well enough he wasn't being patronizing. And he was right. Shawna took a deep breath. "Okay. I'm cool. Now," she licked her lips, "what do we do about this?"

"Nothing," Calhoun said. "Absolutely nothing. We do our jobs, we keep investigating, and we make sure everyone's as safe as we can make them. With that in mind," he stared at the moon-glow coming through the clouds, "I want you to add something to the report before the lab in Houston gets it."

"And what would that be?"

He turned to her. "Possible biohazard or corrosive agent present."

"Biohazard?" she asked. "They're never going to believe it."

"Call it a CYA. Call it being prepared. Call it whatever. Just make sure it gets in the report," he gestured with the cigar. "I don't want them caught flat-footed."

She chuckled at that. "Aren't we already there?"

"And then some," he said. When she left him and walked back to her stateroom, he was still staring at the clouds and puffing away on his cigar.

The report, with the additions, would be ready in the morning. In order to protect PPE's proprietary mud fluid components and their drilling methodology, certain parts of the report had already been redacted. This was SOP in the industry. You only told as much as you had to, especially when exploration was involved. All labs had to sign NDA's about what they were testing and where it had come from, but that didn't mean other companies weren't willing to bribe the shit out of the staff to get a leg up.

Sliding a warning into it would be easy. She'd wake up first thing in the morning and get it taken care of. If, that was, she could sleep at all.

She closed her eyes and imagined she was on a float in the ocean. A mattress of air separated her from the cool water as the sun warmed her belly and legs. Through her imaginary sunglasses, she studied puffy clouds. In a moment, she was finally asleep.

Chapter Five

Mornings were Vraebel's favorite time of day. He loved waking up before the sun and watching it rise over the horizon as he sipped cup after cup of black coffee. When he woke that morning, however, he wasn't happy. Sleep had been fickle to non-existent.

The crazy shit Calhoun and Sigler had written in the report had haunted him all night. He was right to have emailed Simpson and let the exec know there was a possible problem aboard Leaguer. He'd taken great pleasure in pointing out it was Simpson's hires that were the problem. Simpson hadn't responded. Yet.

And that was the other problem. He'd tweaked Calhoun hard last night. Implied the engineer had gone insane, senile, or both. After the man had left the bridge and Vraebel had time to think about his words, a sinking feeling hit the pit of his stomach.

He had met masters of the "career limiting move." Those were people on the rise who shot their mouth off one too many times. Piss off the wrong exec at the top, and you'd never get promoted. If you angered enough of them, they'd give you a window seat or just find a way to fire you. He didn't know Simpson well enough to gauge how the man would react to the email. Calhoun? He didn't know the engineer at all.

At least Harvey didn't seem concerned. The man had volunteered for inspection duty. Belmont and his dive crew were scheduled to perform a routine sweep of the substructure as soon as they arrived at the second spud-site. It would take a few hours at most. As long as Harvey was off the damned rig, Vraebel could relax. A little.

But that didn't make the bad feeling go away. Ocean floors didn't move unless there was magma involved either through eruption or an earthquake. The idea the floor was shifting was insane. He kept trying to imagine it, but his brain wouldn't cooperate. It just sounded…crazy.

And the oil? *It's fucking oil!* That thought bounced in his head all night. But Sigler had looked terrified. When he mentioned they were going to drill another well, the color bleached out of her face. And when she pointed out the spot on the map last night, her hand was shaking.

The bullshit about a possible gas pocket? Yeah, he didn't believe that one either. There was a reason she and Calhoun had chosen the thickest part of the crust. He had a feeling they weren't going to tell him why.

Vraebel stood on the bridge as the morning shift appeared on deck. Gomez was out there, his bright red hard hat making him impossible to miss. The clouds had thickened overnight, and the sun was barely visible through the soup. But that wasn't going to stop the next drill string.

Shouldn't it? a voice said in his mind. *Shouldn't you just stop for a moment and take a look around?* Vraebel shook his head to clear it. Not enough sleep. He was jittery and exhausted.

The numbers from the oil analyses kept running through his mind. An impossible gravity, an impossible water content, and an impossibly sweet crude. All PPE would have to do was filter out any particulates and then they could refine to their heart's content. They sat on top of a goddamned gold mine of oil. And he, Vraebel, would get credit for bringing in the greatest find since Nigeria.

An acidic burp escaped his mouth and his stomach burned. This was bullshit. A goddamned nightmare Calhoun and Sigler had conjured to… To… To what? That's what didn't make any goddamned sense.

There was nothing for them to gain by manufacturing evidence or analyses. He could see Harvey or that asshole

Standlee setting all this in motion just to tweak him, but Calhoun and Sigler?

He took another sip from the mug and realized it was empty. Vraebel swiveled in his chair and eyed the coffee machine. Another burp of heartburn escaped his lips and he sighed. Instead of rising from his chair to get another cup, he rolled the mug between his hands.

Simpson wanted another well. Calhoun and Sigler had told him where to drill. Gomez and the crew were getting ready to build another drill string. And what was Martin Vraebel doing? Martin Vraebel was thinking about how it was a goddamned bad day to be a rig chief.

The radio squawked. "Leaguer, this is Helo 115 Heavy, over," a female voice said.

The acid in his stomach settled at once and a grin filled his face. *At least something is going right today.* He pulled the mic off the clip.

"115 Heavy, this is Leaguer, over."

There was a slight pause and then the voice came back to him, the whine of engines barely audible in the background. "Leaguer. We are thirty minutes out. Please have the cargo ready. We don't have a lot of fuel reserves. Over."

"Understood, 115 Heavy. Should we have anything else ready for you? Over."

The pilot chuckled. "Unless you have some whiskey, we'll just take the cargo. Over."

Vraebel laughed. "Sorry, 115. We have plenty of coffee and anything else you could desire, but that's about it. Over."

"Damn," the voice said. "Oh, well. I tried. Helo 115 out."

For the first time that morning, he felt as though the day might not be a complete shit sandwich. The PPE helicopter was early. That meant the oil sample would get off the rig and head to Houston sooner than he'd hoped. By tomorrow or the next day, they'd be working another drill string.

The fatigue that fogged his brain disappeared. He pulled a yellow telephone receiver from the console. He heard the buzz of the ringer on the other end until someone picked it up.

"Gomez."

"Steve? The helo is about thirty minutes out. Please check the helipad and make sure the sample is ready for them. Sounds like an immediate dust off," Vraebel said.

"Understood, Chief. We'll be ready."

"Vraebel out." He dropped the phone back in its cradle.

He looked down at the deck. Gomez was pointing at several of his men and then to the helipad. The men nodded and then made their way up the superstructure. Vraebel smiled. *Clockwork. Clockwork is how everything should work.*

He stood from the chair, turned toward the coffee machine, and then stopped in his tracks. Standlee stood at the hatch threshold. His hair was clean and tied back in a braid. For once, the man was dressed in a PPE polo shirt and a pair of faded pants. He wore boots instead of sandals.

"You have a moment, Mr. Vraebel?" the tech asked.

The rig chief forced a smile. "Sure."

Standlee cleared his throat. "I'd like permission to send out an AUV."

Vraebel watched the tech's body language. The man was obviously stressed. About what, Vraebel wasn't certain. "May I ask why?"

A slight smile tugged at Standlee's lips. "One last shake out with some new programming. Need to make sure we're ready for the next drill string."

For a moment, the only sounds in the room were the occasional bang or grind from the deck below and the air conditioning. He waited for Standlee to stammer or say something else, but the man didn't.

"Of course," Vraebel said. "I assume you'll want to go with Harvey?"

Standlee shook his head. "No, I'm needed at my console, sir."

"Okay. Tell Harvey to get with someone from Belmont's team. Let me know when it's in the water."

"Will do. Thank you," Standlee said. He left the bridge and headed down the hall at a fast walk.

Vraebel watched him go. The surly tech seemed to have had a major attitude adjustment. Calhoun must have told his team they were on the verge of being fired. Bullshit, of course. While he'd threatened to have Calhoun and Sigler removed, the rig couldn't possibly do its job without an ROV/AUV pilot. At least not in water this deep.

Stomach settled, he pushed the coffee mug into the machine and started the process. He'd thought about finding Calhoun and apologizing, or at least sending another email to Simpson to explain he'd been rash. But neither was a good idea. He'd deal with whatever Simpson threw at him. And Calhoun? If he was finally going to keep his team in line and not spread hysteria among the crew, it would be good to have the man's expertise on board. At least until they were done with two more test wells.

Vraebel walked to the situation board on the wall and studied the schedule. Gomez' crew was calibrating the sensors for the next coordinate. By that afternoon, they should have the laser guidance directed on the exact spot for the new spud site. They'd use Leaguer's thrusters to float the rig on top of the target. Once they started lowering the drill string, Standlee's ROV would hold things steady at 18,000 feet. The ROV could then make any adjustments necessary for the drill string to hit its mark.

It wouldn't take long. A day from now, maybe two, they'd be back to drilling and get another sample. In three to four days they'd probably have the report back from Houston. If it was good news, they could drill two more test wells, and send all three sample barrels back to Houston for confirmation. Once that was done, they'd know it was a gold rush. If this was a success, Vraebel could look forward to manning the production rig that would ultimately replace Leaguer.

If we make it that far, a voice said in his mind.

He ignored it. He was not, *not*, going to let those thoughts control him. He had a job to do and so did everyone else on the rig. With that in mind, he checked the time on the console. In twenty minutes or so, the helo would land. He sipped his coffee and watched as the deck crew inspected the helipad.

Clockwork, he thought.

#

Breakfast had come and gone. Catfish was alone in the drilling office. The man was rapidly going over the diagnostics for each of the remaining AUVs, and, of course, AUV 5 in particular.

The drill string would start its drop tomorrow. It would punch into the ocean floor, then the crew would drop concrete casing and a blowout preventer. Once that happened, they could put the drill bit into action and start drilling. Time to get all that going? Less than 24 hours. Catfish's AUVs would already be sweeping the ocean floor, especially around their target drill point.

Calhoun hoped Shawna's hunch was right about hitting the deepest point in the survey. The bullshit line she'd fed Vraebel about a possible gas pocket was perfect. The rig chief had looked dubious about her explanation, but didn't offer any resistance. The man was convinced anywhere in the trench would bring up a ton of oil. At least that meant he'd stay the fuck out of their way.

When Calhoun logged into his laptop that morning, an email from Simpson had been waiting for him. The engineer had sucked his teeth while he read it, but he didn't get angry. Simpson wanted to know, in his words, "what the hell is going on out there?" Calhoun wanted an answer to that question too.

He responded by explaining the concerns in the report and the fact Vraebel didn't appreciate their conclusions. He also pointed out the possibility that the oil was contaminated, but required further tests in Houston before that was proven. "I'll work with Vraebel," he typed, "until such time as my team's expertise is no longer required. I'll leave that decision to you."

Calhoun was an old hand at dealing with angst-ridden executives. Whether he was an employee or a contractor didn't matter. Eventually, the execs treated him like an indentured servant regardless of his credentials and reputation. They wanted what they wanted. For some reason, many in the industry still hadn't learned the lessons from dead rigs, dead wells, and dead people.

He paused after finishing the email. A quick browse through his bookmarks and seeing the day's news allowed him time to forget the words he'd written. Back in the old days when writing reports or responding to correspondence, he'd learned that once you typed something up, you should always take a few minutes to forget about it before putting it in the mail. It gave you time to consider your words and decide both the impact and possible ramifications. In the industry, there were always consequences to hasty remarks.

While Simpson couldn't destroy his reputation, he could certainly make sure that PPE never hired any of his crew again. Getting blackballed by one company was hardly the end of a career, especially considering every oil company out there had a shortage of staff. But Calhoun didn't want it to get that far. If PPE was successful here, it meant a lot more work and something he could retire on. That was enough to make him play nice. Or want to.

He ended up sending the email without changing a single word. Sometimes you just had to stick to your guns. Simpson would cringe when he saw the implied challenge which amounted to "if you think Vraebel can handle everything, then get us the fuck out of here already." Regardless of the problems Vraebel had with his team and their analyses, Simpson would be smart enough to realize it was a bad idea to remove them while the rig was still drilling holes.

Harobin might be okay, or even great, with the mud logging, but he wasn't a geologist or petrochemist. He had no specialties in those disciplines. Replacing Shawna would be impossible on such short notice. And Catfish? Without a pilot, his robots were useless. And while PPE might have paid for the damned things, the code and design was property of both Catfish and Calhoun.

JP was the only one they could readily replace, but that would leave the rig a diver short. It would only take a few days to get a new face with fins out to the rig, but he imagined the logistics would be a nightmare. Vraebel didn't like being stuck with people he didn't pick. Hence the tension in the first place.

When Calhoun left his room to get some breakfast, he let the thoughts slip away. Instead, he focused on the news. And the weather.

The storm to the south was moving and not in a friendly direction. It could swing up toward the rig at any time. Once that happened, life would get interesting. Vraebel seemed like a stickler for safety, but when a storm like that bore down on an offshore rig, even the most routine operations became more hazardous than usual.

With those thoughts in his mind, he entered the drilling office expecting to see Shawna. When all he saw was Catfish, he started to head back to the personnel cabins.

"Thomas?" Catfish said from his terminal.

"Yeah?" Calhoun replied.

"Can you give a look at AUV 3? I need to run more diagnostics and could use a second pair of eyes."

Heaving a sigh, Calhoun sat at the workstation next to Catfish. After logging in and capturing the diagnostic reports from the shared drive, he lost himself in the reports. He and Catfish worked side by side for over an hour. They barely spoke to one another as they poured over the information.

By the time Calhoun heard the helicopter landing on the rig, he'd forgotten all about Shawna and the report. Both he and Catfish rose from their chairs to look out the windows as the huge bird landed.

In the old days, most rigs had helipads only large enough to take on small helicopters. Since the advent of OSHA rules regarding life-flight and etc., rigs had to be designed with the larger copters in mind. If they had to travel long distances, they had to carry a lot of fuel. That meant larger machines and larger helipads. Calhoun didn't envy the poor bastards who had to give up another forty feet of space to make room for them. Rigs were packed as tight as they could be and that was a precious amount of real estate.

The helo was the size of a coast-guard chopper. Its body was blue and white with a large black PPE logo painted on the tail. As the two of them watched, a man dressed in fatigues and a blue helmet slid open the port side hatch.

Three roughnecks lifted an orange barrel into the helicopter's open door. Calhoun frowned. "Have you seen Shawna today?"

Catfish turned from the window. "Uh, no. Kind of odd actually."

"Hope she made the changes to the report."

"What changes?" Catfish asked.

Calhoun grunted. "The ones where we warn Houston that barrel might be contaminated with something."

Catfish blinked. "You really do believe that, don't you?"

The engineer stepped away from the window and walked back to the workstation. He rubbed his eyes before he crumpled in his chair. "Yeah, Craig, I do. This stuff doesn't act like oil. It doesn't read like oil. And yet the hydrocarbon concentrations are off the charts."

"When I get the reports back from AUV 2," he said, "Macully should be able to get us a bead on what's down there. Or at least what she thinks is down there."

Calhoun shook his head. "The fucking tube worms. The fucking ocean floor. The oil." He rapped his knuckles on the desk. "What the hell is going on in lower midnight?"

A cloud of vapor filled the air above Catfish's head. He was sucking on the e-cig again. "Maybe we're just hitting three for three on the weird-shit-o-meter."

"I don't think these are coincidences," he said. "Have you gone over the footage from AUV 5?"

Catfish shook his head. "I was so busy looking at the diagnostics and restructuring the program for the next drill string, I completely forgot."

"Dammit," Calhoun said. "I need to find Shawna. We need help if we're going to get everyone's eyes on this."

"Calhoun to the bridge," a voice said over the intercom. "Thomas Calhoun to the bridge, please."

"Fuck me," he breathed. "Excuse me, Craig, I have to go deal with Vraebel."

"That should be entertaining," the tech chuckled. "Want me to go find Shawna?"

Calhoun nodded. "Yeah. Get her ass in here. We need to start going over the footage."

#

When it reached the bottom of the trench, AUV 2 slowly turned toward the largest tube worm bed. During AUV 5's survey, Catfish had discovered that the animals were not only spread out along the trench, but that the beds were of increasing size as they reached the trench's middle. He had programmed AUV 2 to head for this specific area.

The shark-like robot remained 10 meters from the ocean floor as it headed across the darkness to its target. It ignored the lantern fish it disturbed. It also ignored the way the tube worms reached for it. AUV 2 had a single goal—capture a sample.

When it reached the coordinates, its cameras started taking blue-light pictures and video. The AUV floated two meters away from the bed. The tube worms slowly moved in its direction, but the robot was out of range.

The AUV paused as it slowly descended to a level just below the approximate height of the worms. It sent a command to the modified sand sampler and the sharpened metal maw opened its jaws. Level and still, the robot's brain sent a signal to the propellers. They whirred at full speed.

The worms shivered from the vibration. It was as if they knew what was coming. They tried to move, but they were too slow. The robot crashed into the bed. Its sharpened lower jaw ripped through the flesh of one of the giant stalks. The flat head of one of the worms separated from its long body and slid into the receptacle. The robot's instruments immediately noticed the weight change and slammed the jaw shut.

Writhing inside the sample chamber, the head bit and snapped. The robot shuddered and emptied its ballasts. It canted toward the top of the ocean for a split second and then it was stuck.

The other heads, four of them, had stabbed out. Maws shut on the propeller casings. They held on with incredible strength. The AUV increased power to the propellers. Jets of water slammed down to the center of the bed and the giant open eye that stared upward.

The eye closed in pain and the "tube worms" let go of their prey. The AUV slipped off course and traveled upward and to the left. Its right propeller had been damaged by the attack and was running at less than half speed.

AUV 2 compensated by throttling back on the left propeller and managed to return to its course. Below it, the ocean floor shook with anger. The tremor started beneath the bed, but slowly radiated outward across the trench. Clouds of sand and rock vibrated off the floor.

If lower midnight had had any light, the ocean floor would have been impossible to see. For ten meters above the huge trench, the water was choked with sediment. Every "tube worm" bed had opened its eyes. Their long tentacles snatched at the ocean as if to catch prey, but the movement was from anger instead of hunger.

AUV 2 sped upward from lower midnight, its seismic sensor tracking the quake. A large bubble of water followed behind it. When the robot reached a depth of eighteen-thousand feet, it squirted a data stream to the closest WiFi receivers. AUV 2 had been programmed to alert the rig if something changed on the ocean floor. AUV 2 was sounding the alarm.

#

The hallways were more or less empty. The rig's thrusters were slowly moving it toward the center of the trench. By nightfall, the crew would no doubt begin dropping the drill string. Tomorrow morning, they'd start drilling all over again. Only this time, it would go faster—PPE didn't even want a core. They wanted another taste of the black.

Catfish hurried to Shawna's room. He hated it when a rig started moving. The larger submersibles weren't nearly as bad as the small ones. The moment the ballasts started emptying, rigs sometimes rose hundreds of feet. When that happened, he always worried the damned things were going to fall over. All it would take was a large wave to knock it a few degrees. After that, recovery was nearly impossible.

He felt the rig swaying beneath his feet as it churned northward toward its target. When he reached Shawna's door, he was nervous and a little seasick. He knocked twice and waited. There was no response. Catfish sighed and double-tapped the door with the flat of his palm.

"Come on, Shawna. We need you at the drilling office." He waited another beat and felt stupid. What if she wasn't in there? Or taking a shit? Or a shower? He'd just be out here talking to himself while—

The door opened a crack. Shawna peered out at him with red, sleep-deprived eyes and a wild tangle of hair. "What?" she croaked.

Catfish blinked at her. "Um, you okay?"

"You woke me up," she yawned.

He grunted. "You do know it's almost noon, right?"

Her eyes opened wide. "What? It can't be noon."

A grin spread over his face. "Did you hide some hooch and tie one on last night? Because you know you have to share."

She shook her head. "Give me a sec. I'll bet Thomas is on the warpath."

Catfish chuckled. "Something like that. See you in the—"

The rig shook and then swayed. A klaxon alarm began its incessant grind. He steadied himself in the doorway. "What the fuck was that?"

"All hands. All hands," Vraebel's voice said through the intercom, "report to action stations. This is not a drill."

"The fuck?" Catfish asked again. That situation he'd been thinking about earlier? Yeah, the rig was listing. He was damned close to pissing his pants. "Get dressed. Calhoun's going to want to know where his team is."

She nodded and closed the door.

Catfish made himself flush with the wall as three rig crew members went running down the hall toward the rig deck. Leaguer shuddered again. Catfish started running toward the deck stairs. Several crew members were in front of him, their heavy boots clanging on the metal.

When he reached the bottom, his ears rang with the groan of heavy machinery, the shouts of men close to panic, and the klaxon. When he and JP had first stepped aboard Leaguer, Gomez had shown them the emergency exits for all portions of the rig as well as the location of the lifeboats.

Catfish had thought that part of the tour rather unnecessary since signs and maps were posted every thirty feet. Now he was glad. Paying no attention to the signs, he jogged toward the non-listing side and grabbed hold of a railing. The red and orange lifeboat was a meter away. He closed his eyes and hoped he wouldn't be getting in the damned thing.

"Ballast! Ballast fucking now!" Gomez' voice screamed from the deck. Catfish tried to see what was going on back there, but he already knew. Gomez wanted the rig crew to refill the ballast. "Port side, goddammit!"

The rig's list increased. He knew in his mind it was barely a few degrees, but that didn't make it less terrifying. Catfish closed his eyes and wished he had a cigarette. Not a goddamned fucking e-cig, but something absolutely stuffed with tar and nicotine.

A grinding noise vibrated his teeth. His feet moved on the deck and his inner ear twitched. The rig was sinking lower into the ocean on the port side. Leaguer started to right itself.

"Starboard! NOW!" Gomez shouted.

The grinding noise increased as the pumps sucked water into the tanks. He had a moment to wonder if JP and the other divers were going to be inspecting the rig's substructure tomorrow. Assuming there was a tomorrow. And then the rig started to compensate. As it sank further into the water, it became stable. Gomez whooped and Catfish heard other men shouting in victory.

"All hands," Vraebel said over the intercom, "Leaguer is safe for now. Remain at action stations until we give the all clear."

He opened his eyes and looked at his left hand. The knuckles were white. Fingers aching, he slowly loosened his grip and let out a sigh. They might be safe for now, but he wasn't moving a goddamned inch until Vraebel gave the all-clear. He stood at the railing and stared at the lifeboat for another hour.

#

Night had fallen. The rig was once again underway toward the center of the trench. Instead of emptying the ballasts and riding high in the water, Vraebel had ordered them half-full. It would be at least 3 am before they reached the spot to drill the second well.

There had been little warning of the bubble. Leaguer had been lucky. Damned lucky. If the bubble had clipped the port ballast instead of merely causing a huge wave, Leaguer would be under water.

Thankfully Gomez was good at his job. When the rig canted to starboard, filling the port side ballast stabilized the floating town. If not for that, Leaguer would have kept listing and they would have lost her.

Vraebel had kept everyone at action stations for another hour after the emergency was over. He'd ordered Terrel to man the sensor arrays and start listening for another seismic event. Once there was one earthquake, after shocks were likely. Had the rig's ballasts been full when the bubble hit, they would have barely noticed.

He sat in the drilling office while the eggheads poured over the readouts. Once he was sure the rig was in safe hands, he'd handed off the bridge to the XO and headed down to talk to Belmont. He'd ordered the diver to get his crew ready for an inspection trip as soon as Leaguer reached her position. He needed to know if the incident had weakened any part of the substructure.

Although the underwater cameras didn't show any bent or warped steel, Vraebel wasn't going to take any chances. Before they started well two, Leaguer had to have a clean bill of health. An inspection would only delay them by another hour or two. Considering what could have happened, it was a small price to pay. And to be sure the rig wasn't damaged? PPE couldn't put a price on that.

He wrote up an incident report, per regulations, and sent it off to PPE. He expected Simpson was probably freaking out back in Houston. Losing a toy this expensive was every company's nightmare. As he filled out the report, noting the time the incident began to when it ended, he made sure to give Gomez credit for saving Leaguer. Vraebel had a feeling Gomez's next check would have a bonus attached to it.

After reports were done and roll call was confirmed, Vraebel headed to his cabin. The adrenaline dump from the incident had left him shaking and exhausted. He'd done his best to hide it from the crew, but he thought for sure Gomez noticed.

Vraebel stripped off his khakis and work shirt and lay down on the bed. He closed his eyes and let himself drift. Focusing on his breathing and heart beat, he managed to calm himself. After ten minutes, he headed to the bathroom and washed his face with cold water. It helped more than he believed it would. After that, he dressed and headed back to the bridge.

Gomez had been waiting for him, a concerned smile on his face. "Okay, Jefe?"

Vraebel managed a grim smile. "Yeah, Steve. As soon as I figure out what the fuck caused that, I'll be much better."

"No shit," Gomez said. "Why didn't we get a warning?"

That was the question. The big question. A rumble large enough to create a disturbance that size should have set off the seismic sensors. Instead? Nothing.

Once he squared things in the bridge, he headed for the drilling office. He clenched and unclenched his fists as he walked. He forced a smile as he greeted his crew in the hallways. It helped ground him and he knew the crew needed to see him confident and in control. If the crew didn't think he was on top of things, another such incident could really cause problems.

The drilling office's air conditioners were a low whoosh below the hum of the computers. He listened to Calhoun, Standlee, and Sigler as they scanned a page of data.

"Here," Standlee said and pointed to the screen. "That's where AUV 2 sent out the alert."

Vraebel leaned forward in his chair. "What alert?"

The tech glanced at him and then back to the screen. "When the bot hit 18k, it started streaming data. One of those packets was an alert."

"What kind of alert?" Vraebel asked. "Alert about the ocean floor jumping?" Standlee nodded. Vraebel stifled the urge to leap at the man. "And why the fuck didn't we get the warning?"

Calhoun cleared his throat. "The alert came in just after I sent him to find Shawna."

Clench. Unclench. He was afraid to look at his knuckles. The rig chief wanted to beat someone's ass. Calhoun's or Standlee's, it didn't matter. He pushed down the anger. "So no one was manning the station?"

"No," Calhoun said. "But look here," he said pointing to the screen. "The alert came in and less than two minutes later, we were hit. We wouldn't exactly have had a lot of time to do anything."

"Bullshit," Vraebel said. "Fucking bullshit. I could have had Gomez readjust the ballasts. We could have made sure no one was going to go flying over the railing! So don't give me that."

Standlee's face was flushed. "Mr. Vraebel, can we please focus on what caused the problem? We missed an alert, yes. But if the AUV hadn't been down there to begin with, we would never gotten it anyway."

The rig chief opened his mouth, and then closed it. Goddammit, the fucker was right. If he hadn't agreed to let Standlee send the thing down there, they would have been even worse off. At least now they had a chance of figuring out what happened.

"Okay," Vraebel said. "Sorry. It's been a rough day and I guess I'm looking for someone to blame."

Calhoun nodded. "Understood. Craig? Have you examined the sample case yet?"

He shook his head. "No. JP said they retrieved AUV 2. It's down there waiting for me, but I wanted to make sure we analyzed the reports first."

"You're getting intelligent finally," Sigler grinned.

Standlee lifted his middle finger and shook it in front of her before smiling back. "That said, AUV 2 didn't notice anything odd as it approached the beds. We need to go through the camera footage, but there was no seismic activity whatsoever."

"Until when?" Vraebel asked.

"Until there," he said and stabbed a key. The screen switched to a time/depth graph. "The spike lasted about ten seconds and then fell off. But AUV 2 was already heading to the surface, so the duration and timing may be a bit off."

Calhoun sucked his teeth. "Can we pull up the camera footage?"

Standlee shook his head. "I still need to transfer it. AUV 2 sent the data, but not the pictures. It's a result of the malfunction."

Vraebel raised his eyes. "What malfunction?"

The tech leaned back in his chair. "One of the propellers was severely damaged," he said. "I haven't taken a look yet, but JP told me it looks like it's been hit with a sledgehammer. Also, one of the ballast tanks is dented."

"What the hell could have done that?" the chief asked. The three eggheads shared a glance. Vraebel rolled his eyes. "Would you guys please tell me what the hell is going on?"

Calhoun sighed. "We would if we could," he said. "Until we get the footage and the data lined up, it's going to be damned difficult to answer that question."

"We're going to reach the site for the second well in five hours," Vraebel said. "Is there any reason we shouldn't set up a drill string, assuming the rig inspection checks out?"

"No," Sigler said. "Besides the fact we ought to wait for the report from Houston."

"Why the hell would we do that?" Vraebel asked.

She blinked and then cast her eyes at the floor. "I'd just feel better if— I'd just feel better if we had a chance to get all the readings. I don't exactly have the best equipment to test here."

The chief stood and put his hands on his hips. "Look, is it oil or isn't it?"

Calhoun narrowed his eyes and stared at him. "It's oil, Martin. All the readings show it as being damned sweet crude. But Shawna's analysis proves the stuff is, well, unique."

"Right," Vraebel said. "Unique. Normal. I don't care. If there's no danger to Leaguer, then we're going to drill. Let me know when you get the data from AUV 2, Standlee. And preferably before we drop the drill string."

Martin spun headed out of the office. His shift was over. He wasn't due back on the bridge until five am. He desperately needed sleep. If he was lucky, he'd pass out when he lay on the bed again. If not, then he was sure he'd still be awake when Belmont and the dive crew began their inspection.

#

With all the lights off and the porthole shade drawn, the room was a tomb. JP shivered and wrapped his legs in the blankets. He normally slept beneath a single sheet with the comforter and blankets kicked off the bed, but that wasn't the case tonight.

He should have been sweating beneath a sheet, two blankets, and a comforter. He should have been miserable and hot enough to set the room on fire. Instead, he was freezing.

The last time he checked the clock, it was 1 am. He'd taken a load of acetaminophen and it seemed to drop the fever a bit. Other than that, the stuff had been fucking useless.

Goddamned oil. Goddamned fucking oil. Three scorching hot showers and he'd barely managed to get the shit off his skin.

When AUV 2 surfaced after the rig nearly capsized, he and Belmont had headed out in the Zodiac to retrieve it. Vraebel had only authorized the trip after he canceled action stations. Which meant, of course, they had to search for the damned thing at dusk. Although it was painted in yellow and reds, the paint wasn't at all fluorescent. They'd had to rely on the GPS beacon.

Catfish had called him on the radio. "JP?"

"Yeah?" he'd asked as they loaded the Zodiac with tow ropes.

There was a brief moment of silence and JP knew Catfish was puffing away on his e-cig. Considering how shaken the tech had been after the bubble hit the rig, he wasn't surprised.

"I'm looking at the reports, and AUV 2 appears to have lost some power to the starboard screw. Can you please check before you hook it up? I don't want to get something even more damaged."

JP and Belmont exchanged a glance. "Damaged?" he asked. "You think it hit something down there?"

"Possibly," Catfish said. "Willing to bet Macully was off in her calculations and it ran into something a little more massive than I'd planned for. Maybe too much speed."

"Roger that," JP said.

"Now we are mechanics," Belmont said in his clipped accent. "How long have you known this man?"

JP chuckled. "Longer than I'd care to admit."

"He is like a father worried about his children," the diver said.

"He is at that."

In silence, they finished loading the Zodiac. JP made sure to bring an extra bumper just in case they had to secure the two ropes to something other than the ballast tanks. He didn't want to tell Belmont, but he was sure they'd have to go extra slow on the return trip.

Luckily, AUV 2 wasn't far from where it was supposed to be. Unlike AUV 5 which was always blowing its approach, the damaged robot was a mere twenty meters from its planned ascent spot. The problem was the rig had been under thrust for several hours. In all the commotion, Catfish had forgotten to reprogram the AUV to compensate for the additional distance.

Once they powered on the boat, Belmont pushed the engine to just twenty percent below the redline. The boat jumped and bumped against the waves as they headed out into the fading light.

JP just knew there were fish below them. Would have been a fine night to go spear-fishing. Oh, well. Maybe later in the week, he and Catfish would have a chance. If, that was, Vraebel wasn't still spooked about another seismic event.

It took them nearly forty minutes to get to the AUV. When the GPS indicated they were almost on top of it, Belmont cut the engine and they glided past its position. The last of the sun was below the horizon. Bruised clouds filled the eastern sky. As they made their slow journey to the north, he could see starlight between the gaps.

Belmont dropped the anchor in the water to slow their movement. He looked at JP. "You down this time?"

JP smiled. "My turn in the drink."

Belmont shook his head. "In the drink? What drink?"

"The ocean," he said. "It's an old idiom."

"Idiom?"

"Forget it," JP chuckled. He put on the air tanks and tested the mask. All the gear was working as expected. He attached a powerful halogen light. "Here we go," he said and dropped backwards off the pontoon.

As soon as he was in the water, JP raised a hand to the mask, found the switch, and turned on the headlamp. A tight cone of white light stabbed through the darkness. There were two splashes and more light flooded the area. Belmont had dropped the two portables into the water.

At first, JP was blinded. When his eyes adjusted he realized Belmont had made the right call. The AUV was more than just a dark shape in the water now. The yellow paint reflected the light back at him. He smiled around his rebreather and swam beneath the AUV.

When he turned his head upward toward its bottom, his eyes widened. Catfish hadn't been kidding. The starboard ballast looked as though a fish had taken a sledgehammer to it. The metal around the screw was bent and there was some damage to its engine. Shaking his head, he ran his gloved hands over the surface.

The metal was pitted from multiple impacts. *Something scaly?* he wondered. That didn't make any sense. No fish he knew of had scales hard enough to dent and scrape metal. Not like this, anyway.

JP surfaced beside the AUV and waved at Belmont. The Ukrainian threw the ropes into the water. Harvey nodded to him, gave him the okay sign, and then slipped back beneath the waves.

He managed to secure the ropes without further disturbing the ballast or the screw housing. The starboard propeller had a bit of something wedged in it, but he wasn't sure what it was. And that didn't matter anyway.

Once he finished making sure they could tow the beast, he swam toward the torpedo-shaped robot's front. The scoop attachment was closed, but just barely. A thin trickle of black liquid drizzled out. Covered in the wet-suit, he was hardly worried about getting any on his skin.

A chunk of flesh dangled and swayed from the scoop's jaws. Even with the powerful halogen aimed at it, he couldn't tell what it was. It twitched and moved upward. *Well,* he thought, *that's something new.*

Catfish had caught himself part of a tube worm and its head might still be alive. JP didn't know they could live without the rest of their bodies, but he guessed it made sense. You could cut certain worms in half and they'd just regenerate. Maybe tube worms had the same kind of biology. JP finished inspecting the ropes and surfaced.

Belmont blinked at him. "Everything okay?"

He swam to the side of the Zodiac and lifted himself into the boat. He turned off the head lamp and pulled off his mask. "Yeah. The AUV took a hell of a hit from something, but I'll be damned if I know what did it."

Belmont's stoic face twitched. "Perhaps the worms were hungry."

"Um, was that a joke?" JP asked.

A thin smile broke across the Ukrainian's face. "Let's hope so."

They towed the AUV back to Leaguer. Instead of keeping the engine near the red-line, Belmont held their speed to less than a quarter. It was a long, long trip. The rig was still under thruster power and while it didn't move very fast, it had put even more distance between itself and their position.

JP spent the time watching the moon as it rose over the eastern horizon and slowly made its way into the sky. The waxing gibbous colored the clouds in shades of yellow that accented their dark, moisture filled hues.

When they finally reached Leaguer, they stowed the Zodiac and then raised the AUV using the crane. Out of the water and bathed by bright work lamps, he took pictures of the robot's belly. The damage looked even worse than it had underwater.

JP snapped dozens of close-up photos of the pitting, scrapes, and dents on the AUV's ballast tanks and propeller housing. If he didn't know better, he'd swear someone had taken a hacksaw to it. Only something really sharp and strong could have done that kind of damage.

He sent Catfish an email describing the damage along with the photos. And then he'd done the dumbest thing of his life.

JP moved to disconnect the sample scoop. Because the AUV was in the air and the scoop was directly in the middle, he had to duck under the damned thing. Because he was more concerned about hitting his head than what his hands were doing, he missed the scoop release and instead dragged his hands across its front.

The scoop rattled as whatever inside it moved. Startled, he tried to pull back his hand just as whatever was in the scoop managed to bite him through the gap. He leaped upwards and slammed his head into the bottom of the ballast tanks. The world became a shade of grey punctured by starlight.

His finger throbbed and he tried to see how bad the cut was. Through the fog, he made out two small puncture wounds. Bright red blood welled out of the holes. He brought it to his lips and sucked on the blood. The taste of copper and rancid castor oil filled his mouth. He spit as a wave of nausea threatened to spew dinner over the metal-grated deck.

"You okay?" he dimly heard a voice say.

Swaying a little, he looked over and saw Belmont. The Ukrainian was trying to hide a smile and failing. "Fuck no."

Belmont's face broke into a grin. "Seriously. You bleeding?"

"Only from my fucking hand," JP said and held up his swollen index finger. He managed to shuffle out from beneath the

AUV. Belmont stepped forward and looked down at the top of JP's head.

The Ukrainian shrugged. "No blood in the hair. But I think you need to go to the medic. Finger doesn't look so good."

JP nodded and regretted it. The mental furniture was doing a bit more than moving around in there. He felt like his head was filled with shattered glass. "Fuck it. I'll get Catfish's goddamned monster later."

Belmont raised his brows. "Monster?"

"Tubeworm sample," JP said and pointed to the scoop. "Damned thing is still alive in there."

"Alive?" Belmont asked and swiveled his head toward the AUV. The color drained from his face. "That should not be. Maybe a fish got in there instead?"

"This look like a fucking fish bite?" JP asked and shook the blood from his finger.

Belmont grunted. "No. Looks like you got forked."

"Got that right," JP said. "Completely forked."

At the time, he hadn't known just how true that was. But now that he was shivering beneath a pile blankets, he knew he'd been poisoned.

The damned rig doc was fucking useless. Dr. Sobkowiak had hit him with a tetanus shot. While the doc had been disinfecting the wounds, the short, balding man had studied the finger.

"You sure you didn't hit a piece of metal?" the doc had asked.

JP had shaken his head. "No clue, man. But I don't think so. The scoop doesn't exactly have teeth. More like pincers."

Sobkowiak continued rubbing alcohol into the wounds. JP ignored the pain. The doctor's fat, pudgy thumbs squeezed on either side of the bites. Blood trickled out, but it was extremely dark. The doc pursed his lips. "What the hell?"

"What?" JP asked and looked down at the finger. A black dot of color rode the narrow stream of crimson. "What is that?" he asked.

Sobkowiak shook his head. "No clue, Mr. Harvey." The white-coated doctor swiveled in his rolling chair and reached for a brown bottle. He pulled off the cap and pointed to the stainless steel sink on the wall. "If you would, Mr. Harvey."

JP stood up and put his hand, palm up, over the sterile metal. The doctor put the bottle close to the finger and squeezed. Thick dark liquid poured out over the puncture wounds. The pain increased in his finger, but the blood stopped flowing.

The doc reached for a sterile pad and slowly wiped off the excess. He grabbed a magnifying glass with a bright LED attached to it. One click, and JP's finger was beneath blazing white light. His finger itched and then started to burn. He tried to ignore it, tried to damp it down. He had been trained to do so, but this was different. It felt like someone had stuck a red hot coal beneath his skin.

He pulled the finger away from the light. The doc looked up at him. "Hey, I need to—"

"It's fine," JP said. "Just give me some antibiotics and I'll go sleep."

The doc had shaken his head. "Mr. Harvey, that could be poison in there. We need to—"

"Just. Do. It."

The lab-coated fat man had shrugged. He'd pulled out a Z-pac and handed it over. "Do you have some anti-inflammatories? Tylenol or something?"

Harvey had nodded. "Yeah. I'm fine, doc." He had taken the small cardboard box from the doctor's hand, and headed back to his room. He'd swallowed the starter tabs for the antibiotics, several pills to handle inflammation, and taken a shower. And another shower. And another. Anything to warm himself up.

And no matter how many times he brushed his teeth, that terrible castor-oil taste wouldn't leave his mouth. He thought about just manning up, putting on a pair of shorts, and heading back to the doc. Fuck that. He hadn't been sick a day in his goddamned life and he wasn't about to let this get to him.

JP continued shivering beneath the blankets until he fell asleep. In his dreams, the scoop opened and something crawled out. It was so black, light just seemed to fold into it. It had the barest shape detectable. The thing moved toward him. He was frozen in fear. Tentacles of black shot out and wrapped his body in their freezing embrace. His skin melted from his body and his bones dissolved. In his sleep, he pissed himself.

While he dreamed, his index finger jerked to and fro. He didn't feel the bone break or the joint collapse. Harvey was too far gone to feel much of anything.

Part Two: The Black

Chapter Six

The inspection team had been underwater for over an hour. Harvey hadn't shown up at 0300 for the briefing or for the dive. Belmont wasn't surprised. The fucking American was probably holed up in his room nursing the itty bitty bite the thing in the scoop had given him.

When he and his team had reached the deck to lower themselves into the water, Belmont had told the others to stay clear of AUV 2. He didn't know what was in that scoop and he didn't want to either. While he and his team finished inspecting their gear before dropping down in the Zodiac, he'd done his best not to look over at the robot, but his eyes had strayed to it anyway.

Without the powerful lights focused on the AUV, whatever protruded from the scoop's jaws looked like rotten meat. Also, it had been shedding a trickle of black liquid that fell through the grates and into the ocean beneath the rig. A shiver had raced up his spine. He'd been glad he was heading into the water. A nice dive and inspection would reset him.

Powerful halogen floods lit the rig's substructure. Every surface of the beams connecting the ballast tanks and supporting the main deck were in tip-top shape. Belmont and his team were tapping their underwater tablets. PPE had given them the toys to help facilitate the accuracy of inspection reports. Belmont hated the damned things, but he had to admit they made life easier.

He lifted the tablet and looked at the screen. When he was happy with the view, he tapped a finger and the table took a photo. He let it drop in the water; the wrist tether caught its weight easily. He swam toward the drill string hole and looked up. His bright headlamp shined on the starter stand. The ballast tanks were nearly one-hundred feet below water and he knew the deck was high above him. Looking up always gave him a moment of vertigo before the perspective righted in his mind.

A few fish swam between the ballasts. The rig had been in the water for less than three months, and barnacles and algae were already growing on every surface. The fish were chewing on the plant matter or chasing one another. Belmont wondered how long before a shark decided to join them.

He took a few photos of the starter stand and then looked down at the other two divers. Grisam was at the lowest point of the starboard ballast tank. His tablet flashed as he took photos. Belmont looked at his dive watch. They had another thirty minutes until they needed to get out of the water.

With a flick of the wrist, he brought the tablet back into his hands. He tapped the messaging icon and punched out four words before hitting send. Grisam's tablet flashed. His head swiveled toward it, read the screen and then looked up at Belmont. Grisam gave the ok sign and swam back up into the substructure.

Belmont tapped another icon and brought up the report. They were 90% done with the inspection. He was surprised it had gone so fast, but he thought Vraebel was worrying about nothing anyway. Belmont knew every inch of Leaguer's undercarriage. It was his job. A single large wave wasn't going to do her in.

He turned and headed to the beams connecting the port ballast. The AUV/ROV/Dive deck was more than a hundred feet above him. With a pang of regret, he knew they'd soon be getting back to the Zodiac and the lift. Once they started drilling well 2, he hoped Vraebel would want eyes in the ocean. Otherwise, he might not get another chance to get in the water for days.

Belmont shined his lamp across the metal beams. Although he was bored, he knew it didn't help to be complacent. If a crack or fissure appeared in the substructure, it could really fuck them later. A red fish swam right across his vision. He smiled around his rebreather. Fuckers were getting a little too comfortable down here.

He took more photos. The tablet's flash attracted more fish. He waved them away and finished the photos. He checked the report progress. Grisam and Shelby had finished their sides. The report blinked at 95% completion. He brought up the section for the port ballast and began tapping the icons.

The tablet's screen turned green. They were done for the day. He dropped the tablet and started to swim away. And then stopped. Something caught his eye. He turned back to a beam that was a little more than ten meters away. Something black was on the metal.

Curious, he swam toward it. Nestled in a gap between the work lamps, it was mostly in shadow. As he approached it, he realized it was an amorphous blob hanging onto the beam. Errant ambient light seemed to, well, just kind of disappear into it. The metal on either side of it shined in the dim light. He turned on his headlamp and pointed it at the shape.

The black blob pulsed and shuddered. Belmont lifted his tablet to snap a pic, and it moved. The thing seemed to flow onto the other side of the beam. Belmont shook his head. The spot where the black blob had been was clean. Not just clean, but brand new. The metal looked as though it had been shined to perfection.

He took a photo of the gleaming steel knowing full well it would be impossible to explain what he'd seen. If there had been more time, he would have swam to the other side and hunted for the creature, but time was a luxury he didn't have. Vraebel wanted reports. Vraebel wanted to make sure he could drill his well. And Belmont would tell him he could.

#

The drill string was dropping. The crew on the deck was making record time. Calhoun hadn't heard any talk of it, but he had a feeling the men wanted to get the well spudded and sampled as quickly as possible. After the previous day's "incident," he wasn't surprised.

He was sure Vraebel hadn't told the men about the changes in the ocean floor or what Shawna had said about the oil, but he didn't need to. These men risked their lives every day to make someone else a lot of money, but that didn't mean they couldn't tell when something was "off." And everything felt wrong.

After a few hours of sleep, he and Catfish headed back to the drilling office. They brought plates of freshly cooked beignets and fruit to their workstations, along with two thermoses of coffee. Calhoun knew Catfish wouldn't want to touch the stuff, but there were only so many energy drinks he could pound.

He let Shawna sleep. She was shaken and exhausted. As for JP? Calhoun heard the man didn't show up for the rig inspection. How had he heard? Vraebel, of course.

As the stands were connected and the drill string started to drop, Vraebel joined them in the drilling office. He told them the inspection was clear and that Belmont and crew were ready to drop the AUVs and the ROV.

"I assume JP will be joining them?" Calhoun asked as he popped another piece of sugary beignet into his mouth.

Vraebel's grin widened. God, but Calhoun hated the man. "Mr. Harvey had an accident last night. He didn't show up for the inspection."

"Accident?" Catfish asked. His normal frown deepened.

The rig chief nodded. "Apparently cut one of his fingers. Doc tells me it was two puncture wounds. Nothing serious, mind you, unless it gets infected."

"So?" Calhoun said. "So his finger got fucked up. Doesn't explain why he didn't make the inspection."

Vraebel shrugged. "Maybe he's sick. I've a couple of other men down as well. Or maybe he lost his nerve and he's cowering in his room."

Catfish stood up so quickly, his knees knocked against the workstation's edge. "Fuck you, Vraebel," he said with clenched fists. "Say that again and I'll beat that fucking smug grin off your ugly fucking face."

"Not my fault the man's a pussy," Vraebel said and took two steps toward Catfish.

The younger man growled in his throat. Calhoun stepped between them and put his arms out. He glared and Catfish backed off. A little.

When he looked at Vraebel, he wanted to smash the man's grin into paste. "I think you should leave now, Martin. Unless there's something important?"

Vraebel sneered. "We'll be below 18k in three hours. I expect your ROV to be down there ready to inspect it. And whatever your AUVs actually do, they should start doing it." He smiled wide. "See you later." The man turned and left the office.

"If JP heard that shit, he'd kill that asshole," Catfish said.

Calhoun turned and stared at his partner. "Do your fucking job, Craig. Let me worry about JP and Shawna. We need to figure out what's going on down there and we need to make sure we don't cause another quake."

Catfish's fists continued to clench and unclench, but he finally took his seat. Calhoun finished his breakfast, fired up his terminal, and started going through his email.

"Holy shit," he said. "The sample is already in Houston."

Catfish harrumphed. "PPE must really want their oil. They must have burned through all the jet fuel in the world."

Calhoun nodded. "I'm sure Simpson found a way to make that happen." Most of the emails were the usual corporate dreck fit to be sent directly to trash. He poured a cup of coffee from the thermos and sipped at it as he brought up the visuals from AUV 2.

Catfish had sent it down to retrieve a sample of the tube worms, but that didn't mean it hadn't captured something near their drill point. Considering the changes in the ocean floor compared to the original survey, Thomas wanted to see the middle of the trench.

He brought up the video of the AUV heading toward the bed. Catfish had programmed the robot to start filming when it was 10 meters away. The preview of the video showed the first frame. The eerie blue-light image was razor sharp even if the color wasn't quite right.

A few meters below the robot, the tube worms moved as one toward the interloper. Calhoun tilted his head. "That's not right," he said. He didn't hear Catfish ask what he was talking about. The AUV lowered itself and then thrust forward at high speed. Just before it hit the bed, Calhoun thought he saw teeth.

The blue-light video was suddenly a cloud of pitch black. The AUV sped upward and then the image stuttered. After a moment, the AUV broke free and started its journey through the swirls of dark liquid.

"Jesus," Calhoun said.

"What are you talking about, Thomas?" Catfish asked.

"Not possible," Calhoun said. He brought up the rear view video and sipped at his coffee. He hit play. The forward camera had shown the robot approaching the target worm bed. The rear, however, showed the other beds in the distance as well as the ocean floor.

He watched as the time/depth counters changed in the video's lower left corner. The image jarred and jumped and then he was looking at the bed beneath the robot.

The worms leaped upward to grab at AUV 2's body. A black, flattened head snapped at the camera. Its maw was filled with what looked like teeth. "Oh, Christ," Calhoun said.

Catfish groaned and stood from his workstation. He peered over Thomas' shoulder as the video jumped upwards. The tube worm heads strained to follow, but couldn't. As the AUV fled upward, the rear camera displayed the ocean floor twitching and then jumping. The ground was further and further away as the AUV dumped its ballast and flew toward daylight.

Before the blue-light video displayed nothing but water, both Calhoun and Catfish watched the other worm beds across the trench. They all pointed upward and writhed in time.

"The fuck?" Catfish asked.

The water far below the AUV was murky with silt and sand. They could see the beginning of the pressure bubble that would hit the surface an hour later.

"What the hell was that?" Calhoun swiveled in his chair as Catfish stepped back. "What the fuck, Craig?"

Catfish shook his head. "Dude, I've never seen anything like that. Tube worms don't act like that."

"I don't know what the fuck those things are, but they're not tube worms," Calhoun said. His deep baritone had risen an octave. His heart rapidly thumped in his chest. "I think we need to check the scoop."

"Yeah," Catfish agreed. "Like right fucking now."

#

Simple, right? Simple. Just walk down the fucking steps to the fucking deck and open the scoop.

Catfish stood on the dive deck wearing heavy jeans, a heavy blue denim shirt, and thick gloves. A large plastic sample jar sat on the corrugated iron. He might as well kick the goddamned thing into the ocean.

AUV 2 hung exactly where JP had left it. The battery and data cables had been attached to charge it up and give Catfish access to its memory and programming interfaces. JP had done his job.

But the scoop wasn't closed—it was open. Wide open. Catfish blinked at it. The scoop's lower jaw had been depressed. The metal was shiny as though it had been lovingly polished. He looked down at the grate below the scoop. The iron, normally black with flecks of rust, gleamed. Whatever crud had covered its surface had disappeared.

"Um, okay," he said aloud. He walked to the equipment lockers and picked up a screwdriver. Adrenaline writhing in his veins, he slowly approached the scoop and shined a flashlight inside it.

The scoop's insides were the same as the lower jaw— immaculate and shining. There was no trace of whatever the AUV had captured; it was as though it had never been there.

He tapped the screwdriver against the lower jaw. Nothing happened. He looked at the end of the screwdriver. It was the same dull gleam as it had been when he picked it up.

Catfish walked to the back of the AUV and looked at the starboard side screw. Sure enough, the damage was severe. Serrated scratches covered the screw's housing and one of the propeller fins was bent. "Jesus," he said. The paint was stripped down to the metal which was just as shiny as the scoop.

This made no fucking sense. Whatever had attacked the robot had also managed to remove any oxidation, not to mention the industrial paint. *A fucking solvent?* he asked himself. *What kind of goddamned animal has that?*

He had nothing to send to Macully but more questions. The idea of tasking another AUV to get a sample was out of the question. Until he knew what had happened to AUV 2, there would be no more close encounters with whatever was down there.

But the other AUVs were already in the water and plummeting toward the spud site. He hoped like hell Shawna and Calhoun had chosen an area clear of the damned things. If not, then instead of recovering the AUVs when the drill string was done, they might be picking up floating debris.

Being completely blind in this much water wasn't an option. If something happened with the ocean floor, they wouldn't be able to stop the drill in time. Last time it was a bubble. This time? Could be a massive system failure on the blowout preventer or something much, much worse.

Catfish detached the scoop with his heavy gloves and lay it on the deck. Inert. Innocuous. Just a hunk of shaped steel.

He squatted and cast his flashlight over the jaw mechanism. The springs were gone. That's why the damned thing was stuck open. The jaws had been pried apart. He jabbed the screwdriver on the side of the jaw and a long sharp crack appeared. Whatever substance had shined the scoop had also weakened the metal.

"Okay, that's bad," he said aloud. He smacked the other side of the scoop with the screwdriver. The metal shattered. Shards of gleaming steel covered the dive deck. Catfish reached over and picked one up with his thick gloved fingers. The piece of metal was normal, except when he turned it sideways. It looked as though the metal was no longer a single layer, but stratified. He pushed his fingers together and the steel crumbled.

Gooseflesh covered his arms beneath the heavy denim shirt. If it did that to the steel, what did it do to the deck? He stared at the corrugated iron grate below AUV 2. Catfish duck walked to it and tapped the screwdriver against the iron. The tool's metal tip clanged, but no cracks appeared. He whistled. Maybe they were in better shape than he thought.

He stood up and tried to walk around the AUV. His left work boot caught the edge of the shining grate. He heard a crunch and leaped sideways, heart racing in his chest. A piece of the iron had disintegrated and fallen into the ocean below.

Fuck. Suddenly he wanted to be on the next helo off the rig. He wanted to be anywhere but above whatever sat below the ocean crust.

#

The portholes glowed with wan light. They were shut, of course, but the sun was relentless in its desire to get in. The ambient light wasn't enough to be anything more than uncomfortable.

If one had shined a light across JP's room, they would have seen nothing but destruction. The center of the bed had melted into little more than particles of fabric, wood, and metal. The bed frame was still intact, but had begun to crack. No matter—It lay on the floor.

The carpet beneath It had ceased to exist. It had burned down to the steel which was something It couldn't absorb, couldn't process. The human shaped liquid had no eyes. It needed some way to see. The creature's neural net activated.

It focused, borrowed mass from Its upper torso, and three tentacles sprouted from its waist. Below the din of the air conditioner, the thing gurgled as it created shapes and manufactured organs as dark as a black hole.

The short tentacles waved in the air as It forced more liquid into them. Its upper body shrank, rendering It into a three-legged tear drop shape. Its humanoid face crumpled as It redistributed more mass. Sensor pods sprouted from the tentacles with a plop.

It saw the world through greys and reds. The tentacles moved to one side. Solid. They moved to the other. More solid. But the enemy was just beyond. The bare glow emanating from the portholes made It nervous. It reacted by rolling over on the floor. Carpet smoked and then dissolved beneath It.

The thing tried to process the concrete and add the substance to Its mass, but again failed. It examined the room. A bright sliver of light shone through the bottom of the door frame. It couldn't get out that way. The thing thought for a moment before Its arms retracted into Itself and became another pair of legs. Its constituent parts reacted as one and It slowly stood.

It moved in undulating waves, the liquid rippling with each step. It approached a wall between the two light sources. It dragged one of the tentacles across it. Paint hissed, sheetrock melted, and then It hit steel.

Instead of turning to the other wall, the tentacles popped out the other side. It walked toward the opposite wall and experimented. Same result.

It examined the room again and finally found something. Air flowed through a rectangular vent high on the wall. A way out. Some kind of exit. Something.

Two of Its legs disappeared, as did the tentacles. The thing reformed itself into a standing tower of liquid. Without eyes, It couldn't see anything, but It "felt" the air rushing through the vent. It found the metal grate and slowly poured itself into the A/C vent.

#

The drill string was well below 25k. The crew was working hard and fast. Vraebel was pleased with their progress. He'd fought the urge to call Gomez on the horn and tell him to slow down. They had time, after all. No reason to rush it. And yet, he wanted this done. So did they.

He'd heard the chatter in the galley. Rig-folk were superstitious. When you were in a profession that frequently ended up costing you fingers, toes, or your fucking life, paying attention to your instincts became second nature.

And everyone's instincts were screaming after the wave. He wasn't sure how it had gotten to the rumor mill, but Sigler's analysis of the oil samples was public knowledge now. He thought for sure it was Harobin's fault since he couldn't believe Calhoun's crew would spread that nonsense. Didn't matter.

Compounding that? He knew Belmont had told his dive crew about AUV 2. And even if he hadn't, they'd no doubt seen the machine on their way to inspect the substructure. That was the kind of thing they were paid to notice. Inspectors inspected, even when they weren't on the clock.

He sipped his coffee and stared at the monitors. Next to a diagram of the drill string was a depth meter and a time estimate of completion. Spudding would happen in a little more than an hour. After that? They'd send down the drill bit. And then the morning crew could get some chow while the night watch started drilling.

Vraebel rubbed his eyes. Rig chiefs didn't get a lot of sleep and he was no exception. PPE may have mandated a 12 hour day, but he often couldn't even get the paperwork done during that time. Then there was the crew to worry about. Sleep was a luxury he could ill afford on an exploration rig. Once he was in command of a production rig, though, life would be much, much better.

The monitor flashed and Vraebel frowned. The white phone rang. He picked it up. "Ops."

"Martin?" Gomez's tinny voice said. The roar of machinery behind him made the words difficult to make out. "We have a problem. Or maybe not."

Vraebel shivered. "What kind of problem?"

"I think we struck the bottom."

The chief blinked and looked at the monitor. The depth chart said 27k. "That's not possible. The survey said it would be over 29k before we hit the floor."

"I know," Gomez said. "But the instruments say we're sitting on top of rock."

He thought for a moment. "Steve? I need to call the drilling office. Stand by."

"Yes, sir."

He typed a few keys on a keypad and waited. With the sounds of the deck machinery in the background, the phone buzzed in his ears.

"Harobin," a voice answered.

"Andy? Gomez says we've hit bottom."

There was a pause. "Yeah, I was going to call you about that. I think he's right."

Vraebel hissed through his teeth. "What should we do here?"

Harobin let out a huff of air and then chuckled. "I think we drill, Martin."

The chief smiled. "Steve? You hear that?"

"Yes, sir. We'll get spudded and I'll let you know when we're ready."

"Good deal, Steve. Tear 'em up. Harobin? Stay on the line." There was a click and the sound of the rig deck disappeared. "Andy? What the hell is going on? The survey off again?"

Harobin laughed. "You that surprised?" Andy's voice dropped to a near whisper. "If the AUVs took the first survey and it was wrong, did you really expect the second to be any different?"

Vraebel shook his head. "That doesn't make sense. Not really. We've got the best technology…" The sentence died in his mouth. "Okay, yeah you're right. Something's obviously goofed with their sensor design."

"Well, it's either that or the ocean floor is alive."

"Alive?" Vraebel asked.

Harobin tittered. "Yeah. Ridiculous, isn't it?"

"Yeah," Martin said. "Okay, if Steve's going to start spudding, I'll need you to get Calhoun in the office. Sigler too. I assume Standlee is down there?"

"No. They've all gone off."

"Figures," Vraebel said. "Okay, I'll track them down. You make sure you keep in touch with Gomez. You see anything that looks wrong, I need you to speak up, okay?"

"Okay, Martin. But we're fine, man. This is going to be the mother lode."

"Right. Talk to you soon." Vraebel hung up the phone. He wanted Harobin to be right.

Alive was the word the geologist had used. And then the man had laughed as if it was the most ridiculous thing he'd ever heard. Vraebel tried to shrug off the image of a giant creature that used the ocean floor like a blanket. He took another sip of coffee suddenly wishing there was plenty of Jameson whiskey in it.

#

Morning had come and gone. She'd skipped breakfast. She'd avoided the drilling office. She was in the last place in the world she wanted to be: the lab.

All night long, she'd dreamed of oil that moved against gravity, that breathed in oxygen and expelled bubbles of CO_2. When she'd finally awakened, the sun was barely visible through a clothing of dark clouds. The bed sheets were moist with sweat and looked as though an alligator had been rolling in them.

She'd pulled off her t-shirt and shorts and threw them to the floor as she stared out the porthole. The rig's thrusters were relatively quiet and for once she could hear the ocean's gravelly whisper. As she stared, the whisper became her father's voice.

What are you afraid of darlin'?

"I don't know, Paw," she said to the ocean.

Ain't nothing to be afraid of, girl, except fear. Got yourself all wound up to the point you can't see the forest for the trees. Get out of your head, Shawna.

"I can't, Paw. Something's wrong."

She heard her father's dusty, coal-choked chuckle. *Something's always wrong, girl. You solve problems. Go solve 'em. Ain't gonna fix nothing by sitting here curled up in a ball.*

She'd opened her mouth to respond to the ghostly voice, and then stopped. It wasn't a spirit talking to her. It was just her subconscious untangling the knots and telling her to get her ass in gear.

Without hesitation, she'd jumped in the shower and dressed as quickly as she could. After that, she'd headed to the lab, wet hair gathered beneath a PPE ball cap. Heavy blue coveralls, her thick lab shirt, work boots…she might as well have been headed for the rig deck.

Instead, she'd entered the lab, closed the hatch, and stood near the wall. The darkness was impenetrable. The lab had no portholes or windows to any adjoining rooms. It had been built to keep in any accidents; the bulkheads were thick and fire proof.

Standing alone in the darkened room, her heart hammered in her chest. The hum of the rig's thrusters was the only sound she could hear. Shawna closed her eyes and fumbled for the light switch. The sun was suddenly in the room with her.

The bright fluorescents bathed the lab in blue-white light. She slowly opened her eyes and allowed them to adjust. It was a lab. The gravity stand's stainless steel frame gleamed. The centrifuge sat on its table, innocuous and innocent. Racks of test tubes, beakers, and other equipment were all set in place. It was as clean as she and Calhoun had left it. Nothing had changed.

She walked to the far wall and donned the heavy lab coat and apron. The apron draped down her body until it met her knees. It was heavy, but heavy was good. Beads of sweat gathered across her forehead and she wiped at them before putting on the black gloves. As her fingers slid inside, the soft neoprene felt familiar. Her heart-rate slowed.

The outer glove shells were made to withstand corrosive chemicals and extreme heat. The only way something was getting through them was if it was radioactive. Finally, she removed her ball cap and replaced it with a shielded helmet. If Calhoun knew what she was planning on doing, he'd no doubt stop her, or at least scream in frustration. But she had to do it. She had to be able to sleep again.

She approached the sample closet. Her heart started pounding again and she waited until it slowed. She popped open the door, took a deep breath, and then peered inside.

The test tube and soiled beaker sat in the dim light. Steeling herself, she reached in and dragged out the beaker. She closed the closet and walked to the stainless-steel lab table. The glassware clinked as she placed it on the shining metal surface.

She stepped back from it. The amber liquid was still. Shawna chewed her lip and thought for a moment. A bubble rose from the bottom of the beaker and popped when it reached the surface. Shawna blinked. Another bubble rose and did the same.

Think, she said to herself. *What is it doing?*

"Why are you bubbling?" she asked the room. The beaker of oil didn't answer.

Think, darlin', her father's voice said in her mind. *What have you tested for?*

She pursed her lip. *UV. Humidity. Sediment. Chemical res—* She stopped and turned. Several decanters sat in racks against the wall. Shawna made her way to the chemicals. She made sure to turn around frequently to watch the beaker.

It took nearly an hour, but she prepared test tubes with samples of the oil and then tried each of the reagents to get a reaction from the liquid. Each attempt resulted in failure. Except for the last one.

Because she was certain the test would fail, she'd placed a single drop of oil in the last Pyrex cylinder. As she reached for another reagent to pour into the tube, she heard a pop. Her eyes snapped back to the tube.

The oil wasn't bubbling. It was practically leaping for the light. She pushed her rolling chair from the table. Before putting the drop into the tube, she'd focused the halogen lamp on the glass. The oil was bathed in bright, white light.

The oil popped again and slid up the sides of the tube. Shawna rubbed her gloves together just to make sure she was wearing them. Her hands went down her lab apron and then touched the safety glass of her hat.

Tendrils of the amber liquid tried to reach the top, but couldn't do it. She watched as the oil turned into a dark brown stain on the glass. It crackled, spit a small tendril of smoke, and then stopped moving.

Shawna let out a deep breath and realized she'd been holding it for quite some time. She stared at the beaker. It bubbled again. All the other test tubes, the ones where she'd poured at least a 1/4 oz. of liquid, were bubbling too.

She slowly walked to the lab table, but leaned far enough back to keep from being over the test tubes or the beaker. When the halogen lamp was in reach, she manipulated the goose neck and pointed it at the nearest test tube with liquid.

The top quarter of the amber liquid frothed and popped. She moved the lamp head closer, making sure she concentrated the light on the bottom of the Pyrex. The oil leaped for the top of the tube and made its way down the sides. She jumped back from the table as lines of amber skated across the table and down one of the table legs.

"Fuck!" she yelled and backed up all the way to the far wall. She could see the thin lines of oil sitting beneath the shade of the lab table. The streams drew together and formed a tiny puddle. It didn't bubble. It didn't move.

Breathing in harsh gasps, she held a hand to her heart. It was thumping loud enough to blot out everything. Slowly, carefully, she reached down for her phone. She had to sweep aside the heavy apron and lab coat. Her gloved fingers touched its metal surface and plucked it from the pocket. Eyes still focused on the liquid, she unlocked the phone with practiced, nimble fingers. She found the round button at the bottom of the phone and held it down.

The phone beeped twice. "Send message," she said in a raspy voice.

"To whom do I send the message?" it responded.

"Thomas Calhoun." The liquid didn't react to her voice.

"Speak your message."

"Thomas," she said, "The oil is alive. I'm trapped in the lab with it. Please help me."

She paused and the phone beeped again. "Send message?" it asked.

"Yes."

The phone beeped again. "Message sent. Would you like to—" She cut the phone off by locking it. There was little to do but wait it out. The liquid was between her and the hatch. She didn't know what the stuff would do if it touched her. She didn't want to either.

#

The usual hum of the computers blanketed the drilling office. Harobin typed at his keyboard and Catfish was doing the same. Harobin was looking for geological anomalies. Catfish was searching for solvents that affected metal. And Calhoun? He was goddamned confused.

Catfish had called him down to the rig deck to show him the stressed and brittle metal. When he'd seen the damage to the AUV as well as the deck, he'd just shaken his head.

"That's not possible," he'd told his long-haired partner. "Just not possible."

Catfish tugged the side of his beard. "Don't you think I fucking know that, Thomas?"

Calhoun took the screwdriver from Catfish and approached the scored propeller housing. He gently brushed the metal with the tool. A flake of silver peeled off. "How much pressure did you use to crack the scoop?"

"Not much," Catfish said. "Not much at all."

Nodding, Calhoun did the same to the propeller. The metal didn't react at all. He increased the pressure, but the steel resisted as it should have. "Okay," he said aloud. "Obviously the propeller wasn't touched."

Catfish blinked. "No?"

"No." Calhoun scraped the screwdriver across the bottom of the propeller housing. It crumbled into flakes of metal. "Holy shit," he said. He flipped the screw driver around, gripped the hard plastic end, and scraped the top of the housing where he'd started. The metal resisted. He increased the pressure, but it remained intact. "Fuck. Me."

"What?" Catfish asked. He'd left his post by the instruments and peered over the larger man's shoulder.

Calhoun shook his head. "It's like the chemical makeup of the metal has changed. Touching it with non-metallic objects doesn't seem to have any effect. But touch it with actual metal, and its hardness is just…well, gone."

"So you've seen this before?"

Calhoun had turned and stared at Catfish's face with gleaming, excited eyes. "No. I haven't. Whatever touched this," he said pointing back to the AUV, "changed the chemical composition of the metal. Rearranged the molecules. Whatever new formation they've taken, they lose cohesion when touched by other metal molecules."

Catfish had cleared his throat. "That's impossible, isn't it?"

"Not impossible," Calhoun had said. "Just damned unlikely. I'm not even sure what would do that. And without a good microscope, it's going to be impossible for me to figure out what happened here."

They'd left the rig deck and headed back to the drilling office. As soon as they reached it, Harobin had grinned at both of them. "We've hit the bottom. They're going to spud."

The engineer had frowned. "They shouldn't hit the bottom for another hour or two," he said. "What's the depth?"

"27k," Harobin had replied. He rubbed at his nose and flicked a green booger against the wall. "A bit short."

"A bit short?" Catfish had crossed his arms. "Try impossibly short. The surveys—"

"Are obviously wrong," Harobin had said. "I'm guessing the sensors need to be recalibrated because something is way off."

"No shit," Catfish had said. He'd flopped down in his chair, unlocked his workstation, and glared at his screen. He hadn't said another word.

Rather than argue with Harobin, Calhoun had sat at Shawna's workstation and started running searches. He had tried everything he could think of to describe the behavior he'd seen, but no articles matched it. He had half a mind to contact a metallurgist. Heat, cold, electromagnetism, all of those factors changed the way metal behaved. Heat spread the molecules apart. Cold forced them closer together. Electrical fields could reorganize the structure and make the metal brittle.

But what the hell would change the structure so much that metal destroyed metal while plastic did nothing? Calhoun had popped the damned thing with the end of the screwdriver to no effect. Hadn't even managed to put a dent in it.

This makes no sense. He listened to himself and a grim smile appeared on his face. That seemed to be the mantra ever since they drilled the first well. Nothing made much sense anymore. Between AUV 5's constant problems, the oil that didn't act like oil, and a changing ocean floor, this particular drilling endeavor defied all logic. Period.

"Well, that was quick," Harobin said. Calhoun looked over at the geologist. The man's eyes were focused on his screen, but his fingers were tapping on the workstation's edge.

"What?" Calhoun asked.

The man turned in his chair and smiled. "Wells been spudded."

Calhoun blinked. "Bullshit. No way they got it done that fast. No way."

"According to Gomez, they're already sending down the drill bit."

Thomas stood from his chair. "Nonsense. They're fucking with you. There's no way—" He paused as his phone beeped. Calhoun sighed and pulled it out of his trouser pocket. "1 message from Shawna Sigler" scrolled across the screen. Frowning, he tapped in the unlock code. The phone's screen filled with text. "The fuck?"

"Problem?" Harobin asked.

Calhoun glared at the geologist. "Catfish?"

The tech turned around in his chair and tilted his head at Calhoun. "Yeah?"

"I have to go help Shawna. Do me a favor and ask Vraebel for a security officer to meet me at the lab." He turned around and rushed out of the office.

Harobin traded stares with Catfish. "Security officer? Was he serious?"

#

Four AUVs circled the second drill site. AUVs 1,3, and 4 traveled in separate orbits around the drill string. Each orbit was further from the ocean floor and wider than the last. AUV 5, on the other hand, hovered a mere ten meters above the rock and sand.

Its cameras and sensors were filming everything. Once the spud bit had been sent down, it detected the RFID signature and a new subroutine kicked into gear. Its rear camera watched the nearest beds of tube worms while its forward camera focused on the spud site.

The drill bit began to turn. It knew this from the frequency generated inside the string. Sand and rock moved aside as the bit started chewing into the earth. AUV 5 activated its seismic sensors. Waves of sound from the disturbance registered as normal. AUV 5 was as happy as a machine could be. It watched as the drill string slowly grew in length.

The robot's sensors suddenly detected something new. The ocean floor rumbled behind it. The tube worm beds had all turned their heads toward the drill string. The rumble grew. AUV 5 continued to film the area. A new subroutine launched and told the robot to begin moving in that direction. It detected new movement in front of it and the routine stopped dead in its tracks.

A long, black tentacle reached upward through the ocean floor. The water around the drill string became an impenetrable cloud of debris, but the robot's thermal imaging continued taking video. The tentacle wrapped around the drill string and pulled. Another reached out and did the same. Then another and another.

The ocean floor shook. A divot formed around the drill string as the tentacles pulled downward. The robot squirted a data stream to AUV 1. AUV 5 continued to watch while AUV 1, the highest in orbit, responded to the alert by emptying its ballasts and ascending as fast as it could. The warning was coming. But it was already too late.

#

Entire universes must have been born, lived their lives, and extinguished themselves between each breath. Afraid to move, afraid to so much as blink, she'd been staring at the thing beneath the table for an eternity.

The black ooze was still motionless. She didn't know how long it had been since she texted Thomas, and she was afraid to look at her phone. The monitors on the wall flashed information, but she didn't dare avert her gaze.

She spent the time thinking about weapons, chemical structures, something she could use. The liquid was light sensitive, but only to high frequencies. Any source that approximated natural sunlight must be deadly to it. Did that include the UV spectrum? It was made of hydrocarbons. Would engineered bacteria eat it? Would it even damage it? What about—

Something tapped on the hatch across the room. Shawna nearly screamed. She'd managed to get her heart rate under control, but it was once again off to the races. The phone in her hand buzzed. She risked a glance at it.

"Can you talk?" a text from Calhoun said.

Her fingers tapped the call icon and she slowly raised the phone to her ear. The ring lasted all of a second.

"Shawna," Calhoun's gravelly voice said, "if you can't talk, don't."

"I can talk," she whispered. She could barely hear her own voice over the thumping of her heart. "I don't think it can hear."

"What's your situation?"

She tried to talk, but there was no saliva in her mouth. She bit the inside of her cheek hard enough to make her wince. Her mouth filled with moisture. "It's between me and the hatch. It's sitting beneath the lab table in the shadows. Thomas, it's sensitive to light. Halogen light. Anything that approximates sunlight."

"Okay, calm down," he said. His voice was even, but she could tell that was forced. He might be as scared as she was. Or maybe he was just humoring her. "Is it sensitive to movement? Vibration?"

"I don't know," she said. "I don't think so."

"Okay," Thomas said. "I'm going to knock on the hatch, okay?"

"Okay."

She prepared herself for the sound, but she jumped anyway when loud bangs erupted outside the hatch. She was sure they were loud enough to echo down the hallways, but through the thick steel, they sounded like distant thunder. The liquid didn't react.

"Nothing," she said.

"Good. I'm coming in."

Before she could find her voice to say anything, there was a loud click and then the hatch squealed open. Shawna kept her eyes focused on the puddle beneath the table.

Calhoun stepped through the hatchway, his head down and eyes scanning the floor. He stopped just inside the room. "I don't—" He paused and his face turned grim. "Okay, I see it." He looked up at Shawna. "You okay?"

"I have to pee," she said.

Thomas opened his mouth, closed it, and then started to chuckle. She joined him, a tear appearing at the corner of her eye. "Well, let's get you out of here so you can do that in privacy."

"Yes," she said. "Let's."

He walked down the side of the room directly in front of the hatch. An extra set of lab clothes hung off the pegs on the wall. He grabbed one of the gloves. "Keep an eye on it for me," he said.

"I don't dare close them," she whispered. "Thomas?" He turned to her. "I'm fucking terrified."

Calhoun nodded. "I know. Tell me what you know. Tell me what it did." He turned back to the wall and seemed to take inventory of everything there.

She swallowed hard. "I poured it into test tubes so I could test it against other chemicals. It didn't react to anything I tried."

"So what kicked it off?" he asked.

"I used the halogen work lamp," she said pointing to the table. "The small sample practically evaporated. A 1/4 oz. of the stuff crawled out of its test tube and went down the table."

He turned and blinked. His eyes went back to the small puddle beneath the table. "That's a quarter ounce?"

She nodded. "Yeah."

"Looks too big for that," he said.

"Tell me about it."

Calhoun donned a lab apron and a mask, but didn't put on the gloves. Instead, he held one of them in his hands. "I ever tell you I was a great pitcher in high school?"

Shawna giggled at the sudden smile on Thomas' face. "No, you didn't."

He nodded. "I was awesome. If I hadn't broken my damned shoulder while skate-boarding," he said, "I could a been a contendah."

She started to laugh and then saw what he was going to do. The sound died in her throat. Thomas threw the glove beneath the table. It hit the floor a foot in front of the amber liquid, slid into it, and stopped.

Nothing happened.

"Well," he said, "that was anti—"

A curl of smoke drifted up from the glove as it dissolved into the oil. The glove was made of polymers with steel woven through it. The polymers had been completely consumed, but she could see the remains of the metal threads sitting on top of the slick.

Calhoun let out a deep breath. "Holy shit."

"Yeah," Shawna agreed. She waited a beat. "Thomas?"

He nodded. "I see it."

The puddle of liquid was no longer a deep amber. It had darkened considerably toward its original black. As they watched, the strange substance spread an inch or two in all directions.

"What in the fuck?" Shawna said. "Did it just… Did it just grow?"

"Yes," Calhoun said, voice shaking. Thomas' fists clenched and unclenched and then he let out a deep breath. Shawna thought she could see the man force himself under control. When he looked at her, his face was set in a gentle smile. "I guess it's hungry."

She swallowed hard. "Got any ideas?"

He thought for a moment. "You said it slid off the metal table?"

"Yeah. Down the leg and everything."

"Okay," Calhoun said. "I have an idea." Tongue in the corner of his cheek, he slowly slid across the wall toward the lab equipment. "You let me know if it starts to move."

"Damned right I will."

He scanned the wall and then grinned. "So it didn't consume the metal. Didn't consume Pyrex. What do those two materials have in common?" He pulled a large metal tray from the wall. Its sides had an inch high lip. Light gleamed off its surface. He held it in his hands and turned to look at her. "Think, Shawna. What do they have in common?"

She let out a breath. "Tightly packed molecular structures."

"Right. So maybe it can't displace them if they're packed a certain way," Calhoun said. He turned to face the table. The puddle was closer to Shawna's side than his. "That would explain why it can only absorb certain materials." The large man lowered himself to his haunches. His joints cracked and he grimaced in pain. He smiled at her. "Fucking age. Catches up with us all."

Thomas looked back down beneath the table. He took a long, slow breath. She could see tremors running down the man's arms. "Be careful, Thomas."

He nodded. Knees creaking, he duck walked around the table and toward the far side. Shawna's eyes were riveted on the liquid. It hadn't moved, hadn't bubbled, hadn't so much as twitched. Calhoun took another deep breath and moved to cover the puddle with the tray.

The rig vibrated. He looked at her, his face a round O of surprise. The floor rumbled and then the rig shook. Calhoun fought to keep his balance. And then the lights went out.

#

Spudding was old hat and nothing special. The drill crew sent down concrete casing. They sent down a large drill bit and then started the damned thing drilling. Very simple. Once the surface hole was made, they'd retract the spud bit and replace it with a regular drill bit. Then they could start bringing up real oil, the real black.

So why was the fucking rig shaking like it was in the middle of a goddamned hurricane? Gomez grabbed on to a railing as two of his men flew overboard.

He yelled an alert to the rest of the crew, but no one was listening. The generators heaved and then went silent, but the rig continued to shimmy from side to side. "Two in the water!" he screamed. "Port side! Get your asses moving!"

Hard hats had tumbled off and slid along the deck as Leaguer shook. "Turn off the fucking drill!" he screamed. When the drill continued rumbling, Gomez turned to look at the control station.

The drill operator wasn't at his post. A large smear of blood covered the back of the station. He could see a motionless leg sticking out from behind the steel platform. Cursing, Gomez shuffled on unsteady feet to the drill controls. T. Reed, the drill operator for the morning shift, was dead. His head had smashed into the metal panel. Fragments of his skull peppered the rig floor like bloody, broken eggshells.

The panel's LEDs were flashing yellow and red. Backflow pressure was redlined. If the drill continued siphoning, they were going to have a blowout. He stabbed his hand on the large emergency button. The rig shook again as the turntable slowed and then stopped.

Heart hammering in his chest, Gomez blew out a long hiss of air and looked up at the deck. Five of his men were at the port side and looking down into the hundred foot chasm that separated the rig deck from the ocean. Gomez's inner ear was still having problems adjusting to the motionless rig. "Where are they?" he yelled as he approached the men.

One turned to him and blinked. Gomez grabbed the front of his shirt. "Where the fuck are my men?"

"They— They didn't make it," the crewman said.

Gomez peered over the railing. When the rig shook and knocked them off, the deck must have been swaying in the other direction. As they fell, it hit them on the way down. Thousands of tons of metal pounded their bodies. The superstructure below the railing was covered in blood.

"Jesu Christie," Gomez breathed. "Roll call! Now!" he screamed. The men near the railing didn't move. "Get the fuck to your stations. Now. And goddammit, section chiefs better have numbers for me in two minutes. Move your fucking asses!"

#

His chest burned. The fresh cup of coffee he'd made had splashed down and inside his shirt. Vraebel was still hissing through his teeth when the power went out. The LED monitors blinked out and the sound of the A/C died. He turned to Terrel, his XO.

"Get to the generators. See what the fuck is going on." Terrel didn't reply as the rig shook again. He ran through the hatch and down the hallway. Vraebel picked up the red phone handle. He didn't know if Gomez would hear it with the chaos he saw below.

He could see Gomez over by the railing with a group of men. They peered down over the side. Vraebel's balls turned to ice. "Answer the goddamned phone!" he screamed. Gomez continued staring over the railing. When he turned back, Vraebel saw the expression on his face. Dead men. The only question was how many.

"Answer the fucking phone!" he yelled again. But it continued ringing. He slammed the handset down. The lights flickered and then came back on. The A/C started to flow again. *One crisis down,* he thought. But he knew that was bullshit.

The drill wasn't moving. Gomez had shut it down. Vraebel had a second to thank God he'd hired the man. The red phone buzzed loud enough to make him jump. Vraebel pulled up the head set. "Bridge," he said.

"It's Gomez, Martin."

"What's your status?"

A long pause followed the question. He stared down at the deck and could see hands and fingers raising. Gomez was taking roll call.

"We have power again," he finally said. "Even to the consoles. But we're missing two men."

Two men. "They're not missing. They're dead, aren't they?" he said in a flat monotone.

"Yes, Martin. I think they hit the ballast on the way—"

"Any other casualties?" Vraebel asked.

Another pause. "Reed is dead. The rest? Scratches and bruises. Harrison has a broken wrist. Other than that, I think we're okay."

My ass, Vraebel thought. "Get Harrison to the doc."

"I sent two men with him. They'll be there ASAP."

"Good. Any idea what the fuck happened?"

"No. No warning. I don't know if we hit a gas pocket or what."

Vraebel shook his head. "If we'd hit a gas pocket that big, we'd either be on fire or sunk."

"True," Gomez said. The sound of his voice was muffled as he covered the receiver. "Check the goddamned stand! See if it's twisted!" The sound of the deck engines and generators returned. "We have to do some checks down here. I'll have a damage report for you as soon as I can."

"Make it happen, Steve."

"Will do," Gomez said. The man sounded exhausted and in shock.

"And Steve?"

"Yeah, boss?"

Vraebel bit his lower lip. "Good job, man. It wasn't your fault."

Another pause. "Thanks, Martin. Talk to you soon."

The phone went dead in Vraebel's hand. He placed it back in its cradle before picking up the white phone. He punched in a few numbers and waited for the other end to pick up.

"Drilling office," a breathless voice said. "Harobin here."

"Andy. What the fuck is going on down there?"

"Martin," Harobin said. "What the fuck is going on period? What the hell was that?"

"You fucking tell me! What did we hit?"

Harobin coughed. "I— I don't know. Readings were good. Everything was good. And then the rig started to shake."

"Is Standlee there?" Martin asked.

"Yeah, he is."

"You tell that fucker to get his ROV down to 18k and find out what the hell happened," Vraebel said.

"I— Hang on a sec." There was a murmur in the background. "Standlee says he'll have a report for you soon."

"Fucking better," Vraebel growled into the phone and hung up.

#

When the lights went out, Calhoun was inches away from the puddle. The shaking rig had almost knocked him to the floor. The clank and rattle of glass and steel hanging from the walls was loud enough to make his ears ring. The sudden plunge into pitch black forced a shriek from his throat. Shawna didn't fare much better. It only lasted a couple of seconds before the emergency lights kicked in, but the darkness seemed to last an eternity.

As the red emergency lights snapped on, Calhoun's eyes were stuck on the space in front of him. The liquid that had been stationary started to slide toward him. He let out a scream and slammed the tray down atop the puddle. He duck walked out from beneath the table and then headed to the far wall.

"Shawna?"

"Yeah?" she said. "I'm okay. What the fuck happened?"

"I don't—" The red lights disappeared as the power returned. His eyes burned from the sudden illumination. "I don't know," he said. When his vision cleared, he was staring at the tray beneath the table. There was no sign of the black liquid. Thomas grabbed two large beakers and headed back to the table. He placed them on either end of the tray to make sure the weight kept it as close to the floor as possible. He didn't want to give the goddamned stuff a chance to slip out between a possible crack.

"Thomas? I think you saved my life," Shawna said from the other side of the room.

He looked up at her and winked. "Well, you can owe me later. Right now," he said, out of breath, "we need to get the fuck out of this lab."

She shook her head. "We need to know what this shit is."

"We'll figure it out," he said. "But right now, we need to find out if we're on a sinking rig."

Calhoun's phone rang and they both jumped. He pulled the phone out of his pocket. "Catfish," the caller id said.

"Tell me we're not sinking," he said into the phone.

"Thomas? Where the fuck are you? I need you down here. Now," Catfish said. Thomas wasn't sure, but he thought he heard fear in the man's voice.

"Okay. Shawna and I had an incident in the lab."

"I don't give a shit," Catfish said. "We got bigger problems. Much bigger."

"We're coming," Calhoun said and hung up. He looked up at Shawna.

"We sinking?" she asked.

"Not yet," he said. "Not yet."

Chapter Seven

There were few things in life Chef "Nutty" Nuchtchas hated more than being on a rig. Syphilis and chlamydia were definitely in the top loathing spaces, but the rig was close behind. If not for the huge child support checks and the ex-wife's ever-hungry lawyer, he would still be in New Orleans cooking the good stuff. Instead he was preparing and cooking what he considered "slop" for a bunch of rednecks.

But the pay was nothing to sneeze at. He couldn't afford to quit the rig. PPE was paying him a damned ransom to keep their workers' bellies full. His sous chef, Robbie Christie, had been let go on their last deployment. The crazy bastard had kept a goddamned ham up in the ceiling tiles. Why would he do that? So he could fuck it. Drilled the core out of the damn thing and then was going to town on it every night. If not for the smell of rancid meat, he wouldn't have been caught.

When Nutty returned from time off, the rig chief had pulled him aside and told him Christie had been fired. When he explained why, Nutty couldn't stop laughing. He'd known Robbie was unhinged, but that was truly going off the goddamned deep end.

That's the kind of shit that happened when you were gone from home for months at a time and then found out your wife had shacked up with your best friend. Oh, well. Christie had been good, but Otto was better.

Otto Hasford was busy chopping vegetables with impeccable skill. Nutty was impressed with the man, but not his command of English. Otto spoke only when he had a question or if you asked him one. The first few days, the only sounds in the kitchen were the gas burners, knives slapping against cutting boards, and water boiling in copper pots. That's why zydeco was playing on the radio.

While Otto probably liked the quiet, Nutty hated it. It made his tour that much more miserable. Another three days, though, and he'd be off the damned rig and headed to town. Maybe find a nice woman at a bar, buy her a few drinks, and then make *her* his ham.

Nutty grinned and continued stirring the sauce. He took a plastic test spoon out and tried a little. It wasn't quiet warm enough yet and still a little too bland. Moving to the crazed accordion on the radio, he popped off the top of his secret blend and started shaking it into the pot.

While he was focused on that, he didn't hear Otto's gasp. He didn't hear the big German struggle for air as something poured itself down his throat. Amidst the sizzling of sausage and beef, he didn't hear the crackle of dissolving flesh and bone. He knew nothing but zydeco and the hot pot until it was his turn.

#

His e-cig was burned out. Ever since the rig had tried to shake itself apart, Catfish had been puffing on the thing. Its aluminum body was hot to the touch and vapor was no longer coming out of it. The atomizer was dead and although he had a spare in his room, leaving the drilling office was a bad idea.

The picture on his workstation was from AUV 5. It had squirted the data to AUV 1. When AUV 1 hit 18k feet, it started transmitting its warnings to the surface. Too bad they were half an hour too late.

The data log from 5's sensors showed more than just a tremor. The video and pictures merely confirmed it. The entire ocean floor had spasmed. But that's not what had broken his flesh out in goose flesh. The picture on the screen had done that.

Even with the surreal coloring of the blue-light cameras, the 8-frame per second video feed was enough to scare him silly.

When he'd first pulled up the video and watched the hi-def pictures scroll across the screen, he'd had to fight not to wet his pants.

AUV 5 had watched the ocean floor divot beneath the spud site. It had filmed tentacles reached out and grabbing the drill string. It had also filmed those same tentacles pulling down on the metal. No wonder the goddamned rig had shaken.

But that wasn't the worst of it. The view from the rear camera showed all the tube worm beds in the trench reaching toward the spud site. Their tentacles waved in something akin to rage. The water exploded into clouds of sand and rock. AUV 5 switched its cameras to thermal imaging at that point to try and cut through the murk. That's when the view went black.

By the time a very pale Calhoun and Shawna arrived in the drilling office, he'd watched the video five different times. He'd applied multiple filters to the frames showing the tentacles leaping from the ocean floor. Each helped clarify contrast and sharpen the image. When they opened the drilling office hatch, he'd nearly jumped out of his chair.

He swiveled around and faced them. Shawna was taking deep breaths and exhaling through her mouth. Thomas looked as though he'd aged twenty years since Catfish had last seen him.

"What— What kind of incident in the lab?" he asked.

Thomas waved his hand. "We'll talk about that soon. Right now, I need to know what the hell is going on."

Catfish jerked his thumb backward toward the screen. "*That* is what's going on."

He watched as their eyes went to the screen. Thomas' face, which had started to gain color, was once again too pale.

"What in the fucking hell is that?" Shawna asked.

"Pretty, isn't it?" Catfish turned in his chair. Another shiver ran down his spine. Thomas leaned in over his shoulder. Catfish could smell urine, but said nothing. He wasn't sure he wanted to know what happened in the goddamned lab. "AUV 5 took this just as they spudded."

He hit the rewind button and the image disappeared. "Now here's the show." His finger tapped the touchpad.

The video played, his filters intact. The trio watched as the drill string moved downward into the ocean floor. The ground below seemed to vibrate and then the entire trench moved. Black tentacles rose from the sand and rock and wrapped around the metal pipes.

"Jesus," Shawna said. "What the fuck are those?"

Catfish pressed the space bar and the image froze. The tentacles strained against the metal, their flat heads jawing at the steel.

"They sure as shit aren't tube worms," he said.

Calhoun shook his head. "What is down there?" he asked. He looked over toward Harobin's station and suddenly realized he'd been smelling vomit. "Where's booger-man?"

Catfish giggled. "He, um, kind of lost his breakfast when the rig started doing its thing. Gotta admire him, though. Ole Andy stayed at his post until a few minutes ago. I think he went to find Vraebel."

"Vraebel?" Shawna said. "Is anyone dead?"

Catfish smoothed a stray lock of hair. "I don't know. I don't know if we took any damage either. But considering our fearless rig chief hasn't been screaming over the PA, I think we're safe. For now."

"Safe," Shawna deadpanned. "We're not safe anywhere."

Catfish looked up at Thomas. "Do I want to know what happened in the lab?"

"No," Thomas said, "but you're going to find out anyway."

He and Shawna told him what happened with the oil and how they trapped it. Shawna went into great detail about its reaction to certain frequencies of light.

He thought for a moment. "Does that make any sense, Thomas?"

The engineer chewed his lip. "I don't know much molecular chemistry. Or biology for that matter. But no. It doesn't make much sense at all."

Shawna stared at the screen. Her eyes darted back and forth between the worm-like appendages. "They have teeth," she said.

"Yeah," Catfish agreed. "Or something like teeth."

Thomas walked to the workstation furthest away from Harobin's. He logged in and the machine immediately began beeping. He raised an eyebrow. "Well someone wants to—" His voice trailed off.

Catfish turned to look at him. Calhoun's eyes were wide. "What?" the tech asked.

The engineer looked over at Catfish and Shawna. "It's the lab in Houston. They've been quarantined."

"What?" Shawna asked. "What do you mean, Thomas? Quarantined? For what?"

"Goddammit," Calhoun said. "We sent them a fucking plague."

Catfish pulled up his email. He'd been ignoring it for the last hour while he worked on data analysis and ROV diagnostics. That was back when they were about to spud the well. After the rig-quake, his email seemed about the least important thing in the world. But now…

He pulled up his email client and sped by the urgent emails from Macully. Instead, he brought up the one Calhoun was looking at.

"To all PPE contractors and employees on Leaguer," he read aloud, "due to biological contaminants in sample 1-J4X and an outbreak in the Houston lab, all drilling must be stopped immediately. Further information will be made available soon. Please stay safe and avoid interaction with the oil at all costs. Rig personnel should prepare for possible evacuation."

Calhoun nodded. "We let it loose," he said, his voice just audible above the whoosh of the air conditioner. "Goddammit. Goddammit!"

"Evacuation?" Shawna asked. "Who the hell are they kidding?" Catfish and Calhoun turned to her. "They're not going to evacuate shit."

"No," Calhoun said. He opened a web browser and then cursed. "Shit. The satellite just went down."

Catfish tried to connect to the internet. The console told him the link was unavailable. "Oh, fuck," he said. "Did they just cut us off?"

Thomas rose from the chair and stretched. The shotgun pop of his joints startled everyone in the room, including himself. "I need to talk to Vraebel. Fast." He traded glances with Catfish and Shawna. "I need y'all to start putting this together. Something. Anything. I need ideas. We need them fast."

He turned and left the room. Catfish shook his head. "Just what the fuck does that mean?"

"It means," Shawna said, "he's looking for a way out of this. And the only one I see is hitting the life boats and getting the fuck out of here."

"With the storm possibly heading toward us? Or with whatever that thing might have put in the water?" he asked.

"Yup," she said. She stared at his screen, her lips moving as she read the email line by line. When she was done, her fists clenched and unclenched. Catfish could see the whites of her knuckles. "And the sooner, the better."

#

To say it was a strange day was an understatement. Vraebel had logged the casualty reports. The XO had reported no damage to the thrusters or the generators. The blip in power from the rig-quake was nothing more than the result of loose connections. The engineering team had taken care of that situation. Now all they had to do was hope the storm didn't come north and kick their ass.

Except that was the least of their worries. And Vraebel knew it. He was waiting on a damage assessment from Standlee's AUVs. Considering the robots weren't due to surface until later that night, it would be a long time before the man could reprogram them. Unless, of course, one of them had already filmed the string.

Gomez had wanted to try and bring the string back up, but Vraebel had nixed the idea. He knew there was little chance of a blowout since there was little to no pressure coming through the pipes. But until they knew exactly what had happened, he was loathe to risk tearing apart the joint stand.

Vraebel had sent Belmont and his crew of divers to search for the two bodies. He held out hope the frogmen would find the corpses and bring them back, but he didn't believe the Ukrainian would find even a shred. The bodies had been in the water for nearly an hour now. If the fish or sharks hadn't yet chewed them to pieces, it was likely the weight of their gear had taken them down.

He was checking the weather when an email alert popped up on his console. Vraebel sighed, knowing it was Simpson replying to the situation reports. The VP was no doubt having kittens over the casualties, let alone the possible damage to the rig. He clicked the mail icon and started to read.

A fist rapped at the hatch. Vraebel was lost in the email and hardly noticed. He didn't hear the hatch open.

"Fuck," he said, eyes glaring at the screen.

"I assume," Vraebel jumped at Calhoun's baritone voice, "you've just read the email."

The rig chief turned in his chair, heart thumping in his ears. Calhoun looked as though he'd aged since they'd last seen one another. Of course, Vraebel felt ten years older himself. "Yeah," Martin said. He stood and headed to the coffee machine. "I'll start getting the rig ready for evacuation."

Calhoun shook his head. "I think you need to see what I've seen before you start thinking about evacuation."

He turned from the coffee machine and looked back at the older man. "What are you talking about?"

"AUV 1 hit 18k right after the quake. It streamed data and images from AUV 5."

Vraebel blinked. "Is the drill string damaged?"

"Martin," Calhoun said, "I need you to come to the drilling office. Now."

"But I have—"

"You have an executive officer," Calhoun hissed. "Use him."

He walked out of the hatchway. Vraebel, feeling queasy, followed.

#

A goddamned conga line. That was the phrase that kept repeating itself in his mind. It had been over an hour and the line just kept getting longer. He wanted to find Gomez and pop the man's head off. He knew this was revenge for quarantining three of his men when they got sick; he'd sent everyone who was on the rig deck during the quake for a physical. Everyone, that was, except himself.

Despite the constant flow of air conditioning, Doc Sobkowiak was sweating. For the past hour, he'd seen dozens of large men with their shirts off, smelled the stench of their unwashed clothes, and examined every inch of their bodies. Bruises, scratches, sprains, but nothing serious. Harrison had been the first, but that was a simple broken wrist. He'd set the bones, put him in a cast, and sent the man to his cabin with pain killers.

Sobkowiak finished examining a roughneck named Menendez. The man had scar tissue down one side of his face, presumably from a knife wound or some other sharp instrument. Doc figured it had been at least 15 years since the man suffered the injury. Other than that? The usual contusions from the rig-quake.

"Get out of here. You're fine," he said with a forced smile. Menendez grunted. "Take some ibuprofen or something if you're in pain."

"Right," the man said. He headed out the door.

Sobkowiak looked at the line. It had finally thinned down to three men. He heaved a huge sigh and wiped the sheen of sweat from his forehead. Instead of dealing with these three, he should be checking on the three men who'd come down with the flu or whatever it was. Today he'd have to make the decision as to whether or not he needed to call in an evac chopper. If the antibiotics hadn't started to kill whatever they had, they needed to get the hell off the rig. He didn't want anyone dying on his watch and he was completely unequipped to deal with anything viral.

That was the whole point of having the supply ships running up the coasts and traveling between the rigs. If something really bad happened, they could send a chopper out to a rig and get seriously injured people to better medical care. PPE's supply ship had a real medical center aboard. And if they couldn't handle the situation, then they'd be able to handle a chopper large enough to spirit the injured workers away to the mainland.

Leaguer just didn't have room for the facilities. Hell, he didn't even have a goddamned nurse. As he ran the next roughneck through the physical, all he could think about was returning to his GP practice in Austin. If not for the goddamned stock market and malpractice insurance costs, he'd still be there lancing boils, performing summer camp and sports physicals, and setting bones. Instead? He was thousands of miles from fucking nowhere.

His phone rang. Sobkowiak lifted the black cordless from its station. "Medical."

"This is Gomez. You checked on my men yet?"

He bit his tongue and forced a cheery voice. "Almost. Just got two more to go."

"No, Doc. I mean the three you let off duty. If they're better, I need them on the deck ASAP."

He sighed. "I planned to check on them as soon as I got through the physicals."

"Good. About that. Anyone hurt?"

"Besides Harrison? No. Contusions, scratches, some bruised ribs, but that's about it." Sobkowiak glanced up at the naked man in front of him and waved him away. The roughneck grunted and pulled on his clothes. "In about twenty minutes or so, I should be able to check on the rest of the men."

"Let me know," Gomez said and then the line went dead.

Sobkowiak sighed again. Two more. Just two more and then he could check and see if his patients would remain his patients. They wouldn't.

#

Twenty roughnecks. Twenty men of the morning shift. They had headed to the commissary for a meal, some trash talk, and the usual camaraderie. Red was last to head up the stairs. After the physical with the doc, he'd wanted a shower. That man gave him the creeps.

He'd winced as he'd pulled off his grease covered shirt. He knew he'd damaged his rotator cuff and hoped it was only a sprain. When the quake had happened, he'd ended up tripping over the joint lines and falling on his side. And for that little mistake? His body was covered in bruises and his right arm screamed at him when he tried to lift it above his shoulder. *Great fucking day,* he'd thought.

After struggling just to get his shirt on, his stomach had growled at him. He imagined Rodriguez was already dealing cards for the poker game. Nutty would have something good to eat.

Probably his frou-frou noodles and sweet sausage. Red had grinned at the thought. And then he opened the doors.

The first thing to hit him was the smell. Burned meat, spoiled food, and something not quite discernible. His nostril hairs wilted beneath the stench. When he had a moment to recover from the eye-watering smell, his brain denied what he was seeing.

The floor near the tables was covered in black ooze. Steel zippers, buttons, the occasional pocket knife, belt clasp, and earring sat atop the ocean of black. In one corner of the room, the steel toe of a boot shined beneath the commissary lights.

"What the—" Red asked.

The floor shivered. The substance rippled as the edges pulled back from the walls. It concentrated itself and then something rose from the goo.

As Red watched, a tentacle of black solidified and popped out of the muck. Another crackling sound and an eye-stalk emerged. The nearly black orb stared at him.

"Fuck," Red said. He turned to run. He turned to scream. He turned to leap down the steps, but something grabbed his foot. Caught in mid-jump, he fell to the stairwell landing with a crunch. His right shoulder was definitely broken now. But the lance of pain from his upper body was immediately drowned out by the screaming nerves in his foot.

He twisted over so he could see what was burning his leg and shrieked as bones snapped. Red peered at his foot. Smoke curled from the black ooze crawling up his pant leg. The heavy denim disintegrated beneath the substance.

Howling in pain, Red used his hands to pull himself to the first step. A stream of tears fell from his eyes and blurred his vision. God, the pain! He pulled with his gnarled, strong fingers and dragged himself forward. There was another snap and he knew, somehow knew, his left leg was gone at the knee.

He heard the plodding of heavy boots on the staircase. Through his tears, he saw Harobin's balding head as the man headed toward the landing.

"Help me!" Red screamed.

Harobin lifted his eyes to the landing and froze. Color drained from his face and his mouth opened in a wide "O".

"Help me!"

The geologist blinked at him and then fled. Harobin stumbled and had to hold the railing as he took the steps two at a time.

Red screamed again. Against every instinct he had, he looked back at his leg. Streams of ooze had wrapped around his thigh in a rising spiral. He could see bone and exposed muscle between the gaps. Red pulled as hard as he could, but his strength was going. His body shivered as he went into shock. The adrenaline surge wasn't enough to keep him going.

He watched as the tendrils met. A gurgling sound met his ears as the liquid rushed from the floor and swept up his other leg. The smell of burning hair and flesh made him vomit. Red's breathing became labored and his vision grew dim. The blanket of black slowly covered him as he lost consciousness.

#

Have you learned your lesson? He asked himself. *Yes, never play the fucking stock market again.* Sobkowiak headed down the hall to the staterooms. Gomez had demanded he check in on the three sick mud specialists. What the deck chief didn't seem to understand was that Sobkowiak had been trying to check on them for the past several hours. He'd been on his way to do just that when the rig-quake happened.

Instead of checking on them, he'd been forced to give the deck crew physicals. More delays. More time lost. Sobkowiak sighed as he reached Richardson's room.

Richardson was a balding brit with a hawk nose and a congenial smile. When he'd come to Doc a day after the first well had been drilled, he'd complained about coughing and rattling in his chest. Sobkowiak had been alarmed at the man's 102° fever. He'd given him the usual fever suppressants and a Z-pac. While Sobkowiak didn't believe in handing out antibiotics like they were candy, Richardson had all the symptoms of pneumonia.

The two other mudders, Jameson and Parker, had visited him later the same day with the same symptoms. He'd filed reports with PPE as soon as he'd sent the men back to their rooms armed with meds. SOP was to alert the company in the event of a of dangerous illness spreading through the crew. PPE hadn't bothered to do more than acknowledge their receipt and send him the standard quarantine/evac policies.

Before ever stepping foot on Leaguer, he'd made sure he was familiar with them. He knew PPE sent the policies to him just to make sure he was aware of them, but it had been unnecessary. Sobkowiak wanted to make sure he didn't end up dead because of some aerosolized VD the roughnecks were likely to bring back from shore leave.

The black leather bag in his hand seemed to weigh a ton. He'd had to keep changing his grip on the handles to keep the sweat from causing them to slide out of his grasp. The bag thumped to the floor and rattled. He donned a surgical mask, fiddled with the straps until it was comfortable, and then let his hands drop to his sides. The paper filter would keep him safe from all but the smallest microbes. *Just a precaution*, he told himself.

He rapped on the door. There was no response. "Mr. Richardson? It's Doctor Sobkowiak. Can I come in?" No response.

Sobkowiak rubbed his bald head. He didn't want to do it, but regulations were regulations. He reached into the pocket of his khakis and brought out a key ring. Only two people on the rig had a master key—the rig doctor and the rig-chief. It was only supposed to be used in times of emergency, either medical or rig-related.

He slotted it into the door lock, took a deep breath, and turned the key. The bolt slid back with an audible click. Doc returned it to his pocket and swung open the door.

The well-oiled hinges were silent as the door opened inward. There were no lights on. The portholes were covered and he stared into utter darkness. The light from the hallway barely illuminated the first few feet inside. "Mr. Richardson? Are you in here?"

The darkness in the corner of the room shifted. He listened for the tell-tale rattle of labored breathing, but there was nothing but the sound of the A/C. "Andrew?" he asked the room. It didn't respond. "I'm going to turn on the lights, Mr. Richardson. I need to see how you're doing."

At the touch of his fingers, strong fluorescent lights glared down on the room. Doc's eyes adjusted and then he blinked as he took in the destruction. The bed was little more than a metal frame.

The pillows were crusted with blood and shoved against the wall. In the center of the bed, the comforter, sheets, and mattress had dissolved into nothing. The remains of the fabric looked as though its edges had been burned by a flame. After a beat, he realized the hole in the bed was man-shaped.

Something moved in his peripheral vision. Doc turned and stared at the far corner. Beneath the desk and covered in shadow, something rippled. "Richardson?" Doc's voice was a barely audible tremor.

He stepped into the room, his leather bag forgotten. The ghostly scent of cooked flesh and spoiled meat wrinkled his nose. There was some other smell, something like metal, but he couldn't place it. He kept his eyes on the darkness beneath the desk until he reached the bed.

His breath stopped as he peered down into the hole in the mattress. Metal glinted at him. Surgical steel. Pins and a plate. "What the fuck?" he asked the room. There was no reply.

Richardson had broken his leg in a rugby match at university. The man's medical records had described the location of the plate and pins. And there they were. On the floor.

He cast his eyes back to the desk and the shadow beneath it. The dark pool rippled again. *What the fuck are you?*

Richardson's dead, you old fool, a voice said in his mind. *Get the fuck out of here!*

Doc swallowed hard. He didn't want to check on the other men. He didn't want to be on the rig. He didn't want to be anywhere but back in Austin lancing boils and popping kids with vaccinations.

He stepped backwards away from the bed, eyes firmly fixed on the desk and the thing beneath it. It had stopped moving. When he reached the doorway, he closed the door and didn't bother turning off the lights. Whatever was in there could stay in there. Forever.

Taking deep breaths, he picked up his leather bag and headed down the hall. He needed to get back to his office. He had to call PPE. They needed an evac. They'd never believe what he saw, but he'd say the men were near death. That would get them a chopper. Or a boat. Anything to get the fuck off the rig.

#

The drilling office was cool and dark. Standlee had turned off the lights so they could all bask in the glory of his monster movie. Vraebel was still trying to process what he'd seen.

As he and Calhoun had made their way to the drilling office, the engineer had said he and Shawna had been attacked by the oil sample. Vraebel wanted to yell "bullshit" as loud as he could. The man had clearly gone insane. He'd considered ignoring Calhoun and simply heading back to the bridge. But then Calhoun had said the AUV had filmed what happened to the drill string. That was enough to keep Vraebel from bolting.

The email from Simpson regarding quarantine of the Houston lab, coupled with what Calhoun said, had set him on edge. When Standlee had shown him the film? Yeah, that's when the wheels of reality started to come off.

"The tube worms aren't tube worms," Vraebel finally said.

Calhoun, Sigler, and Standlee were all staring at him and had been for several seconds.

Calhoun cleared his throat. He rubbed his hands together. Vraebel was sure the man was going to tell him it was all a joke, but the big engineer's face turned stony. "No, Martin. They're not." He sighed and jerked a thumb at the screen. "That's what grabbed the drill string. You can see it as clear as day."

"No," Vraebel said. "Simply not possible."

Sigler and Standlee exchanged a glance. A strange look came over her face and when she met Vraebel's eyes, they glittered with something akin to madness. "If you don't believe us, I can always take you in the lab, give you a flashlight, and then turn off the overheads. Then maybe you'll understand."

"Is that a threat?" Martin asked. His pulse pounded in his ears. None of this made any sense. Maybe in the fucking Twilight Zone or some goddamned Jake Bible book, but this shit didn't belong in reality. Period. "You threatening to lock me in your lab?"

She shook her head. "You don't get it, do you?" She turned and pointed at the screen. "That fucking happened, Martin. That is fucking real!"

Sigler was obviously close to panic. Whatever had happened, or she imagined happened, had addled her brain. There was no other explanation for a rational person, a fucking scientist no less, to take this seriously.

Vraebel tapped his foot and raised his hands. "I don't believe it. I simply do not accept this."

Calhoun's face flushed. "Martin," he said in a low even voice, "do you accept that the Houston lab has been quarantined?"

"Of course," Vraebel said. "I mean, Simpson wouldn't fuck with us. Would he?"

Calhoun shook his head. "No, Simpson wouldn't. And I'm telling you that we're not fucking with you either. What would be the purpose?"

He opened his mouth, and then closed it. He didn't know what to say to that. What *would* be the purpose? Vraebel couldn't believe he was going to say the words that popped into his mind. "Say I believe that," he said and pointed at the screen. "The fuck am I supposed to do about it? What do you suggest? We pull the string back up?"

Standlee shook his head. "We don't know how it would react."

"It. You mean the drill string?"

"Fuck," Standlee hissed. "No, goddammit. Whatever the fuck that is beneath the goddamned ocean floor!"

"It," Vraebel said. He rubbed at his temples. A headache was definitely in his future. "I think we need to evacuate the rig. Right fucking now. Let PPE decide what to do."

Calhoun looked at Standlee. "Show him."

The tech turned in his chair and brought up a web-browser. A dialog box popped up. "DNS Failure. Network Unavailable."

"See that?" Standlee asked. "We no longer have an internet connection via the satellite."

Vraebel blinked. "Bullshit. Unless something's wrong with the antenna."

"There's nothing wrong with the antenna," Calhoun grimaced. "If there was, GPS wouldn't be working."

"Okay, so it's just an outage. Sunspots or something."

Calhoun slammed a hand down on the desk. "Martin? You're in denial. And if you want to save your goddamned men and this fucking rig, you need to snap out of it. They've isolated us. They shut us off from the network. And there's not going to be any fucking evacuation."

"You don't know that!" Vraebel yelled. "You're just jumping to conclusions. You're scared, I get that. After watching...that," he said, "I'm a little shaken too. But PPE isn't just going to leave us out here."

Sigler nodded. "Yes, they will. If the CDC has already gotten involved in Houston, and they know where the sample came from, they're going to assume we've all been exposed to the agent."

"What agent?" he asked. "You have no proof anything has happened to anyone on this fucking rig."

Calhoun walked away from the desk, hands clasped behind his back. "The problem," he said to the monitors hanging from the ceiling, "is we don't know what it does when it encounters a human being."

"We can find out," Standlee said. "We need to go see JP."

"Right," Sigler said. She looked at Calhoun. "Have you talked to him today?"

Calhoun shook his head. "No. Catfish?"

"Nope. I figured he was out with the dive crew."

Vraebel pursed his lips. "You think what? That he was bitten?"

Standlee shrugged. "That's what he said. And JP's a tough bastard. He wouldn't hide in his bunk unless it was something pretty damned serious."

"Okay," Calhoun said. "Let's go see JP. Maybe he knows something. Or at least we can find out if this shit is lethal."

"And if it is?" Vraebel asked.

Calhoun paused. He headed to the door. "I'd rather not think about it."

#

The world was rendered in shades of grey. He'd nearly fallen down the steps as he ran away from...well, from whatever the fuck that was in the commissary. When he reached the bottom steps, he just kept running until he was in his stateroom.

Once he closed the door, locked it, and propped a chair beneath the door handle, he stood with his back against the wall huffing and puffing. His lungs burned and his heart was trip-hammering in his chest. But he was safe.

He stood there until the stars floating before his eyes departed and the world returned to full color. His fucking GP had told him he needed to lose weight. Harobin hoped he'd have a chance to get healthy.

After he'd left the drilling office to take a shower and clean up, he'd realized he hadn't eaten lunch. That was when he went to the commissary. He wasn't sure he'd ever eat again.

Red, he thought that's what the man's name was, was lying on the landing outside the commissary. The man's face was white as a sheet and trails of blood were trickling from his nose. When the man screamed for help, Andy had been caught off guard. He hadn't even noticed him until then. And then...

The black. A large puddle was consuming the guy. Even though he was still on the steps, he could see Red was missing the lower half of one leg. But that wasn't the terrible part. The terrible part was the appetizing scent of cooking meat and then realizing the source was the dissolving flesh of one of your coworkers.

Harobin closed his eyes and willed himself not to puke. On top of the rig quake, this was too much. Just too goddamned much. He was a coward. He'd run. He'd said "fuck you" to Red by high-tailing it down the steps to save his own skin. But what else was he supposed to do?

If Red had seen what was behind him in the commissary, he'd understand. Shit, he'd probably have screamed at Andy to get away. Yeah, that's how it would have gone down.

The commissary floor was nothing but black oil and floating bits of metal. Except for the thing sticking out of the mess. It looked like a tentacle that ended in eyes. Harobin shivered as the image flashed through his mind. *Fucking aliens have fucking landed,* he said to himself.

Or, maybe Shawna was right. Maybe there was something odd about the oil. Maybe it wasn't oil at all.

Something banged in the hall and he froze. The ooze was in the hallway. It was going to slide under the door and--

"JP? Open the fucking door!"

He exhaled a deep breath. Ears pounding with the sound of his heart, he peered through the peephole. Calhoun and Vraebel stood in front of the door across the hall. Harobin pulled the chair from beneath the door, unlocked it, and opened it. The two men turned toward him.

"Mr. Vraebel," he gasped, "there's something you need to know."

The rig-chief's forehead furrowed as he squinted. "Harobin? You look like shit. Why weren't you in the drilling office?"

Calhoun sniffed the air and grimaced. "And what the hell have you been into?"

"I saw—" He took in a deep breath. "I saw it. It ate Red."

Vraebel glanced at Calhoun and then turned back to Harobin. "What are you talking about?"

"The commissary," Harobin said. "It's in the commissary."

Calhoun stepped forward so he was face to face with the geologist. "What is *it*?"

"The oil," he said. "Or, um, I don't fucking know what it is!" He tried to take another deep breath and realized he was panting. "It took Red. It was eating him."

"Eating him?" Vraebel asked. "The fuck you—"

"Absorbing him! I don't know! It just…it was crawling up his legs. And he was screaming."

"Jesus," Vraebel said. "Did you get him out of there?"

Harobin shook his head. "I ran, Martin." Andy started to cry. "I couldn't save him. He was already gone."

Calhoun placed his hands on Harobin's slight shoulders. "Andy, I need you to calm down. You're starting to hyperventilate."

A sharp stabbing pain ran up his left arm. Harobin's lungs froze and suddenly there wasn't enough air in the world. His eyes grew wide and drool fell from his mouth. The floor of the hallway rushed toward him and he smashed into it head first.

#

CPR had no effect. Harobin was dead. Calhoun stared down at the corpse. "Martin? We have to get out of here."

Vraebel shook his head. "Four dead men, Thomas. I have four dead men. Possibly five, if what he said about Red wasn't just crazy talk."

Calhoun looked down the hallway. He thought he'd heard something, but wasn't sure. "Where's the doc?"

Vraebel said nothing.

"Martin?" Calhoun placed a hand on the man's shoulder. The rig-chief's eyes broke out of their distant stare and flashed to him. "Where is the doctor?"

"I— I'll get him," Vraebel said. He pulled out his phone and started typing. The phone's digital clicks sounded too damned loud.

"We still have Wi-Fi?"

Vraebel nodded. "On the internal network only. At least PPE was smart enough to make sure *that* wouldn't go down." He pressed the screen and the phone made a whooshing sound. "Okay, message sent."

"I take it you can't just call him?" Calhoun asked.

"No," Martin placed the phone in his shirt pocket. "We don't have local VOIP if the satellite is down."

Thomas nodded. He turned back to JP's door. He knew there was nothing in there. Nothing human, at least. What Harobin had said before he died made no sense and all the sense in the world. Shawna had wanted to know what happened when the oil touched human flesh. Now they knew.

"Martin," he said, "we need to get everyone to the life boats."

Vraebel laughed, but it sounded dangerously close to a scream. "Life boats? Are you fucking serious? You have any idea what's in that water?"

"Besides sharks?"

"That's not what I'm talking about, asshole," Martin said. "How do we know that, that thing, from the ocean floor isn't out there?"

"We don't," Calhoun said. "But we need to get everyone off this platform."

"That's a shitty idea," Martin said.

"Have a better one?"

The rig chief thought for a moment and then shook his head. "No." He walked down the hall to a red box. He punched through the plastic glass and pulled the switch.

Klaxon alarms echoed around the rig. The lights in the hallway flashed red. "That'll get everyone to the deck."

Calhoun shouted above the din. "Let's go."

He and Vraebel turned and headed for the stairs. The commissary was a floor above them. At least they wouldn't have to go near it. He fought the urge to look back at the dead geologist or Harvey's door. They were both dead, but they deserved better than just being left behind.

When they reached the stairwell, Vraebel stopped so quickly that Thomas ended up running into the back of him. Martin's body moved forward but he managed to keep his feet. Calhoun, taller than the rig chief, peered over his shoulder at what had made him stop.

The flight of stairs leading to the next floor was covered in black ooze. The black had five more steps to slide down before it reached the landing. "The fuck?" Vraebel asked.

Calhoun hit him on the shoulder. "Move, goddammit!"

A ripping sound echoed in the stairwell and something rose out of the thick river of oil. Vraebel hadn't twitched. Calhoun hit him again and then pushed him toward the flight of stairs leading to the deck. Finally, Martin started to run. Calhoun watched as a tentacle waved and then reached for him.

He followed Vraebel as fast as he could, his heavy boots thudding on the metal steps. They followed the twists and turns of the stair case as they headed toward the deck. Thomas slowed and chanced a look back. The black wasn't on the stairs.

As he took the next turn, metal creaked. He looked up and froze. The black was no longer bothering with the stairs. Instead, it was a solid mass extending downward and weaving through the rails. Calhoun ran as fast as he could. He could hear it behind him as he descended. It was moving slowly, but not slowly enough.

The stairs finally led them outside. The sun was still high enough in the sky to blanket the world in gauzy light. Calhoun, lungs burning and legs threatening to give out, reached the deck. He looked back at the way they had come. The entrance to the rig's superstructure was clothed in darkness. Whatever the thing was, it had followed them down but would not come out in the light.

Vraebel puked on the deck. Calhoun fought down his own nausea and bent over. Hands on his knees, he forced himself to take deep breaths. *Getting too old to run marathons,* he told himself. *Too fucking old for it.*

"Thomas!" Shawna's voice yelled from other side of the deck. He looked up. Shawna and Catfish were running to him. Catfish had his laptop cradled under one arm.

Calhoun managed a wave, let out an acidic burp, and then tried to stand. His knees popped like firecrackers.

"You okay?" Shawna asked as she reached him.

He shook his head. "Not in any way possible," he said. "Although," he slapped Vraebel on the back, "we're alive. And that's something."

Catfish stared up at the rig stairs. He and Shawna had obviously come down the other way from the drilling office. "What the fuck is up there?" he asked.

"The black," Calhoun wheezed. "It's alive."

Shawna blinked and then followed Catfish's stare. She saw the same thing he did. "It's covered the entrance to the rig."

Calhoun shook his head. "I don't think it's covering it. I think it can't come out into the sunlight."

"Fucking fucking fuck!" Vraebel yelled. He wiped his mouth on his sleeve. "That's the fucking oil?"

"About time you got with the program, asshole," Catfish said.

The rig-chief's fists clenched and he started to walk toward Catfish. Calhoun grabbed his arm and pushed him back. "Quit it. Now." He glanced at each man in turn. "We don't have time for this."

Vraebel's phone let out a beep. He pulled it from his pocket, looked at the screen. "Shit," he said. "Doc says he's trapped in medical."

Catfish sat down, crossed his legs, and propped the laptop on his thighs. He typed a few keys and looked up at Calhoun. "While you two were busy finding JP, I ran some network tests. Email is still working, both outbound and inbound."

Calhoun blinked. "What does that mean?"

"We can call for help," Shawna said. She glanced around the deck. Calhoun followed her gaze. A little over a dozen roughnecks stood with wild, confused eyes. "If this is all that made it, then we have plenty of room in the lifeboats."

Calhoun nodded. "Worth a try."

Shawna looked down at Catfish. "You got the addresses?"

He smiled. "In my address book. Where else would they be?"

The day darkened and Thomas looked up into the sky. The fluffy clouds that had blanketed the horizon for days were growing darker. The first rain bands from the storm might be heading toward them. Or maybe it was just a typical day on the ocean.

"Light. We need light," Calhoun said. "Martin. We have lamps out here? High-powered halogens? Something like that?"

Vraebel didn't respond. His eyes were riveted to the deck.

"Martin!" Calhoun shouted. The rig-chief looked up at him. The man was terrified and lost. "Keep it together. Do we have lights?"

"Yeah," Martin said. He turned and looked at the remaining crew. "Gomez? You down here?" There was no response. He looked over at the roughnecks. "You guys seen him?" They all shook their heads. "Fuck. Okay, I need you guys to grab the deck lamps. I need them out here and hooked up." The men just stared at him. He took a deep breath. "MOVE!"

The deck crew jogged toward the supply sheds. Vraebel turned and looked at Calhoun. "What are you thinking?"

The engineer chewed his bottom lip. "If Shawna is right, the black can't handle a certain UV spectrum. That means the halogens should protect us when night falls." He looked up at the sky again. "Or it gets dark enough for it to feel safe out here."

Vraebel nodded and started typing on his phone. "I'll try and locate Gomez. If he's still alive, he should respond."

"If," Shawna said. "How come this is all that's left of the deck crew?"

"Shift change," Vraebel said without looking away from his phone. "Most of the night shift was headed for their breakfast and the morning shift was heading for dinner." He finished typing his message and the phone whooshed. He made eye contact with her. "Those men either finished early or hadn't yet left their posts."

"Jesus," Shawna looked at Calhoun. "Eighty people on this rig and this is all that's left?"

Vraebel nodded. "Harobin said the commissary was empty. I think it killed them all."

"Where is Harobin?" Shawna said as she gazed around the deck.

Vraebel swallowed hard. "He didn't make it." She blinked at him and then looked down.

"Catfish? How's it coming?" Calhoun asked.

The tech's grim face melted into a grin. "Got it. What do you want to say?"

"Request immediate evacuation. Hostiles on board the rig," Vraebel said. "Tell them we're under attack by pirates, North Koreans, gang-bangers, I don't give a shit. Just get us off the goddamned rig!" Catfish nodded and started typing.

The crew started to return. Some carried large tripods, others held rectangular light heads. Vraebel had them place the five lights in a large semi-circle. He looked over at Calhoun. "We're going to be fucking blinded by this."

Calhoun nodded. "Yeah. We won't really be able to see beyond the circle." He tapped his foot. "Catfish? When you get done sending that email, I need you to try and get the video feeds from the rig."

"On it," the tech said.

The sun was dying and not just from the blankets of clouds. It would hit the horizon in less than an hour and then they'd be defenseless.

#

When the klaxons started, he was still praying. His late father's Saint Christopher's medallion felt warm and moist in his palm. He had been muttering over it for the past thirty minutes. Whenever he prayed, he felt the world calm around him and the presence of God. But not today.

Gomez sat in a chair at the bridge. He'd cycled the hatch and locked it from the inside. If someone tried to get in, they'd meet an impenetrable metal shield. At least that was the theory.

Everything went to shit when he'd headed to the bridge to find his boss. The deck crew had been between shifts and he'd taken a break. Too much had happened. Way too much. Steve was afraid if he didn't get a break, he'd freeze up. So he'd decided to go see Vraebel.

The idea the rig-chief wouldn't be on the bridge had never crossed his mind. He'd slowly taken the stairs up past the drilling office and kept going into the main hallways. As he'd turned toward the bridge, he heard something and turned around.

The long hallway was empty except for the drink machine. Gomez licked his lips and walked toward it. He realized he hadn't had anything to eat or drink in at least six hours. No wonder he felt like he was about to pass out.

Talking to Vraebel while he polished off a Snickers and an energy drink wasn't exactly too informal, but it was pretty damned close. Considering the kind of day they'd had, though, he thought Vraebel would forgive him.

PPE wasn't the only company to stock free food and beverages for its people. That was pretty much standard. But PPE only stocked the good stuff. His stomach growled as he approached the standing metal vending machines Someone had pasted a picture of Jules from the movie "Pulp Fiction" over the coin slot. It read "You mind if I have some of your tasty beverage?" Gomez smiled at it.

He scanned the choices of drinks and finally decided to go for purple today. He slapped his hand against the plastic rectangle. The machine whirred and a pint can dropped to the slot with a bang. He picked it up, flipped open the top and took a long pull.

The acidic carbonation hit his palate and he smiled around the can. He'd planned to sip it, but fuck it, he was thirsty. He guzzled the entire can, belched loud enough for it to echo in the hallway and moved to toss the aluminum into the recycle bin. His hand froze in mid-throw.

The A/C duct over the snack machine was covered in black ooze. The stuff bubbled and rippled as it moved through the grate and drizzled down the wall. The can dropped from his hands and clanged on the hard floor.

He took a step back into the hallway. The thick, black ooze flowed faster through the grate. A crunching sound echoed in the hallway as the stuff rippled and quaked like shaken pudding.

Something rose from the black. A large tube-like appendage shot out of the stuff. An eye popped out from it and stared at him.

Steve ran. He pelted down the hallway as fast as he could. When he reached the bridge hatch, he swung open the door and turned to close it. The ooze was in the hallway now and speeding toward him. Gomez had closed the hatch with a shriek and turned the lock wheel to barricade the door. He'd turned around and stared into the XO's wide, panicked eyes.

"What the fuck was that?" Terrel had asked.

Gomez had pulled the medallion from its chain and palmed it. He'd stepped back from the door as close to the bridge windows as he could get. "I don't know," he'd said. "But I think we're fucked."

When his phone went off, a stream of urine jetted into his boxers. The medallion nearly flipped out of his hands. The XO looked at him and then started to laugh.

"Scared the shit out of me," the man said.

Scared the piss out of me, Gomez thought. He reached into the pocket of his dungarees and brought out the phone. He heaved a sigh of relief.

"Where are you?" the message asked.

Gomez typed in his answer and sent it. He looked up at the XO. "It's Vraebel. He's alive."

Terrel hissed through his teeth. "Thank, God. Ask him what the fuck is going on."

Gomez held up a hand. *We'll get to that,* he thought. The seconds drew out like taffy as he waited for Vraebel's response.

The phone buzzed in his hands. He read the message, and then peered out of the windows onto the deck. Twilight was falling, but he could still see the deck without a problem. Halogen work lamps were arranged in a large semi-circle. Over a dozen people stood inside the ring with a portable generator.

"Jesu Christi," he said.

The XO followed his gaze. "What the fuck are they doing?"

"Preparing," Gomez said.

"For what?" Terrel's voice trembled.

"For nightfall." The phone buzzed again. He looked down at the bridge control board. "Terrel? Vraebel's asking if we can get coms up and running."

Terrel blinked. "They're still up. We're just not getting anything."

Gomez looked at him. "You're the fucking XO, Terrel. You're supposed to know how everything works up here. Vraebel says make it happen."

The man thought for a moment. "Okay. What does he want?"

Gomez read the message. "He wants you to check the satellite link. If it's down or we can't send, he wants you to do a patch on the Wi-Fi. Try and get VOIP up on the local network."

Terrel blinked. "I have no idea how to do that."

Useless fucking bendajo, Steve thought. He typed in the message back to Vraebel and waited. When the phone buzzed again, Gomez couldn't help but grin. "Catfish is going to walk you through it."

"Who?" Terrel asked.

"Standlee."

The XO groaned. "That asshole doesn't know shit!"

"More than you, apparently," Gomez chuckled.

#

Cigar smoke drifted from the deck. It swirled upwards around the bright, white halogen lights before the ocean breeze spirited the smoke away. Calhoun pulled the Macanudo from his lips and exhaled through his nostrils.

Shawna wrinkled her nose, but said nothing. Catfish sat in the middle of the circle, a laptop propped on his knees. The lid was closed and his fingers kept tapping against its aluminum surface. She fought the urge to look behind her. She knew if she saw anything, she'd scream.

They'd been exposed to the night for three hours now. The work lamps were so bright, she couldn't even see the moon. With all the clouds racing across the sky, she wasn't surprised. The last weather report Gomez had listened to on the bridge said the storm was coming. The first bands of rain would probably hit them before dawn.

Shawna shivered. Cold wind, cold rain… That was going to be so much fun around 4 am. If they survived that long.

While everyone was sitting in the circle of light, that didn't mean everyone believed what Vraebel and Calhoun had told them. She thought at least half the remaining deck crew thought the two men had gone off their collective rockers. Four of them lay sleeping on the deck. The others sat staring at one another or out into the darkness. They hadn't spoken a word in over an hour.

"The fuck are we doing here, chief?" a burly blond man asked once darkness had fallen.

Vraebel glanced at him. "Waiting out the night, Bill. Waiting out the night."

"The fuck does that mean, boss?"

Vraebel sighed. "You wouldn't believe me if I told you."

One of the other men, a rail-thin, red-haired man with huge biceps snorted. "Rig quake? That fucked up oil?" He shook his head. "I'll believe anything right now."

So he told them. After that, they'd just checked out. Bill looked afraid to say anything. Jack, the red-haired man, had been the same way. The rest? While Vraebel told the story, they'd rolled their eyes. Some had even chuckled and only stopped when the chief glared at them.

Shawna checked her watch. Six hours until dawn. She looked over at Vraebel. He was staring at the deck, his lips moving in silent words.

"I have an idea," Calhoun said. The circle of people all looked at him in startled surprise. Thomas ignored the stares, eyes fixed firmly on Shawna. "Assuming the light keeps it away, we should be able to move about during the day without a problem."

"Big assumption," Shawna said. "Although since the samples in the lab reacted so violently to it, I think it's correct."

Vraebel harrumphed. "What makes you think these halogens," he said pointing at the tripods, "are doing anything like that?"

Shawna noticed that Thomas' fingers were trembling. He took a deep drag on the cigar and let the smoke creep out of his mouth. He glanced over Vraebel's shoulder. "Because it hasn't attacked."

She slowly turned her head and looked where her boss' eyes were fixed. "I don't see—" She stopped, the words dying in her throat. It was difficult to make out, but there was a shadow a few feet away from the circle of light. She squinted and then nearly screamed.

A shape, blacker than the darkness, stood behind Vraebel. It was solid, but amorphous at the same time. It stood on three legs, its body squat and low to the ground. Appendages waved from its top half. She couldn't be sure, but she thought it was the size of three men. Maybe more. It seemed to stretch out into the distance, but it was impossible to tell how far.

"Oh. My. God," Shawna said. She stared back at Calhoun.

Vraebel was looking over his shoulder. The ruddy color in his cheeks had faded. "Is that—" he started to say and then gulped hard. The rest of the men in the circle were looking too. One by one, they seemed to see it, jaws dropping open.

Thomas patted his knee and took another drag on the nearly spent cigar. "I think it has us surrounded." Jack got to his knees and then stood. "Don't leave the circle," Calhoun said to the red-headed man.

The lanky rough-neck blinked at him and then faced the darkness. "What the fuck is it?" he asked.

"I don't know," Calhoun said. "Something old. Very old. And I don't think the oil is all of it. I think it's part of it. But something else is down in the ocean. I've no idea what."

Jack glanced back at him. "Something like what?"

Thomas shook his head. "Like I said, I don't know."

Vraebel's phone rang making everyone jump. He pulled it out of his pocket and stared at it. He slid his finger across the screen and put it to his ear. "Gomez?" he said. Shawna watched as Vraebel's eyes widened. The man bit his lip. "Okay. Thanks," he said and put the phone down. He pointed to the bridge above them. "Steve says we're fucked."

Catfish grunted. "Like we didn't already know that."

Vraebel glared at the tech and then stared around the circle. "It's getting closer," he said. His eyes found Calhoun's. "You're right about us being surrounded."

"How's Gomez holding up?" Thomas asked.

"I guess he and Terrel are safe." He chuckled. "Safer than us anyway. That bridge is made of steel and glass. Nothing's getting in there."

"So he can see it?" Shawna asked. "I mean around us?"

"Yeah," Vraebel said. He looked up at Jack. "Sit down, man. You're— You're attracting it."

Jack glanced at the rig chief. "I don't know what—"

Something shot out of the darkness and splatted against Jack's chest. He turned to the others in horror as they scrambled away from him. The smell of cooking flesh and something fetid filled the air. He clutched at his chest as his clothes caught fire.

Bill grabbed the man's legs, pulled him to the deck, and patted at the flames. "Jack!" he yelled and rolled him over, chest to the light. Jack's mouth opened in a silent scream. Tendrils of black flashed out of the darkness and grabbed the burning man's head. The sound of pine-knots combusting in a fire place was barely audible beneath Bill's shouts. The tentacles caught fire as they pulled the burning man's body out of the circle.

"Jack!" Bill screamed again. There was no response. Out in the darkness, they could hear the sound of bacon frying in a pan and the crackling of bones breaking. Bill reached a hand beyond the circle of light. Catfish grabbed his leg and pulled him back to the center of the circle. The man flung a fist and smashed the side of Catfish's head.

He shook it off and kept pulling until Bill was safely in the center. Vraebel and one of the other deck-workers tackled the man, keeping him still. Bill was still yelling. Vraebel looked down at him. "He's gone!" the rig chief screamed. "He's gone!"

Bill's eyes went wide. "What— What the fuck was that?"

Calhoun's cigar had fallen to the deck. It looked like a brown turd. The end was still smoking. He shuffled a little closer to the inner circle. As did everyone else, including Shawna.

Thomas was shaking. Shawna put her arm around his shoulder.

Vraebel looked at each of the roughnecks. "Everyone believe us now?"

No one said a word.

\#

Tequila. That was the cure. A bottle of Tres Generaciones Anejo was exactly what he needed. Too fucking bad there was no booze allowed on the ship.

Gomez sat in the captain's chair, eyes riveted on the circle of light on the deck below. Terrel sat in the corner of the room, head in his hands. As they watched the attack, the man's resolve had folded like a cheap tortilla. Gomez couldn't blame him. He had clutched the medallion in his palm tight enough to draw blood.

Jack Hosley was dead. That much was certain. From high above the circle of light, he and Terrel watched as the shadows gathered on the light's edge before it attacked. Whatever it was. When it dragged Hosley's body into the darkness, clouds of whitish smoke wafted upward into the breeze.

He'd tried to warn them. Even made the phone call Vraebel had told him NOT to make unless it was absolutely dire. Once Standlee walked Terrel through setting up a VOIP stream via the Wi-Fi, they'd decided conversation would only kill the phone batteries. Trapped on the deck, Vraebel and his circle had no way to recharge them.

Now Jack Hosley was dead. Gomez couldn't tell, but it looked like Bill Christian was hurt too. And dawn was still hours away.

They'd heard something scratching at the hatch over an hour ago. Whatever it was gave up after ten minutes or so. He thought both he and Terrel were going to shit themselves when it started. Now? That seemed laughable after what they'd seen down on the deck.

Gomez brought up the computer. The Wi-Fi was live, but there was still no connection to the outside world. Except for corporate email. All other ports had been closed off. Catfish had tried to carry SSH traffic over 587 and connect to another server outside the corporate firewall, but hit a dead end. PPE wasn't allowing any traffic that wasn't mail.

And they weren't exactly getting any of that either. Gomez, Vraebel, and Calhoun had all sent messages to Simpson and other PPE executives requesting evac. Thus far? Nothing. No response. It was as if the mails had never been sent.

He'd asked Vraebel via text why PPE wasn't responding. His assessment? "They're deciding what to do with us."

The email regarding the Houston quarantine had been vague to say the least. The line commanding Vraebel to prepare for evacuation seemed like a lie to give them hope. Hope. Gomez fingered the medallion. Hope was all but gone.

The air on the bridge was souring. He didn't know if the A/C intakes were picking up rotten food from the kitchen or... Gomez decided he didn't want to know. Whatever that shit was he'd seen in the hallway and on the deck, he didn't want to know what it did to its victims.

Gomez jumped in his chair as the computer dinged. "New Message," the screen said. "Dios mio," he muttered under his breath. His shaking fingers clicked the mouse button and the email text filled the screen.

"To crew of PPE Rig #2785 Leaguer:
Send status report and known head count of crew. All documents related to oil extraction and any incidents are needed by emergency personnel in Houston.

The Center for Disease Control is now in charge of all matters related to PPE Rig #2785 Leaguer.

In order to plan a successful evacuation scenario, we require as much data as possible."

Terrel was reading over his shoulder. "Holy shit," he giggled. "They're coming for us."

Gomez turned to him. "Maybe."

"What do you mean maybe?" the XO said and clapped him on the back. "It's right there!" he pointed at the screen.

"So is the fact the CDC is now in charge." Gomez rubbed his fingers across the medallion's face.

Terrel's manic smile faltered. "So?"

Gomez shrugged. "I don't know, but I—"

Something scratched on the wall. Gomez and Terrel turned toward the starboard side. The fetid stench flowing through the

A/C duct intensified. Gomez's heart rate increased. The scratching noise came again.

"Fuck," Gomez said. "Where the hell is that coming from?"

Terrel's frightened eyes scanned the ceiling. "You think it's trying to get in from above us?"

Gomez shook his head. "Can't. Vraebel said it can't go through metal or glass."

"I don't think—"

The metal A/C vent cover rattled.

"Fuck me," Gomez said. He backed away from the wall and grabbed his phone. "We need to get out of here."

A thin line of black ooze drizzled through the grate. It touched the hard floor and sizzled. Gomez ran to the supply cabinet and threw it open. He grabbed a heavy black cylinder and turned back toward the far wall.

Terrel stood frozen in front of the captain's chair. "Move, bendajo!" Gomez yelled. The XO didn't move. His eyes were fixed on the vent. "Move!" he screamed.

A river of ooze poured through the grate and puddled on the floor. The puddle started to crackle and ripple. Gomez pushed Terrel to the side and pointed the halogen flashlight at the black. The puddle contracted as a jagged tube rose from the surface. It waved toward the two men and an eye popped into existence. It blinked and then the tentacle reached for them.

Steve flicked on the flashlight. A narrow beam of strong white light shot out and hit the tentacle in its eye. The puddle of black slunk away as the tentacle smoked. Its eye disappeared back into the tentacle. Terrel screamed. He stumbled over his own feet and fell to the floor. Gomez tried to keep the flashlight pointed at the base of the tentacle as he grabbed Terrel by the shirt collar and dragged him across the floor.

The beam of light wobbled and then moved off the target. The puddle stopped smoking and began moving forward again. The tentacle raised in the air and smashed down into the floor with a heavy plop. Gomez shifted his gaze from Terrel's screaming, trembling body. The tentacle no longer had an eye. Instead, its end tapered to a fine point with jagged edges.

Gomez shouted as it raised and hit the floor again mere inches from his heavy boots. He loosened his grip on Terrel and aimed the flashlight back at the puddle. The sound of bacon frying in deep grease filled the room. The tentacle slashed down again and this time caught Terrel in the meat of his bicep.

The XO shrieked as the tentacle drew him backward. Gomez dropped the flashlight and pulled on Terrel's boot. "No, fucker!" he shouted. Terrel screamed in pain as he was caught between the tentacle pulling him one way and Gomez the other. Blood geysered out of Terrel's arm as the jagged tentacle ripped through flesh, muscle, and bone. Crimson droplets pattered into the puddle where they pulsed and then disappeared. The tentacle severed the arm near the shoulder and dragged its prize back into itself.

The remaining skin sizzled and dissolved. Tissue and bone were the last to go, but it was finished in seconds. Gomez continued dragging Terrel's screaming, shaking body toward the port side. The puddle rippled and then slid forward, its tentacle searching for a new target.

Gomez dropped his charge and scrambled for the flashlight. His fingers came within an inch of it before the tentacle slammed down into the floor. The puddle rippled and popped again. A smaller tentacle rose from its surface, a green and black eye staring from the end of the stalk. The blade shaped tentacle wavered in the air and then pointed at him as the eye found him.

He lunged for the flashlight just as the tentacle slammed down beside it. His left pinky finger touched the side of the tentacle. Flesh started to melt from his hand. Screaming, he lifted the flashlight with his other hand and pointed the beam straight at the eye.

The orb smoked before vaporizing in a flash of light and white smoke. The jagged tentacle whipped around and sliced through the front of his shirt. He shrieked louder as he held his ruined left hand against the cut in his chest, but still managed to keep the flashlight's beam pointed at the eyestalk. It retreated into the puddle and then the entire mess of goo slid backwards toward the shadows beneath the coffee table.

He advanced toward it, the flashlight shaking in his hands. The black ooze hit the wall and then slid upwards back into A/C vent. It disappeared leaving smoke and scorched drywall in its wake.

"Help. Me," a voice said from behind.

Gomez whirled, the flashlight beam lighting Terrel's face. Blood poured from the stump where his bicep should have been. Gomez pulled off his belt and cinched it around Terrel's arm. "Jesu Christi," he muttered. The blood slowed, but not enough.

Terrel's eyes fluttered. His weather-beaten skin was no longer tan, but pale.

"Don't you fucking die on me, bendajo!" Gomez yelled in Terrel's face. The XO's eyes closed. He took in a large shuddering breath as his body bucked and shook. The smell of shit and piss wrinkled his nose and then Terrel's body relaxed. The man's eyes stared up at the ceiling, but there was nothing in them.

The sudden silence on the bridge was enough to let him hear the puddle sliding in the ductwork. It was gone. For now. Gomez sat on his ass next to Terrel's corpse, tears welling from his eyes. "Fucking bendajo," he said. His breathing was too fast and his heart raced. Gomez pulled off his shirt and looked down. A long line of burned flesh spread from beneath his left underarm and to the right side of his waist. Blood didn't seep from the wound, but it hurt like hell.

Gomez held up his left hand. His pinky had been cut in half lengthwise. Bone protruded from missing skin and muscle. He shuffled backward to the wall and turned off the flashlight. The thing would be back. He was sure of it. He pulled the phone out of his pocket and started to type, his eyes jumping back to the grate with each word. He wasn't sure how long he could stay conscious. But he had to. Or it was all over.

#

It was outside the hatch. Every few minutes, he heard it sliding against the metal as it tried to find a crack, a crevice, any gap it could use to get through. But he was safe. For now.

Sobkowiak lay on the examination table, a scalpel in one hand. He knew the knife wouldn't do anything against what he'd seen, but it still made him feel better. If nothing else, he could slit his own throat before it got to him.

He'd eyed the prescriptions and tranquilizers when he'd run back from the hallway. It would be a painless way to go. Inject an overdose of morphine and simply slip off into... The black? He shivered.

It was a word. Just a word. But it was the absence of color. The absence of light. The absence of everything. But the black moved. The black was alive.

Sobkowiak tapped the scalpel against his knee. When the CDC email had come in, he'd stared at it and reread it so many times, he knew every syllable it contained.

"We require as much data as possible," the email had said.

"Bullshit," Sobkowiak said aloud. It didn't take a fucking PhD to read between the lines. If they were willing to admit the Houston lab had been quarantined, requesting data from ground zero meant they had no idea what it was or how to stop it. Evacuation? "Bullshit."

He brought the scalpel up before his eyes. The blade was bright steel and incredibly sharp. The rig was like a gangrenous limb. You could clean it, you could cut out the diseased parts, but the rot would just spread. And in the end, you'd have to amputate.

Amputation was the answer. It was the only answer. If the CDC didn't understand that, they would soon. And then what? Would they drop a fuel-air bomb on the rig? Or send a submarine to sink it with a torpedo?

Sobkowiak chuckled. How pissed off would Greenpeace be if the American government sank a fucking oil rig?

There would be a cover up. PPE would likely go bankrupt under mysterious circumstances. The executives would be sworn to silence, paid off, God only knows what. The world couldn't afford to know about the black. It would bring the oil industry to a complete and utter halt. The world economy would collapse. No more cars. No more trucks. No more gas stations.

Sobkowiak touched the cold blade to the tip of his finger. A person could survive without a finger. Hell, remove all four limbs and a person would be able to live. It would be hellish, certainly, but life would remain. But cut out the heart of business and locomotion? It would be a cut the world couldn't afford.

Something scratched at the hatch. Sobkowiak glanced over at it. The white rectangular steel door didn't move. The scratching sound continued. He shifted his legs off the bed and stood. With slow steps, he approached the door.

He reached it and put his ear against the metal. The scratching sound was something else. Sizzling. Frying. White noise from a television tuned to a dead station. The metal door grew warm.

The doctor pulled away from the hatch and walked back to his desk. He turned on the computer and sat down in the black ergonomic chair. The screen lit up as the hard drive whirred. He put on his glasses and stared at the screen.

He brought up the email client, found the message from the CDC, and hit reply. He typed as the thing continued scratching at the door. Before he sent the email, he said a prayer to a God he didn't believe in.

#

Two hours had passed since the attack. The group was pushed together so closely, their feet touched. Within the center of the circle, bathed in light, they were fairly safe. Or so Calhoun hoped.

They could hear it sliding around on the deck. At one point, they heard what sounded like footsteps, but the creature didn't appear. When they'd moved further into the light, their night vision was completely shot. Beyond the tripods was little more than shadows and utter darkness.

The moon was high in the sky, but its wan light barely penetrated the blanket of clouds that raced from horizon to horizon. Calhoun wanted to check his phone again, see if there was another response from PPE or the CDC or whoever the fuck was now in charge. But his battery was already down to 15%. Best to save it.

Catfish had opened his laptop several times to check on the AUVs. The three that remained in the water had surfaced hours ago. Calhoun had asked him if they could look at the image data, but Catfish didn't want to waste the battery. Instead, he brought up the seismic reports. What they said made little sense, like every other fucking thing that had happened.

Once the thing below the ocean floor had attacked the drill string, the trench had shifted again. The data didn't tell them how it had reconfigured itself, but Calhoun didn't need to know.

AUV 5 had reported that the drill string was still in the ground. How far it had punched through the ocean floor was still unknown. When the rig quake happened, those sensors had been damaged. Harobin knew how far they had drilled, but he was gone.

Calhoun wished he had another cigar and a single malt. Or better yet, a port. He grunted at the thought. They were surrounded by something malevolent that could tear them to pieces or dissolve their flesh and he was thinking about his favorite after dinner routine. He looked up from the deck and out into the darkness.

Three hours. Three more hours and the sun would start to rise in the east. The clouds may have blanketed the sky, but he was sure enough UV light would make it through to harm the thing. Maybe even kill it. But only if they could keep it from getting back inside the rig structure. Once inside, it would have plenty of places to hide.

"Once inside," he said aloud.

"What?" Shawna asked.

He looked over at her and grinned. "Nothing. Just thinking."

"About what?" Her face was lined with worry, but her eyes were steely.

Calhoun once again patted himself on the back for hiring her. "I do have a question for you."

"Okay. Shoot."

He pointed up to the bridge. "Gomez said they were attacked by something much smaller than what we have out here."

"Yeah. So?"

"What if," he said, "each person that was, well, infected, became a different entity?"

Shawna opened her mouth and then closed it. She raised her eyes to the sky, tongue clicking against her teeth. "That would mean there are..." She paused and then looked back at him. "At least four other creatures. All smaller than the one out here."

Calhoun nodded. "I think that's a fair assumption. Harvey and the three mud workers were infected. However this thing reproduces, it must have used them for food to grow."

"And this one," she pointed into the darkness, "had a huge meal."

Catfish tapped on his laptop. "Then why aren't they out here joining the fun?"

"Good question," Calhoun said. "Maybe they just haven't gotten around to it yet."

"Like they need to," Vraebel said. "Doc and Gomez are still in there. Maybe some others."

Goddammit, he wanted a cigar. Calhoun rubbed a hand across his forehead. He was getting a migraine and it didn't seem like sleep was in his future. "At least it didn't get Terrel."

Vraebel hissed. "Oh, I beg to fucking differ. The man's dead."

"Sorry," Calhoun said, "that's not what I meant. I meant that what attacked him and Gomez didn't get to feed. At least not much."

The rig chief looked up at the bridge. "Steve is trapped up there and we can't get to him. He could be fucking dying and there's nothing we can do."

Calhoun nodded. "We'll get him come daylight."

"Just how the fuck are we going to do that?" one of the deck crew asked. Calhoun turned to the large black man sitting across from him. "Those things could be anywhere in there."

A smile tugged at the corners of Calhoun's lips. "We have weapons," he said and pointed to the tripods. The rest of the group followed his gaze.

"You're kidding," Vraebel said. "Tell me you're kidding."

"I think we're going to have to light the way," Calhoun said. "Catfish?"

The tech looked up from the deck and to his boss. "Yeah?"

"We need to send the CDC some info. You and Shawna get started on a report. Tell them everything we know. But don't tell them how many are presumed infected."

"Why?" Shawna asked.

"Because if they know," Calhoun frowned, "they'll just blow us out of the water."

Chapter Eight

The generator sputtered and the lights flickered. Calhoun looked up at them with a nervous smile. A dim rosy glow had appeared on the eastern horizon. Even behind the thick, bruised cloud cover, it was enough light to dispel some of the shadows on the rig. In a way, that was worse.

Several meters away from the flickering circle of light, he could see the glint of a belt buckle, rivets from blue jeans, and a pocket knife. That was all that remained of Jack Hosley. As if that wasn't bad enough, they could see the black.

It no longer surrounded them. It had pulled itself around the edges of the western side of the circle. It seemed to know light was coming. He wasn't sure how it would react when sunlight finally kissed the rig and chased away the shadows, but he had a feeling it wouldn't stick around very long.

A single half-meter high eye-stalk rose from its flat, obsidian surface. The circle of people had all turned to watch it. The stalk wavered in the freshening wind. The smell of rain had filled their noses. The storm was coming, or at least its outer bands.

The black rippled and shook as a single ray of sunlight broke through the cloud cover. The eastern side of the rig brightened for a moment, and the puddle slid further away from them.

Both Calhoun and Shawna had gotten over their shock at seeing the thing. Ever since dawn had started and the black was visible, they had watched it, studied it. It hadn't shown any aggression since it took Jack. Calhoun figured the damage it took from the bright lights had been enough to keep it at bay. That and the fact they had all moved to the center of the circle.

It couldn't attack them without suffering damage. On the one hand, that meant it felt pain and they could fight it. On the other, that meant it was capable of strategy and going on more than simple instinct. Calhoun didn't like that at all.

The clouds brightened as the sun rose over the horizon. A tendril of smoke erupted from the eye stalk. The puddle shook like pudding and retreated another meter. The deck was larger than a football field and the black covered at least half of it. Calhoun couldn't tell how thick it was, but he thought it had spread itself thin to cover as much ground as possible.

Another white finger of smoke filled the air above the puddle. The eye-stalk quivered and shrank back into the black. The eye was no more than a few centimeters above its surface. The black receded into itself, thickening and shrinking in size at the same time. It started to move.

The circle of trapped people watched as it traveled to the western stairs. It moved to the bottom step and then a reverse river of black rose up the stairs and into the superstructure.

Vraebel blew out a sigh. "Are we safe?"

Calhoun shook his head. "Not until we're off the rig or that thing has been burned into nothing."

Bill moved to stand up and Vraebel raised a hand. "Not yet, Bill. Let's wait until the rig is in full sunlight. I don't like the idea of that thing playing possum." The large man's face wrinkled in frustration and then he sat back down. "Thomas?" Martin asked. "You agree?"

"Absolutely. Catfish?"

"Hmm?" Craig said as he opened his eyes. The tech had been asleep for the last hour. "What?" he looked around and then smiled. "It's gone?"

Calhoun nodded. "We need to get the AUVs powered up and ready. We're going to need to reprogram them for something special."

Running his fingers through his dirty blond hair, Catfish looked even more confused. "For what?"

Calhoun grinned and turned to Vraebel. "We have explosives?"

Vraebel blinked. "Yeah. Of course. To fracture the strata below the ocean floor if we're having trouble getting the oil flowing." A frown crossed his face. "You're not fucking serious."

"What?" Catfish asked. "What the hell are you talking about, Thomas?"

The engineer clasped his hands together. "We have two things we have to take care of. We have to get rid of that," he said pointing to the superstructure, "and make sure it doesn't get back in the ocean."

"And how the fuck are we going to do that? Blow up the goddamned rig?" Catfish asked.

Calhoun shook his head. "No. We'll have to do something less, um, violent. I'm still working on that." He paused. "But we need to make sure whatever's below the ocean floor stays there. We can't let that shit get out of the trench."

"If we take out both," Shawna said, "they won't have a reason to nuke us. Or whatever they might do."

"Right," Calhoun said. "But we can't have anyone else infected. And we'll have to track down the other entities and destroy them too."

"What does that have to do with the AUVs?" Vraebel asked. "We can use an explosive shot down through the drill string. That would blow up the well and..." He paused. "Wait, why do you think an explosion is going to do anything?"

"Because," Shawna said with a smile, "this stuff is damned volatile to flame and bright light." She pointed at Thomas. "He thinks we can set the whole trench on fire. Burn it all up."

Calhoun nodded. "I do. It's obviously contained. There's no water reservoir to keep the fire from spreading. It should cause a chain reaction."

Vraebel shook his head. "You don't understand, Thomas. Those shots are meant to blow a hole, not start a goddamned inferno. You don't even know if there's going to be enough flame to catch anything on fire."

Catfish groaned. "How big of a hole can we make at the spud site?"

"Well," Vraebel said, "if we put down a huge shot, we'll blow the drill string, but we could probably knock through enough rock to fit something big. We just won't know if it's enough to go through to the oil."

"It will be," Shawna said. "It's not dense down there. It's almost like a blanket wrapped around something else." She thought for a second and then clapped her hands. "Fuck me," she said. Her eyes widened and gleamed. "Thomas? The spongy stuff in the core sample. What do you think that is?"

"Its prison," Thomas said. "Or something a little more disquieting."

"Like what?" Vraebel asked. "What the hell could contain that shit?"

Calhoun licked his chapped lips. God, but he needed a cigar. And a lot of water. "Remember how the entire trench moved? I don't think that was the black flowing beneath the surface. I think it was something else."

Shawna gulped. "You think there's something else down there?"

Catfish sighed. "Fucking sea monsters now? Are you serious?"

"Bear with me," Calhoun said. "What if the strange substance in the core sample is skin? Flesh? The body of some other creature? What if the black is something other than what we've seen? What if it's the organism's blood?"

The circle all blinked, but said nothing. The light had grown. Those facing the east squinted against the dawn's orange rays.

"You're fucking crazy," Vraebel said. "Certifiably fucking crazy."

Calhoun nodded. "I know, Martin. I know how it sounds."

The dim light covered the deck. The sun continued its rise into the sky, but the massive buildup of clouds kept it from drenching the deck in brightness.

"That's not everything, either," Catfish said. "I need to get into the drilling office."

"Oh, we're going there too," Calhoun said. "But we have to get Steve Gomez off the bridge."

"Just how the fuck are we going to do that?" Vraebel asked.

The generator coughed, and then went silent. "First, we need to get that refueled. Do you have another one up here?"

Vraebel blinked. "We have three."

"Good," Calhoun said. He looked up at the sky. "And then we're going to need something to carry them around."

#

The storm was moving in. In a few hours, the wind was going to increase and the rain would begin falling from the sky. The waves were going to become swells. And when that happened, the rig was going to buck like a bronco.

Gomez looked at the weather radar. He'd been staring at it for the last hour, watching as the bands of red continued driving toward them. Grim entertainment, but it was better than looking at Terrel's corpse. Which, by the way, was getting a little ripe.

At first, he'd thought the black sludge had returned. He'd sat against the wall, flashlight pointed at the grate, for nearly ten minutes before he noticed Terrel's belly swelling up like a balloon. Instead of suffering with the stench, he'd dragged the corpse to the far corner of the room. A smear of bodily fluids soiled the floor in long lines of brown, red, and gray.

When the light first started to rise over the horizon, he'd peered out the bridge windows to view the deck. He'd watched as the light started to touch the rig and the sea of black retreated to the western staircase. That meant the monstrous thing was back inside the superstructure. He wondered how long he had before it showed up. He had a bad feeling a halogen flashlight wasn't going to be enough to fight it off.

His phone beeped. He sighed and picked it up. Vraebel. His finger slid across the screen and the message appeared.

"Hang tight. We're coming for you."

Steve read the words twice before they sunk in. A grim smile lit his face. He looked around the bridge. Vraebel's satchel sat in the wall locker. Steve picked it up and rifled through it looking for something useful. He found Martin's phone charger, his wallet, a set of keys, a spare shirt, and an emergency medical kit.

He shoved the flashlight inside and pulled out the medical kit. He smothered the wounds on his left hand with burn cream and then wrapped it in heavy gauze. He had no illusions it would hold, but at least the pain receded.

Wound tended, he packed up the supplies and put them back in the satchel. The locker had three life vests, a flare gun, and several rounds. Gomez smiled at the red plastic gun. He cracked its breech and loaded a flare inside. He put three more of the flares inside his pants pocket and stuck the gun in his belt.

He zipped up the satchel and put it next to his feet. When he looked back down at the rig deck, the circle of people was gone, the halogens were gone, and so was the generator.

"Dios mio," he said. "You fuckers are crazy." He didn't know exactly what they were planning, but he hoped they'd be here soon. He didn't know how much longer he could stay conscious.

#

The lights were on inside. At least that much was going according to Calhoun's plan. As for the rest of it, she thought he was nuts. But since no one had a better idea…

Three burly roughnecks and Martin Vraebel dragged a generator up the stairs. There was a cargo elevator, but it was on the other side of the rig. Besides, she didn't think anyone wanted to be trapped in there in case the lights went out. Or worse.

When they climbed the top of the stairs, they set the gas generator on the landing and then ran down the stairs to grab the halogens and a hand truck. Once everyone was positioned, they hooked the halogens up to the generator and kicked it on.

Maneuvering the hand truck past the narrow corner leading to the main hallway was hellish. It took two of the roughnecks to shimmy it into position. The bridge was down two corridors and then to the left.

Bill, the roughneck who had tried to save Jack Hosley, demanded to be in the lead. He held the heavy work light in his hands. "If that fucking thing comes out, I want to make sure it gets what's coming to it," Bill growled as he lifted the light.

Shawna was behind the hand truck. Another worker, a tall thick, bald man named Robert Creely brought up the rear. In a way, she thought his job was the most difficult. He covered the rear by holding another lamp and walking backwards behind the generator. Martin and Dick Green carried their lamps as well, but theirs were off. When they reached points in the hall with vents or exposed ducts, they turned them on and shined the brilliant light at them until the party went past.

It was slow going. Despite the chill air coming from the A/C, Shawna and the group were sweating. Her job, making sure the cables didn't get tangled while pushing the hand truck, was more difficult than she'd imagined. Meter by meter, they traveled down the main hallway to the first corridor.

Bill held up his hand when he was near it. He slowly pulled on the extension cord until he had enough slack, and then shined the light down the left hallway. Martin did the same, but pointed his to the right. The two men were breathing hard and Shawna could tell their adrenaline had spiked. At any moment, the creature could drop down through a panel in the roof, come pouring out of a ventilation duct, or just be waiting for them.

"Clear," Martin said. His voice was soft, but distinct.

"Clear," Bill said. "Going left." He advanced a meter down the hall and then waited while Shawna pushed the handcart. Martin kept his light pointed down the other side of the hall until Robert had enough slack to cover the rear. Martin then shuffled past the hand truck to follow Bill.

Sweat poured off the group. The smell of rot and mildew whooshed through the A/C vents. Shawna felt like she was going to vomit. A look around at the others told her they were having the same problem with the air.

"Come out, come out wherever you are," Bill said. "You fucker." He continued down the hall, the group in tow. Doors to storage and equipment rooms lined the corridor. As he came to each, Martin shined his light at the cracks between the door frame and the floor. Shawna suddenly wished all the rooms had hatches.

They could see the next turn up ahead. After that, it would be relatively easy to get to the bridge. As they neared the next hall, Bill held up his hand for the group to stop. Shawna brushed a sheen of sweat from her forehead and wiped her moist hands on her khakis. Her clothes reeked of salt air, diesel, and sweat. And she wasn't the only one with Ea Du stinky. The whole group needed a dip in the ocean, if not a hot shower.

Bill peered around the wall and froze. "Jesus," he said.

Martin was already covering the other side of the hallway. Without turning around he asked "What is it?"

Bill shook his head. "Fucking sheetrock is gone. All the way down the hall. Just studs and metal."

"You see anything else?" Shawna asked.

Bill was silent for a moment. "I've never seen the floor so shiny."

Shawna groaned. "It's been here. It dissolved whatever was on the floor as well as the sheetrock. Are the studs damaged too?"

"Can't tell," Bill said. "You guys ready to move up?"

"Clear here," Martin said. "Watch the vents up ahead, Bill."

"Got it," the roughneck said. "Robert? You ready?"

"Yeah," his baritone voice boomed.

Shawna pushed the hand truck and awkwardly maneuvered it behind Bill. He waited until he felt the edge of the generator against his ass and then started forward. Robert carefully walked past the generator and into the hallway, his light covering the rear.

Martin pointed his light at the upper edge of the left wall. Green's light covered the right. Shawna pushed the hand truck slowly behind Bill.

Above the generator's din, she heard a scratching sound. "Bill?" she asked.

"Yeah," he said. "I hear it."

"The fuck is that?" Robert yelled.

Shawna fought the urge to turn around.

"What's going on, Robert?" Martin asked.

The scratching sound was louder. Something clanged to the floor behind her.

"Goddammit!" Robert shouted.

Her resolve broke and she turned around. Her breath stopped in her throat. Three ceiling tiles had disintegrated. The lights at the other end of the hallway were going out one by one as the sizzling sound increased in volume. The right wall's sheetrock dissolved beneath the dead lights.

Bill growled. "Let's move it, people. We've got to get Gomez out of there."

He continued forward. Shawna turned back around, her skin covered in gooseflesh and her breathing labored. She felt like her heart was going to leap out of her throat.

The hand truck was getting heavier. Her lips upturned in a grim smile. *Of course the fucking thing isn't getting heavier. You're just tired.* They still had to make it to the bridge. The return trip was going to be hell. *If there is one,* a voice said in her mind. She did her best to drown it out by focusing on the cables.

Creely hissed through his teeth. "I can see it."

God, but she wanted to turn and see what he was seeing. As she continued following Bill, she imagined the black ooze creeping down the hall and nipping at her boots. "How big is it?" she asked.

"Fucking big enough!" Robert yelled.

Bill walked faster. Shawna quickened the pace, but her arms burned with fatigue. Before too long, she simply wouldn't be able to push anymore. She knew she was running on adrenaline and little else.

The extension cord feeding Robert cinched taught. The generator tried to slide off the handcart. "Keep up!" she yelled.

Slack, glorious slack, showed up in the line, but she could hear Robert puffing behind her. It sounded like he was going to have a heart attack.

Up ahead, Bill took the left turn to the bridge hatch. He didn't slow before taking the corner. She imagined him falling backwards, a large creature of black dissolving his clothes, flesh, and bones. Instead, she heard him banging on the hatch.

"Steve! It's Bill! Open up!"

For a moment, nothing happened. She turned her head to look behind them. The hallway was dark. The black had chewed through wall panels, ceiling tiles, and the light fixtures. She was willing to bet there was plenty of metal up there still holding the florescent tubes together, but the wires were most likely stripped and the plastic dissolved into atoms.

She followed the light as Robert waved it around the hallway. Sure enough, the halogen bounced off metal fasteners, screws, and sheets. The floor, however, was empty.

"Where did it go?" she asked.

Robert shook his head, but didn't turn around. "I don't know," he said. "I saw it back there at the end of the hall, and now it's gone. I tried to get a bead on it with the light, but it's just not strong enough to reach."

Shawna flinched when she heard the hatch open with a grinding groan.

"Gomez?" Bill said, "You look like shit." She turned back to the hall to see Bill bear hug the short Hispanic man. Bill was right. Steve Gomez looked ragged and barely alive. The man was dazed and stared with glazed eyes. "Here," Bill said and offered his arm, "hang on to me. We're getting you the fuck out of here."

Something sizzled behind the walls.They all froze. Shawna gulped as both Martin and Dick shined their halogens near the ceiling tiles. She placed a hand against the wall. It was warm to the touch.

"Guys? Something very bad is happening."

Martin turned to her and snarled. "And that would be something new?"

She ignored his sarcasm. "I think it's in the walls. It must—" Her words were cut off as Dick started screaming.

#

Walking through the halls was eerier than he'd imagined. With his laptop bag dangling off one shoulder, Catfish really wished he had an entire pack of cigarettes stuffed in his mouth. This trip was right out of the video game Doom.

The lights down the main hallway had been flickering since they entered the superstructure. The walls had large holes in them, the edges scorched as if burned. Polished metal gleamed from behind the damaged sheetrock. The hard floor reflected back their halogen lights as though it had just been waxed.

As with Vraebel's team, they'd loaded a generator on a hand truck and connected the remaining halogen work lamps to it. Two roughnecks who Catfish didn't know were at the front of the cart. Another was in the rear. Calhoun walked next to Catfish. Catfish and his boss carried high power flashlights. Calhoun had said they would do the trick, but Catfish wasn't so sure; he wished the engineer hadn't insisted on keeping so many lights back on the deck. Then again, the sun would eventually go down and they needed to make sure they had something to fend off the creatures.

Now that the fluorescents were on the verge of going out in the hallway, he wondered if they shouldn't be rethinking this plan. Big time. To get to the drilling office, they were going to have to pass the stairwell that led to the living quarters as well as the commissary. That big fucking puddle of black could be anywhere in the rig. Not to mention its smaller brethren.

Vraebel had taken his team to the eastern stairs to gain easier access to the bridge. He hoped they were having better luck with the lights. If anything happened to Shawna, he'd personally blow the rig up as a final fuck you to whatever was on it.

They crept slowly toward the stairwell. The two men in front had their halogens pointed straight down the hall. As they neared it, one of them said "Stop" in a low voice.

Catfish and Calhoun stopped the hand truck and waited. The roughneck walked sideways across the entrance and bathed the landing in light. "Fuck," he whispered.

"What is it?" Calhoun asked.

The man didn't turn around. "Stairwell metal is shining damned bright. The sheetrock is gone. Completely. Only things left are burned wood and metal.

"That tracks," Calhoun said. "It could be in the walls now, guys, as well as the vents." He turned on his flashlight and shined it up at the ceiling tiles down the hall. Vents were spaced out every four meters or so. "We need to be damned careful."

"No shit," the roughneck behind them said.

What's his name? Jake? Jim? Fuck, Catfish thought.

Calhoun didn't respond or turn to the man. "Ready when you are, Terry."

The roughneck staring into the stairwell flinched a little at his name, and then stepped past the entrance. They kept moving. Catfish peered into the stairwell as they passed. As Terry said, the landing was a goddamned mess, and yet clean as a whistle. The usual detritus of rig grime from boots was completely absent. The sheetrock was gone all right, and the wooden studs looked as though they'd met a flamethrower. Well, now they knew the thing could consume wood too.

Catfish kept one hand on the dolly to help push while held the halogen flashlight in the other. He and Thomas flashed their lights up at the vents as they had before, but something felt off. The deeper they walked into the superstructure, the more fetid the air.

The drilling office entrance was close. Catfish went over in his mind what he needed to do. It was simple, really. He needed to hook up the laptop, download a few files, and reconfigure the rig cameras to talk to his laptop. Once that was done, they'd be able to see what was going on as they executed Calhoun's plan.

When they reached the door to the drilling office, Terry blew a sigh out between his teeth. "Now what?" he asked.

The door was open. Not because someone had left it open, but because it had been dissolved into nothing. A gleaming brass door-knob and locking mechanism sat at the threshold.

Calhoun scanned the debris. He cursed and then waved his flashlight toward the drilling office entrance. "We go in," he said. He turned to Catfish. "You take the left side, I'll take the right."

Catfish nodded. The sight of the damaged walls, the flickering lights, and the damned door knob on the floor, had sent his pulse racing. "If I see it, I'll make sure I hurt it."

"Good," Calhoun said. "Terry? Aaron? We need you to go in first and give the all clear. Then we'll push the generator past the threshold. Once we're inside, we'll need y'all to cover us while Catfish punches some keys. Got it?"

"Yeah," the two men grumbled.

Calhoun glanced over his shoulder. "Joel? Guard the door. Keep the light pointed out into the hall."

The large bearded man nodded. Catfish wasn't sure if Joel was mute or just didn't like to talk. Or maybe he was as terrified as the rest of them and didn't want anyone to hear it in his voice. Didn't matter. Catfish could tell the man would do his job. He'd volunteered to take the rear guard and in some ways, Catfish thought that was more dangerous than being up front.

Terry walked through the entryway first, Aaron close behind. Their cords stretched as they traveled a few feet inside. He could hear whispered cursing, but little else. "Clear," a voice called.

Catfish ground his teeth as he and Calhoun pushed the generator into the office. There was barely enough room for the hand truck and it took some work to get it inside. If the door had still been attached, it would have been impossible. As it was, they dug huge gouges in the remains of the wooden frame.

The drilling office was quiet except for the hum of the computers. Catfish glanced over at Harobin's workstation. He wished the man was still there, talking to himself and picking green gold from his nostrils. He sighed and took another long look around the room. He swept all the nooks and crannies with the high powered light. No sign of the black.

He let out a sigh, released the hand truck, and headed to his workstation. Terry walked beside him and kept the light shining on the area in front of the computers. If the things wanted somewhere to hide, the actual server room was the perfect place. Although under a desk or printer stand would do just as well.

Calhoun had read his mind. The engineer squatted a meter away from the line of workstations, his light stabbing into the darkness beneath the computer desks. That was good. At least someone had some common sense.

Catfish hit the keyboard and then logged in. He brought up a console and connected to the control server. Vraebel had given him the username and password he'd need to reconfigure the camera feeds. He added his laptop's MAC address to the push list and then reloaded the camera service configuration. A green "OK" appeared on the console.

He dug his laptop out of the bag, opened the lid, and then hit the camera service IP address. His browser immediately filled with six real-time images. He felt someone staring and turned to Calhoun. The engineer's eyebrows were raised. Catfish nodded to him.

The keys clacked beneath his nimble fingers as he traversed to the directory he needed. He transferred the latest AUV configuration files to his laptop, and checked to make sure they were there and in good shape. The last thing he needed was for them to have made this trip for nothing.

"Okay," Catfish said. "I think I have what I need."

Calhoun nodded. "Let's get the fuck out of here," he said. Both his eyes and his light were fixed on a spot above the workstation.

Catfish slowly turned his head and saw what his boss had seen. High on the wall, an A/C vent was darker than it should have been. Its once white painted face now shined beneath Thomas' light. There was something in the vent, something the light couldn't quite reach.

He slipped the laptop back in its case, stood, and threw the bag over his shoulder. Once the heavy flashlight was back in his hands, he felt a little better. But whatever was in that vent had chilled his blood.

He walked over and stood next to Calhoun. "It's in there," he said.

Thomas nodded. "The only question," he said, "is which one."

"We ready to get out of here?" Joel asked from the doorway. The man's light was still facing the doorway, but he'd turned around to stare at them.

"Joel!" Calhoun yelled. But it was too late.

While he was turned to them, a black tendril of ooze grew from the top of the door frame. As Joel's head turned back to the hallway, the tendril reached forward and wrapped around his neck. Joel dropped the halogen light and it shattered when it hit the floor. He wrapped his hands around his neck to try and pull the thing off. Severed fingers dropped to the floor like sliced sausages. The tendril ripped him off his feet. The sizzle and stench of burned flesh filled the drilling office. Joel's screams were cut off as his body disappeared into the hallway.

Both Terry and Aaron stood frozen just a few meters away from the doorway. Catfish breathed in shallow gasps. "Jesus."

Calhoun looked back up at the vent. "It's still there. Aaron? Terry?" The two men kept staring at the empty doorway. "Guys!" Calhoun yelled. The two roughnecks turned to him. "Keep your fucking lights aimed on that door way. One high, one low."

Catfish pointed his light at the vent. The black thing was still in there. "Jesus. You think those two are working together?"

"I don't know," Calhoun said. "Not sure I want that to be true."

"Me neither." Catfish gulped. "Back into the hall?"

"Yes. Back into the hall." Calhoun walked toward the hand truck. The air had turned hazy from the generator's exhaust. It was getting hard to breathe. "We need to keep moving," Calhoun said. He pointed to Aaron. "You. Cover our backs. Terry? You take point. Craig?"

"Yeah, I'll cover the vents."

"Good." Terry got in front of the hand truck and Aaron took his position behind Calhoun. "Let's go," the engineer said.

Catfish lingered for a second to make sure the thing in the vent stayed there. As he turned and got behind Terry, he wished like hell they could close a hatch behind them.

#

Steel buckled with a shriek. The entire left side of the hallway bowed outward as wooden studs disintegrated. A pair of black tentacles struck out through large gouges and wrapped around Dick. The man's shoulders smoked and sizzled at the black's touch.

Dick's lamp crashed to the floor and the light went out. Creely shouted and pointed the high-powered light at Dick's shaking and twitching body. Smoke curled up from the black tentacles, but they refused to let go of their prize. They dragged Dick's screaming body into the wall with a crunch. Blood splattered against the walls and Shawna's face as Dick's head popped off his shoulders and rolled to the ground.

"Green!" Creely yelled. From behind the shattered wall, they heard the sounds of frying bacon. "Green!" Bob yelled again. He held his head in his hands and wailed.

Sigler could barely hear anything over the sound of her heart. She turned and stared back at the bridge hatch. Bill helped Gomez limp toward the generator. Vraebel stared down the hallway. She turned back and realized she was far too close to the buckled wall.

She stepped backward until her ass hit the hand truck. "I need a light!" she yelled. No more than a second later, Vraebel was beside her, his light pointed at the wall.

"Wipe your face," he said.

Shawna brought a hand up and wiped the wetness away from her left cheek. As difficult as it was, she did her best not to look at her palm. She rubbed it against her moist and soiled khakis. "How the fuck are we going to get past that," she pointed at the wall.

Vraebel grunted. "We shine our lights. We go forward."

"Martin," Gomez said from behind them.

"Glad you're still alive, Steve," he said without turning around.

"I have something for you," Gomez said.

Shawna turned as he produced a large red gun from his trouser pocket. She saw his ruined hand. The pinky had been bisected along with part of his palm. The skin was scorched and blistering where the black had touched him. Gomez handed the weapon to Bill and he held it out to Shawna. She took it.

"Flare gun?" she asked.

Gomez nodded. His undamaged hand slipped into his pocket and he lifted out several rounds. Bill took them and passed them to Shawna. She placed them in her shirt pocket. "Be careful," Gomez said. "That thing's loaded."

"Good to know," she said. Vraebel's light was still pointing at the wall. Diesel exhaust choked the hallway. "We have to move," she said, "or we're all gonna pass out."

"Right. Bill?" Vraebel asked.

"Ready, boss."

Vraebel looked at Creely. "Cover our ass." Creely still looked as though he was in shock, but he nodded. With that, Martin took the lead.

Shawna got behind the hand truck and started to push. Her arms felt like overcooked noodles, but they had to make it out of the rig and back to the deck. Once they were down the stairs, they'd be in natural light again, although that didn't seem to deter it too much. As they passed the blood drenched wall, she forced herself not to look.

The hallway ahead was dark. The creature had destroyed enough of the electronics in the ceiling to short them out. Vraebel's halogen beam spread out before them in a rectangle of white light, but the hallway's length seemed to eat the light before it hit the back wall. Shawna wanted to run. She wanted to push the cart as fast as she could while Vraebel sprinted ahead. She wanted—

Vraebel held up a hand and cocked his head to one side. She stopped pushing and took a deep breath. She listened. The wind outside buffeted against the raised superstructure. But that's not what had stopped Vraebel in his tracks.

Somewhere up ahead, or maybe around one of the corridors, something made a tapping noise. "Is someone trapped?" she asked.

Vraebel shrugged. The tapping sound increased to a metallic rattle. He lowered his hand and continued down the hall. Shawna followed with the hand truck. She could hear Gomez' heavy breathing. There was a shudder in his exhales and she wondered if one of his lungs was filling with blood.

The sounds in the other corridor stopped. Vraebel paused in his steps and cocked his head to listen. Shawna heard nothing. Whatever those sounds were, they were gone now.

The rig chief started moving again and the battered entourage followed. Creely's light constantly shifted from the left to the right as he illuminated the upper vents. Shawna kept listening for that sizzling sound or the rending of metal. If the creature learned that it could dissolve the wooden studs that supported the metal framing, they could be in big trouble. With that in mind, the first level of the rig's superstructure could collapse at any time.

After an eternity of slow steps, Vraebel reached the corner. He held up a hand and Shawna stopped. Her eyes watered from the generator's exhaust. Vraebel leaped into the adjoining hallway, light held out before him. "Oh, fuck," he said.

"What is it?" she asked.

"Guys? We have to find another way."

Bill cursed. "Got to be fucking kidding me, boss. What the hell's the problem?"

Shawna walked around the hand truck and peered around the corner. The ceiling was a disaster. The lights were off, but she could see twisted metal dangling from where ceiling tiles and light fixtures once hung. The floor was clean, but warped.

"Shit," she said. "I think it ate the supports beneath the floor."

Vraebel nodded. "Yeah. I'm guessing the floor's not going to support our weight. Not to mention it has plenty of places to drop down on us now." He shook his head. "How smart are these fucking things?"

Shawna clucked her tongue. "Smart enough," she said. "It's got us trapped."

"Creely?" Vraebel shouted.

"Yeah, boss?"

"Check the other corridor," the rig chief said.

Shawna watched the large, bald man walk forward, and then turn in the other direction. His halogen lit up the other end of the adjoining hallway. "Dammit," she said.

"We're totally fucked, boss," Bob said.

The other hallway was a shambles. In addition to the ceiling being a complete mess and the warped floor, the black had eaten large enough holes in the walls for the ductwork to come loose and point at the floor. The ooze could pour out of the vents like a faucet.

Vraebel panted. "I think we need to—" The walls started to make that sizzling sound. "Get back to the bridge!"

Shawna didn't wait. She bolted back to the hand truck and started to pull it down the long hallway. Gomez and Bill had already started to move in that direction, but Bob's extension cord was taut. She turned her head. "Let's go!"

Martin appeared from around the corner, his light aimed behind him. "Bob! Cover the rear!" he said and ran toward Shawna with his light held high. She was blinded by the sudden stabbing brightness. "I've got you, Shawna," Vraebel said as he reached the other side of the hand truck. Creely's cord was still taut. "Creely! Move it!"

Bob stepped backwards from the hallway, his light kissing the walls and then the ceiling. Something above them groaned. "Bob! Run!" Shawna yelled. But it was too late.

Creely raised his head to look up, and then a pool of black poured from the ceiling and swallowed him. The sound of frying flesh filled the hallway. His light popped and exploded as the ooze shorted out the electronics.

The generator growled loudly and then Vraebel's light started to flicker. "Fuck!" he shouted. "Fuck the lights! Run!" He pushed her away from the hand truck and leaped over it. She pelted down the hallway toward the wan light coming through the open bridge hatch. She heard Vraebel's heavy foot steps behind her.

Bill and Gomez disappeared into the bridge just as she cleared the threshold. She turned, the flare gun in her hands.

Vraebel's halogen pointed down the hallway. He finally ran out of slack and the light jerked from his hands. It hit the floor with a thud. Vraebel stopped running and turned to grab the lamp.

The white light bounced off the metal beams and created a dim pool of light around the generator. As Vraebel's hands scrabbled for the light, the barely illuminated portion of the hallway turned black.

"Forget the light! Run!" she screamed.

Vraebel raised his eyes, saw what she saw, and then started to sprint. His right boot tangled in the cord from Bill's dropped lamp and he fell face-first with a thud. Shawna ran forward and put her left hand around his outstretched arm. She pulled as hard as she could. His limp body started to move forward, but the black was closing in.

She fell backward on her ass, took aim, and pulled the trigger. The hallway exploded into red and orange light as the flare raced past the generator and slammed into the floor. Flames shot out of the pool of black. It trembled and shook like pudding as the fire spread. The entire hallway was ablaze.

Shawna used both hands to pull Vraebel forward. The man moaned in pain. The flames were going to reach the generator. It was going to explode and they were both going to die.

"Run, dammit," Bill yelled from behind her. He bent and took Martin's hands. His strong biceps bulged as he pulled the man toward the bridge. Shawna didn't have to be told twice. She ran as fast as she could through the hatch. Seconds later, Bill carried Vraebel into the room.

Shawna shut the hatch and swiveled the wheel. Through the walls, they heard the sound of a roaring fire. Tendrils of smoke curled through the A/C vents. She didn't know if she'd killed the black, but they might die in this room anyway. The sprinkler systems weren't working. And there was no telling how far the fire would spread.

#

They were walking away from the drilling office when the lights stopped flickering and went dead. He and Catfish took out their flashlights and continued pushing the cart. The close walled corridors made the diesel exhaust that much more pungent.

Calhoun hoped they made it to some fresh air soon, or they'd risk carbon monoxide poisoning.

Terry and Aaron hadn't said a word since Joel's death. What he'd seen on their faces told him they'd already given up. Considering one was on point and the other covering their rear, that didn't exactly fill him with confidence. If they didn't do their jobs, the whole mission was fucked.

From the other side of the rig walls, they heard the sounds of banging, ripping metal, and screams. Calhoun gritted his teeth. Shawna's team was in trouble, but there wasn't a damned thing he could do about it. Not yet.

The men they'd left on the deck should be preparing for the explosive shots. He hoped Vraebel had chosen the right crew for that. Wireline could be tricky. And the amount of concrete they'd have to pour after the shots was going to be intense. Of course if the thing below the ocean surface decided to get nasty, it wouldn't matter—the rig would be matchsticks.

Terry's lamp filled the corridor with light. The group was moving a little faster than they had before. The roughneck up front was either too terrified to stay still or he just didn't care anymore. Neither possibility boded well.

As they passed a door marked "Storage," Calhoun called a halt. "Terry? You have a key to this room?"

Terry shook his head. "Gomez, Vraebel, and the quartermaster have those."

Calhoun pointed his light at the lock and grinned. He stepped far enough away for a kick and then planted his boot right at the lock. His leg shook with the recoil of hitting steel, but the door popped open.

"Guess nothing in there is too important," Catfish said.

Thomas said nothing as he examined the room with his flashlight. Two cases of D-cell batteries were stacked in the corner alongside bottled water and a case of energy bars. He trained the light over the rest of the boxes. "More flashlights in here," he said. "We probably need to stock up."

He opened the box and pulled out five of the heavy flashlights. He turned each on to make sure their batteries were good and then handed them backwards to Catfish. "Find a place for those."

"A place? Like where? My fucking pants pockets?"

Calhoun turned and glared at the tech. Catfish brushed away a stray lock of hair and took the black cylinders.

"We also need to figure out how to get these batteries out of here," Calhoun said. Then he saw what he really wanted and grinned. "Perfect." Coils of heavy nylon rope hung from pegs on the wall. Calhoun took one and put his head through its center. It would be awkward, but he could take at least two. He handed the others to Catfish.

There was an emergency medical kit as well. Calhoun grabbed it and handed it backwards to Catfish.

"What are we doing here?" Catfish asked. "This isn't fucking Wal-Mart."

"Shut up, Craig," Calhoun said. Boxes, boxes, and more boxes. He scanned the labels. There was a box of canned food, one marked "coffee," and another whose label was torn. Thomas frowned at the cardboard box and then opened it. "Bingo." He pulled out three duffel bags, the PPE logo emblazoned on their sides. He didn't know what fabric they were made of, but they seemed heavy enough.

He placed the medical kit, and the energy bars in one and handed it back to Catfish. "Put the lights in there too." Catfish grabbed the duffel, but didn't say anything. Calhoun was glad the man was finally shutting the fuck up.

Calhoun went over chemical recipes in his mind. If he could just find the right ingredients, he could fashion a bomb or... A bead of sweat fell from his brow. The room was getting warm. He reached forward and put his hand against the wall. The sheetrock was hot to the touch. "Shit," he said. He stepped back out of the small area. "We need to move. Now."

"What's wrong?" Catfish asked.

"The rig is on fire," Calhoun said. "Might be electrical, I don't know. Doesn't matter. We're fucked if we don't get to the other side." Thomas closed the door to the storage room and looked at Terry. "Let's go."

Catfish coughed. "Getting hard to breathe, boss."

"I know," Calhoun said. "Start moving. Now."

He and Catfish pushed the generator cart, their flashlights on and at the ready. They took turns shining their lights up at the vents as they moved forward.

They came to a junction and Terry stopped. "Holy fuck," he said. "Can't go starboard. The floor is all buckled. And I see smoke and fire at the other end."

"Coming toward us?" Calhoun asked.

Terry nodded. "We gotta go the other way."

"Then move." Even Calhoun was surprised by the growl that came out of his mouth. The fire meant Shawna's team was trapped in the bridge if they hadn't already gotten out. He gritted his teeth and hoped they were still alive.

#

Black smoke wafted through the A/C vents. Shawna and the others could barely breathe. The room was already uncomfortably warm. The bridge shook as something exploded out in the hall. She was sure it was the generator. If nothing else, burning diesel fuel was adding to the flames burning up the black. Or at least that one.

But it didn't matter unless they found a way off the bridge. She looked at the windows. "Bill? Can we break those?"

He turned and looked at them. A maniacal grin spread across his face. "We can sure as hell try." The roughneck picked up one of the heavy rolling chairs from the bridge console. He lifted it into the air and swung it into the middle window.

The wheel-base smashed into the heavy Plexiglas with a crash of metal. The transparent glass spider-webbed with cracks. Bill pulled the chair back for another swing and slammed the chair forward.

The glass detonated outward with a crackle. Shards fell to the deck over a hundred feet below. "Fucker," Bill said. He made his way to the next window. It disappeared with a crunch.

Smoke escaped through the wide windows. Shawna stuck her head near the opening and breathed deep. The air smelled of diesel, rain, and salt. Compared to the stench of acrid smoke and unwashed bodies, it was a glorious scent.

"That's going to pull the fire toward us," Gomez said. His face was ashen. She wasn't sure why he kept clutching his chest, but she could tell his wounds were damned severe.

She nodded. "That's why we have to get the fuck out of here." She peered out the window. The dark clouds veiled the deck in twilight. Powerful work lamps cast their white glow over the men working near the drill string rotator. "Up here! Hey!" she yelled.

The men didn't look up. Shawna ground her teeth. They couldn't hear her over the roar of machinery. She thought for a moment and looked at the flare gun in her hands. "Gomez? How the fuck do we get out of here?"

He blinked and then his eyes went glassy. She stepped forward and slapped him across the face. His eyes crossed and then focused on her. "What?"

"How do we get out of here?" she asked again. Gomez pointed at the wall. She followed his finger and saw the wrapped coil of fire hose behind glass. "You have to be fucking kidding me."

"Use it as rope," he said. "Maybe it'll reach."

"No fucking way it will reach," she said. "We'd break our legs in the fall."

He shook his head. "Not if you hit the ledge."

Shawna stuck her head out the window. The bridge protruded from the rest of the rig superstructure, but only by a few feet. All she could see was the deck. "Bill? Grab my legs."

The roughneck put his strong hands around her calves and she climbed through the window. She looked down. There was a ledge. It was at least fifty feet down.

"Okay," she said. "Bring me back."

Bill pulled her back from the window. Jagged shards of Plexiglas cut through her khakis but she ignored the pain. She stared back at the fire hose.

"No way that thing's going to hold our weight," Bill said. "Have to go one at a time. And even then, it'll probably snap out of the wall."

"We'll need to cut it and tie it to something," she said.

Vraebel groaned from the floor. He sat up and wiped an ooze of blood from his forehead. His nose was crooked and his lip split.

Shawna wasn't sure, but he might have broken a tooth. "We safe?" he asked.

"Not really," she said. "But this is better than the hallway."

He shook his head and winced. "Goddamn, that floor is hard."

"Yeah," Bill said. "Lucky you're alive, boss."

"Can you move?" Shawna asked the rig chief.

He flexed his fingers and slowly got to his feet. He wobbled for a second and Bill moved to catch him. Vraebel waved him away and managed to stabilize himself. "I can move. Just don't ask me to run very fast."

"May not be an option," Shawna said. "Bill? Let's see how long that hose is."

He nodded and hit the glass door release. The fire hose spindle swung wide. He inspected the bolts holding it to the wall. "Man, I really don't know if this is going to hold."

Outside the hatch, something crashed. "Not sure we have a choice," she said. "Hurry. We need to count it out."

They spun the wheel and pulled the fire hose off the wall. She estimated it was fifty to sixty feet in length. It was just enough to get them down to the ledge. Maybe.

"We're going to lose at least ten feet if we keep it attached to the wall," she said.

Vraebel's eyes stared around the room and then he smiled. "There," he pointed at the console. A steel support leg was bolted to both the console and the floor. "We can wrap it around that."

Bill nodded, produced a knife from his belt, and began cutting and tearing at the hose fitting. A moment later, he had the hose ripped apart at the coupling. He grabbed the chewed, ripped end and tied it around the support.

"Ladies first?" he asked.

Shawna shrugged. "No offense, but I am the lightest. We're going to have to figure out a way to move Steve."

Gomez shook his head. "I'll make it. Just get down there."

Bill wrapped the hose around her waist. "Try not to fall. If you do, you're fucked."

"Then why wrap it around me?"

He grinned. "Just in case it doesn't kill you."

"Great." She turned to the bridge windows, took a deep breath, and then slowly climbed up onto the console. She clenched her hands around the hose and slowly lowered herself into the air.

Bill held the hose in his large hands. Vraebel had taken up station behind him and held the slack in case Bill lost his grip. They lowered her.

Exhausted from pushing the hand truck through the halls, her arms screamed in pain. She grunted and held on. The rough hose bit into her flesh making it difficult to keep her grip. A whimper escaped her lips as strips of skin on her palms ripped away.

She kept descending and was past the lip of the bridge. "How much slack?" she yelled upward.

"You got a little!" Bill yelled back. "Just swing out and get to the goddamned ledge!"

They lowered her another meter. Her feet were nearly parallel with the ledge. Shawna shifted her weight and started to swing. Her feet hit the wall and slowed her swing. She waited until she was just above the ledge and let the hose slip through her grip. Her feet touched down on the ledge. She exhaled a sigh of relief and unwrapped the hose from her waist.

"I'm good!" she yelled upward.

After a moment, the hose slithered upward beyond the overhang. The ledge lip was no more than a meter wide. She held out her arms, put her back against the wall, and slowly made her way to the starboard side. She didn't want the next person to smack into her when they started their swing.

"Coming down!" a voice yelled from above. Shawna waited. A light rain fell from the sky punctuated by flashes of lightning and the roar of thunder. A gust of wind hit her skin and gooseflesh broke out on her arms. After the hot box of the bridge, it felt like heaven.

She stared at her palms. The skin was red, puffy, and bleeding in places. She was going to have a hell of a set of blisters. She heard something clank and looked upward. A pair of scuffed and stained work boots dangled near the center of the overhang. Vraebel appeared a moment later. His face was red and strained. The cut on his forehead had opened again and a thin line of blood trickled from his scalp.

He swung until he could put his feet on the ledge. He groaned and started untying the hose from his waist. "We're losing Gomez," he said. "Pretty sure he's dying."

"How's Bill going to get him down here?" she asked.

Vraebel shrugged. "I don't know. I fought to be the last man out, but Bill said I couldn't hold the hose." Martin touched the top of his head and winced. "I think he was right. But I don't know how the fuck he's going to—"

There was a scream from above them. They looked at one another. Shawna's blood went cold. "What the fuck was that?"

Something clanged off the overhang. A pair of large boots came into view along with droplets of blood falling past them. Bill was climbing down the hose as fast as he could. He swung himself to the ledge and managed to get his footing. He pushed against the wall. "We are so fucked," he said.

"What happened? Where's Gomez?"

Bill shook his head. "It ate him. From the inside, I think." He wiped his bloody hands on his heavy denim pants. "He started coughing up sludge and then his skin just…" Bill paused to cough. "Just bubbled away. I got the fuck out of there."

"Goddammit," Vraebel said. His face had drained of color. "Steve was my friend!"

The big man nodded. "I know, boss. Mine too." Something crackled above them. "We need to get the fuck off this thing. And right fucking now."

Shawna didn't wait to be told twice. Back against the steel wall, she shuffled starboard. Vraebel and Bill followed. When she reached the end of the superstructure, she turned her head around the corner. "Right back where we fucking started," she said. The flight of stairs they'd climbed to start their failed mission rose upward. She stared at it for a moment. The steel supports holding up the stairs was at least a meter away from the lip.

"Goddammit," she said and continued shuffling toward it. Bill and Vraebel rounded the corner and saw what she saw. Bill cursed from behind her. "Anyone good at jumping?"

Vraebel panted. "You have to be fucking kidding me. I can barely see straight."

"We can't switch positions, girl," Bill said. "There's not enough room. You're going to have to jump first."

#

The staircase leading down to the deck was in the other direction. The fire was blocking their way. That meant there was only one way back down—the elevator.

Terry panted as he stabbed the down arrow on the metal shell. The sound of cables and machinery vibrated the metal doors.

"We don't want to use the fucking elevator," Catfish said. "Wasn't that the whole goddamned point of coming up those stairs?"

Aaron's lips turned into a snarl. "Got a better idea, asshole? There are two stairwells. And we can't get to either." He jerked a thumb in the direction they'd come. "Unless you want to face off with that thing."

Catfish shook his head. "If we get trapped, there's no where to go."

"It's solid steel," Terry said. "Even if it was in the shaft, it can't get in."

"Man," Catfish said, "I don't think you get it. If that thing isn't airtight, it can come through the vents. Through the top. Shit, it could squeeze through the electronics!"

The elevator dinged. The four men pointed their lights at the door as it slid open. "Kill the generator," Calhoun said.

"Fuck," Catfish said and turned it off. The generator died with a wheeze. The air in the hall had grown foul. Between the diesel exhaust and the fumes from the fire in the other hallway, the superstructure was becoming uninhabitable. At least for humans.

Thomas opened up the duffel bag and handed two of the heavy flashlights to Terry and Aaron. "Use these," he said. "Let's move."

Catfish pushed the generator inside the elevator. The roughnecks put their work lamps on the floor next to it and stepped inside. Calhoun flashed his light down the way they'd come. His eyes widened and he stepped into the elevator. "Punch it!"

Terry hit the button for floor one. The doors started to close. When there was still a sliver of an opening, Catfish saw something moving in the hallway. "Fuck. Me. Was it following us?"

Thomas nodded.

The elevator started its descent. The generator creaked with the change in gravity. The car's lights still functioned at least. Their halogens cast bright circles on the metal walls.

No one spoke. The only sounds were the machinery above them and their own heavy breathing. The car smelled of unwashed bodies and diesel fumes.

"You guys need a shower," Catfish said.

Terry chuckled. "So do you."

The elevator stopped with a slight bump. The four men pointed their flashlights at the door. It slowly creaked open into a lit hallway. Terry stepped forward, his light pointing to the right side. Aaron followed suit to the left. Calhoun and Catfish aimed their lights at the far wall.

"Clear," Terry said.

Aaron nodded. "It's clear."

"How come the lights are still on?" Catfish asked.

Calhoun grunted. "I guess those things haven't gotten around to fucking up the first floor."

"Thank, God," Aaron said. "Let's get the hell out of here before that changes."

Catfish pushed the hand truck out of the elevator and then pulled the starter cord. The generator sputtered to life and the large halogen lamps lit up with glaring light. Terry and Aaron pocketed their flashlights and groaned as they picked up the heavy lamps. "Here we go again," Catfish said.

Terry took point, Aaron in back. Calhoun and Catfish once again shared duties on pushing the hand truck while their flashlights bore into the vents near the ceiling.

As they made their way down the corridor, Catfish noticed the floor. It had grime and boot prints on it. "Wow. Those things haven't made it down here yet."

"Either that," Calhoun said, "or they're in the walls."

Catfish shivered at the thought. The image of one of those things bursting through the sheet rock with their tentacles was enough to make him quicken his pace.

"Slow down, dammit," Terry said as the hand truck bumped him in the ass. "I'm going as fast as I can here."

"Sorry," Catfish said. Calhoun glanced at him, eyebrows raised. "Just want to get the fuck out of—"

The maze of metal pipes above them groaned. Behind them, something smashed in the hallway. "The fuck?" Aaron asked. "Oh, shit! Get moving!"

Terry set the pace and soon they were jogging down the corridor. Catfish wanted to look at what Aaron had seen, but he was afraid to turn his head.

"Goddamned thing has legs!" Aaron screamed.

The hallway filled with the sound of sizzling. Suddenly his fatigue disappeared. Catfish's blood filled with adrenaline and all he could hear was the thumping of his own heart. Behind him, he could hear Aaron yelling, but it was distant and incomprehensible.

Calhoun was chuffing away. The engineer was having trouble keeping pace. Terry turned a corner in the hallway to reach the exit. The line connecting the halogen lamp jerked hard and flew out of the electrical outlet on the generator. Terry's shriek made his blood run cold.

"Stop!" Calhoun yelled and let go of the hand truck. The sizzling sound was louder. Catfish turned. Aaron hadn't been kidding about legs. A squat thing lumbered toward them. The triped creature's limbs ended in sharp talons. Two tentacles spread from its bulk reaching toward them like arms. An eyestalk rose from its center and swung in time with its steps. The creature was so black, it was almost impossible to make out any other details. Catfish froze.

Calhoun shouted something. Aaron's lamp was pointed straight at the thing. Its black shell was smoking from the light, but it kept coming. Calhoun pointed his flashlight at the eyestalk. The thing twitched and shuffled sideways, the long stalk swerving to try and avoid the light.

Catfish found his wits and pointed his light at the thing. Between him and Calhoun, they had the eyestalk trapped in overlapping circles of white. A gout of flame shot from the stalk and then the creature's legs were running the opposite direction. The three lights bore into its back until it was out of range. The thing shuffled around the far corner and was gone.

Calhoun turned around and yelled in surprise. Catfish turned as well. A large puddle of black approached them from around the corridor. Thomas and Catfish immediately pointed their lights at the edges of the thing. It immediately began bubbling and flowed back around the corner and out of sight.

"Jesus," Aaron said. "Terry dead?"

"If he ain't," Catfish said, "it'll be a fucking miracle." Calhoun exhaled and inhaled in deep breaths. His face was far too red, far too spent. "You okay, Thomas?"

"Not really," the engineer said. "Okay, Aaron. You keep covering our asses with the lamp. Catfish and I will take the corner and let you know if it's clear."

"Fuck," Aaron said. "How the hell can it be clear?"

"Just do it," Calhoun said.

Catfish gulped. He knew what Thomas had in mind. It was going to suck balls too. He tightened his grip on the flashlight. "You ready?" Thomas didn't reply. He moved around the generator and stood against the wall. Catfish kept his light pointed low at the corner and slowly moved around the generator.

Calhoun's light shined on a spot less than a quarter meter away in the hall. If the black decided to come flowing in, it would meet the halogen weapon. Catfish took a deep breath and then moved forward. As he crept into the hallway, he pointed his light directly ahead. The hallway was lit with fluorescents, but the lights were buzzing and flickering. He didn't see any sign of the black. What he did see was a belt buckle and several metal buttons.

He was about to give the all clear when something shifted at the end of the hall. Something was on the floor back there. It looked like a black block had been placed on the white tiled floor. The door to the deck was in the middle of the hallway, halfway between he and it.

"I don't know how fast those things can move," Catfish said without turning around, "but it's at the end of the hallway. Over by the decon room."

Calhoun sighed. "You check the ceiling?"

"Yeah. Nothing there," Catfish said. "But I see Terry's belt buckle." Aaron groaned from the hall. "Can you push the generator, boss?"

Calhoun paused. "Yes. I can push it past the corner."

Catfish gritted his teeth. "You don't sound good."

"Fucking shut up. I'm coming."

The generator's motor filled the hallway with sound as Calhoun pushed it forward. Catfish walked a few steps closer to the door, eyes firmly fixed on the shape at the end of the hall. If Aaron managed to get close to it, he could torch it with his much stronger light. But if they got through the doorway unharmed, Catfish wouldn't bother the creature.

"We still good?" Calhoun asked.

"Yeah. I'm walking." Catfish took one slow step after the other as he headed for the deck hatch. Calhoun's flashlight flicked up toward the vents and then to the ceiling in a constant swing of motion. However bad off the old man was, he was keeping to the plan.

The thing at the end of the hall shifted. It had looked like a solid block, but now it was morphing, changing. Something stuck up out of its melting rectangular form. "Move!" Catfish yelled.

He ran toward the door, his flashlight bobbing up and down as he tried to keep it focused on the shape. Calhoun was huffing and puffing behind him. A pair of tentacles plopped out of the melted thing and began dragging itself toward them. He reached the hatch and spun the wheel. The door popped open into a stiff breeze and falling rain. He ran through it and turned.

Calhoun struggled to get the generator over the lip.

"Fuck that thing! Move!" he yelled at the old man.

Calhoun dropped the hand truck handle and shuffled past it and into the open. Aaron appeared in the doorway and tried to jump the cart. His foot landed awkwardly atop the generator and he slipped. His body tumbled over and hit the deck with a splat.

A black tentacle rushed out of the doorway and smacked into the hand truck. It jostled, but didn't move. Catfish ran to Aaron and pulled him away from the door. The tentacle kept waving until a bright light settled on its base. Sizzling and smoking, the thing pulled itself back behind the door.

Catfish rushed forward and slammed the hatch close. He cycled the wheel until he was sure it was sealed. "Goddammit," he said.

Calhoun was barely standing. The old man was spent. "Thomas? Go find Shawna and sit the fuck down. Get someone to help me with this guy."

The engineer nodded and slowly backed away from him. Calhoun finally turned and walked toward the drill table. Catfish sighed and rolled Aaron over. He wished he hadn't.

Aaron's head was caved in on the left side. One of his eyes was open, but the pupil was so small it might as well be non-existent. He held the man's wrist and searched for a pulse. Nothing. They'd lost the entire team except for Thomas and him.

The light and the generator were both behind that hatch. They wouldn't be able to get either of them back out unless they were willing to let that thing loose. He hoped they had plenty more lights.

#

The sky was getting darker, not lighter. It was only 9 am and she felt like the day had lasted a year. She sat on a tool chest some six meters away from the roughnecks who were working on the drill string. Red and Vraebel sat near her. The three of them had sucked down bottled water, but there was no food on the deck. Her stomach rumbled. She was nauseous and on the verge of passing out.

She raised her eyes to the bridge. Black smoke billowed out of the windows. She wondered how long it would be before the fire destroyed the superstructure. And when that happened, where would they go?

Vraebel had told her the fire systems must have been damaged by the creatures. When they shorted out the lights in the hallways, they no doubt damaged the sprinklers as well.

"With any luck," he'd said, "the lower and upper floors still work and maybe we'll only lose the bridge level."

Only she thought. She knew what Vraebel wasn't saying. Without the bridge, there was no radio. Without the bridge, there were no thrusters, no control over the helm. The only controls they had access to were those on the deck. And besides the emergency ballast instruments, they didn't have fuck all else.

She wondered what the creature that was once Steve Gomez was doing. Was it trapped on the bridge, too terrified to come out into the dim sunlight? Or had it already found a way to escape down the burning vents? Or maybe, just maybe, the fire was already spreading into the bridge and would kill it.

Gomez. Creely. Green. They were gone. The team had gone into the rig to save Gomez. They'd failed and two men had died in the process. Shawna felt like crying, but she was too damned tired. Too damned frustrated.

At least they knew for sure what happened when the black encountered fire. As Thomas had postulated, the liquid was extremely flammable. Sunlight, a swath of the UV spectrum, and fire were the only weapons they could use against it. Sunlight was cheap and safe, but it only lasted so many hours. In this storm, there was no guarantee the black wouldn't risk joining them on the deck. The UV spectrum delivered by the halogens certainly damaged it, but again, she wasn't certain how long the flashlights and lamps would deter it. Fire was easy to create and deploy, but they were sitting on a goddamned powder keg. One look at the superstructure was enough to know that.

The men working the drill string hadn't asked questions. They'd seen the cuts, Vraebel's thousand yard stare, and thought better of saying much of anything. The fact Creely, Green, and Gomez hadn't returned with them was more than enough proof they'd failed.

Shawna studied the men's body language as they prepared the wire lines. They were exhausted and defeated. If Calhoun's team didn't come through with a miracle, they were all going to die here.

She shook water from her hair and then gave Bill an apologetic smile. He grinned and wiped a sheen of rain from his thick, black beard. "We have any umbrellas out here?" she asked.

Bill grunted. "No, ma'am. There are some emergency slickers inside. But," he said and popped his back with a groan of satisfaction, "I don't think you want to go in there."

"Um, no, not really." Vraebel glanced at her. The man hadn't said more than three words since they'd leapt for their lives. Like Bill had said, she'd had to jump first.

The stairs were steep and met the platform more than four meters above her. She'd stared at the wet metal stairs and aimed for the bottom railing. It was only a meter or two away from the ledge, but it seemed like miles away. After a deep breath, she pistoned her legs with a shriek. As her body neared the railing, she knew she was too low. She threw her arms out and snapped them shut over the railing.

Pain rocked up her arms and back. She felt something give in her shoulder, ignored it, and swung by her hands over the deck. Shawna flung her leg up and caught the edge of the railing. As carefully as she could, she pulled herself up onto the stairs. She lay there, the steps biting into her back, and panted.

"You okay?" Bill yelled from the ledge. She popped her head around the rail and nodded. "Okay. Vraebel's coming next."

Shawna forced herself to stand and walked a few steps down. She crouched and waited. If Vraebel couldn't hold on to the railing, she might be able to pull him up. Her arms shrieked at the thought. Of course if he missed the railing, there wasn't a damned thing she could do.

She watched as the rig chief gathered himself. He took a deep breath and swung his arms back and forth. Then he leaped.

Unlike Shawna, he went too high instead of too low. His chest hit the lower rail. His hands missed the upper rail and then he started to fall backwards. His left arm wrapped around the lower metal bar and took all his weight. Vraebel screamed.

Shawna reached down and took his other hand. She lifted as hard as she could and felt something give in her back. The two of them yelled in pain as she helped him over the railing and on to the steps. They lay panting as rain pattered down upon their heads.

"That. Was too close," Vraebel said.

"No, shit," Shawna grinned.

"Y'all okay?" Bill asked from the ledge.

"No," Vraebel yelled back, "but we're alive."

"Let me know when you're ready," Bill said.

Meters above them, a wall of black smoke funneled through the doorway. Shawna wrinkled her nose. "We need to get moving."

Vraebel nodded. "Yeah. Okay."

He used a rail to push himself upright. He offered Shawna a hand and helped her stand. The wide stairs gave them enough room to stand side by side and watch as Bill made the crossing.

His jump was perfect. The metal groaned under the big man's weight as his hands wrapped around the railing. Bill pulled himself up on to the stairs. Red-faced and panting a little, he grinned at them. "No sweat."

Something crashed above them. Shawna turned to look at the doorway. A flame leaped out and then disappeared. "Fuck this. Let's go. Now."

The three of them ran down the steps as fast as they could. When they hit the deck, the rain started coming down harder. Forks of lightning flashed in the sky followed by booming thunder. For a moment, the sound of grinding machinery and engines were lost in the din.

Shawna stared out into the ocean and watched as the waves seemed to grow larger before her eyes. Her arms were bruised and cut from where she'd slammed into the grated stairs. She rubbed a hand against her shoulder. "How long before we—" She stopped in mid-sentence as a figure appeared out of the shadows next to the superstructure.

She smiled. "Thomas." She stood up and quickly walked to him. He was carrying a flashlight and three PPE duffel bags. The closer she came to him, the more worried she became. His skin didn't look good and he was rasping for breath.

"Give me the duffels," she said.

He waved her away and kept walking toward Bill and Vraebel. The two men looked up at him as he unwound the bags from his shoulders and lay them on the deck. He unzipped one and pulled out a cardboard box. "I come bearing food," he said. He split open the box, took one of the bars and handed the rest to Vraebel.

Shawna stared at the open duffel. Batteries. Flashlights. And food? She grinned. "Looks like you had a successful scavenger hunt."

Calhoun shook his head. He more collapsed on the bench than sat down. "Bill? Catfish needs some help with Aaron. I think—"

"Forget it," Catfish said from behind her.

Shawna turned and watched as Catfish wrung out his soaked hair. A stream of water hit the deck. He stared up into the sky for a second and let the rain wash down upon his face.

"Where's Aaron?" Vraebel asked.

Catfish shook his head. "Didn't make it. Slipped and hit the deck head first."

"Fuck," Bill said. His giant fists clenched and unclenched. "You guys get chased?"

Catfish and Thomas exchanged a glance. "You could say that," the old man said. "I'm going to sit here, eat this energy bar, and rest."

"Yeah," Shawna said, "you do that." She looked at Catfish. "Get what you need?"

"Besides a new pair of pants? Yeah." He looked around and sighed. "Gomez didn't make it either."

"No. He didn't," Vraebel said. "Neither did Creely or Green."

Catfish sucked his cheeks hollow. "We have enough deck hands to do what needs to be done?"

Vraebel shrugged. "I guess. If we all help. Since we're not exactly worried about tight seals, I think we can manage."

"Okay, good," Catfish said. He dropped his duffel bag to the floor and pocketed the flashlight. "I'm going to eat something. We should probably call those guys over too. Ain't much, but it'll have to do."

Lightning crisscrossed the sky and the rig lit up in the twilight. Thunder shook the world two seconds later. "Storm's getting closer."

"Yeah," Catfish said as he tore open one of the energy bar wrappers, "I think we've been in it for days."

Chapter Nine

They'd started out with a crew of 80. Now? They were down to five roughnecks, a wounded rig chief, a geologist, an engineer, and a smart ass tech. Losing Gomez was the worst of it. Vraebel still couldn't believe his old friend was gone. And worse, couldn't believe he wasn't able to save him.

But like Sigler had said, Gomez had been dead for hours—he just hadn't known it. The geologist sat next to him as he downed a bottle of water and consumed one of the energy bars.

"I don't know how it happened," she said. "But JP was infected. Your three mud specialists were infected. Somehow Gomez was infected when it...touched him."

Vraebel tried to focus on her words. His mind still felt barely attached to his body. Every few minutes, the world tried to swim away from him and he bit his tongue to keep hold of it. The water cooled his throat and made the faux peanut-buttery, chalky taste of the energy bar somehow palatable. "You think anyone that comes in contact with this stuff gets infected?"

She shrugged. "I don't know. But I think we need to be more careful. I'm not a biologist and when I examined the oil in the lab, I wasn't looking for biological markers. Also, I didn't exactly have access to the right equipment."

Vraebel chuckled. "PPE spent all this money and they didn't provide a large enough lab for you? Lady, you are hard to please."

She grinned. "Sorry. I'll make sure Thomas puts a request in for the next rig."

"'Next rig.' I'm never fucking leaving land again," Vraebel said.

Even Calhoun laughed at that. The old man had started to look better. Vraebel guessed the engineer just needed a rest and some food.

It was past afternoon now. The storm was bearing down on them. The sky was so dark, there was barely any light at all. They'd surrounded the drill table with the remaining halogens. As Bill and the remaining crew began the wire-line operations in earnest, Vraebel and Catfish had loaded the explosive shots on a dolly and pushed them over to the drill table.

Shawna and Calhoun kept watch over the superstructure, their flashlights dancing in the darkness. He knew they couldn't hurt the black from this distance, but at least they could give the drill crew a heads up. Considering the things seemed to be less and less afraid of the light, Vraebel wasn't sure how they were going to survive the storm. When the light completely died in the sky, the dinner bell would start ringing.

He tried not to think about it as he stood off to the side and watched his men. *My men,* he thought. *What's left of them anyway.*

They hadn't heard from Sobkowiak since last night. Vraebel had to assume the portly doctor was dead. Belmont and his crew had been off-shift. Had the black gotten them as well?

Catfish sat cross-legged beneath one of the platforms, fingers dancing over his laptop. The rain barely touched him where he sat, but Vraebel had noticed him wiping the screen more than once. He really hoped the long-haired asshole knew what he was doing. If Calhoun was right, they might at least be able to take care of what was below the ocean floor.

What the engineer had postulated was insane. Cthulu-type shit. But he was right about one thing—if they weren't able to give the CDC the all-clear, they were fucked. After what he'd seen and experienced, no one could afford to allow the black onto land. Hell, it couldn't even be allowed back in the ocean. If Vraebel was in charge of the CDC, he'd drop a goddamned bomb on the rig. One of those fuel-air things that nuked every living thing.

Living thing, he thought. *Yes, that's what the black was.*

The five remaining deck crew members loaded another explosive shot into the pipe. Considering the drill string was over 5 miles long, it took a long time for the shots to drop to the bottom. He figured they had time for one more before the storm finally killed the remaining daylight.

He glanced over at Catfish. The man was perspiring as he typed. He might be a shit-bag, but Vraebel didn't envy him his task. If the tech didn't program his robot-friends correctly, then none of this would work.

"Martin?" Calhoun asked.

Over the sounds of the engines and the storm, his voice seemed less gruff and less confident. Vraebel turned and stared at the older man. Calhoun's eyes were bright and focused, but he still didn't look well. "Thomas? What's up?"

The large man tapped his foot on the deck. "You ready to help with the flares?"

He hissed through his teeth. "This plan of yours is fucking crazy."

Calhoun nodded. "I know. But you didn't answer my question."

A grin slowly spread across Martin's face. "I just wanted to say that again before I started taking part in it."

"I can live with that," Calhoun said. "Come on."

They walked out from the drill string area and toward the storage bunkers at the rig's edge. A workbench for fixing pipe problems and cleaning tools was affixed to one of the steel structures. At least the overhang would protect them from the rain.

Five flares were spread across the bench's rubber mat. "How do you know they won't, like, catch fire when we start doing this?"

"Because magnesium needs a flame. Just make sure you don't cause sparks while we're cutting into them," Calhoun said.

Vraebel chuckled. "I'll do my fucking best." He clapped Calhoun on the shoulder. "Let's get to work."

#

The AUV bay was far enough beneath the rig for him to actually hear himself think. Coding while sitting next to the drill table had been tough, but he'd managed to at least get most of the new instructions ready. He still thought Calhoun was out of his fucking mind, but what was the harm in trying to kill a subterranean ocean floor monster? *We can only die once right?*

He rubbed at his eyes. God, he was tired. Every few minutes, the code on the screen became blurry gibberish and he had to close his eyes to reset his brain. Considering what they were about to do, and how long it was going to take, sleep wasn't on the agenda anytime soon. Besides, who the fuck could sleep while those things were looking for a meal?

Shawna stood behind him on the platform staring up the steps to the rig deck. She was the lookout. The AUV bay was one of the brightest parts of the ship when the lights were turned on. If one of those things came down the steps, it was going to meet something akin to sunlight.

AUV 2 was permanently fucked. With the damaged ballast and screw housing, it wasn't going back in the water. It was good for nothing except parts and testing. Testing is exactly why he'd removed its outer casing.

He loaded the program into its brain and checked for data corruption. Nope, all good. AUV 2 sent back a ping it was ready for insertion. Catfish told the AUV to start its dive.

He'd set the engine driving the propellers into diagnostic mode to trick the AUV into thinking the engines were working. The laptop sent false pressure readings to its sensors; the robot thought it was descending beneath the ocean.

The screen lit up with a three-D depth/pressure grid including the robot's position. The AUV thought it was nose down and diving like hell for the bottom. Catfish raised his arms above his head and yawned.

"Stay awake, code boy," Shawna called from behind him.

He shook his head. "Sleep? Here? Why the fuck would I want to do that?" He put the laptop on its stand and turned to her. Shawna's clothes were grimy and stained. Her khakis were torn in more than a few places. Streaks of blood had welled from her skin onto both her shirt and pants. "You look like shit."

"Whatever," she grinned. "You're just as much a mess as I am."

"Uh-huh," he said. "There's blood in your hair."

Her grin faded. "Yeah. I tried to wash it out in the rain, but I guess I just didn't get it all."

He shook his head. "I wish someone could wash what I saw out of my brain."

She didn't reply. Shawna glanced upward at the deck and Catfish followed her gaze. The roughnecks had been working for hours now and night might as well have fallen. Somewhere up in the sky, behind the thick blankets of black clouds, the sun still shined. But down here, there was nothing but murk and water.

"You understand what they're doing?" he asked.

"Yes," she said. "And what they're doing is probably going to blow the drill string."

"Fuck, that's the best idea I've heard all day."

She turned and her smile was back. A little sad, but still a smile. "The shots are weighted and so is the drill string. When they rotate the table and drop the weight, the drill bit will sink back into the spud site. Then I guess they'll hit the button and 'boom.' If Thomas is right, it should blow the bit down further and possibly rip a hole large enough for your AUV."

"'If,'" he said. "That's a wonderful word, isn't it? It means 'this could work. Or, we could be fucked.'"

She giggled. "That's what I love about you, Catfish. You're a charter member of the 'we're on the verge of getting killed' club."

He sighed and turned back to the laptop. The timer showed another ten minutes. He wasn't sure he could wait that long, but he needed to let the sim run. If he was wrong, they really would be fucked.

"You think this will work?" he asked. "I mean the flares?"

"Magnesium burns. It doesn't care about water. It cares about a flashpoint. And once it starts, it's damned difficult to get it to stop. So yeah, I think it'll work."

"I smell an 'if,'" he said.

She rolled her eyes. "Okay, fine. IF your robot does its job. IF the hole is big enough. And IF something else doesn't go wrong."

He smiled. "See? That's what I wanted to hear. So, Ms. Geologist, still interested in rocks?"

"Yes," she said. "But only if they're on dry land and a thousand miles away from the ocean."

"Thomas thinks it's some prehistoric creature. What do you think?"

"I don't know," she said. "I'd have a better idea if I knew what Houston found." She shook her head. "Let me rephrase that. I'd love to know the results of their tests."

"You mean before the quarantine."

"Right," she said. "Before it...did whatever it did."

The image of some poor lab tech opening a barrel filled with tentacles, pincers, and teeth made him shudder. He suddenly didn't feel like talking anymore. From the look on Shawna's face, he was pretty damned sure she'd imagined the same thing.

Catfish tried to clear his mind, but JP's face kept sliding across his vision. His friend, the man who'd taught him how to dive, spear fish, and enjoy the ocean, had been that thing's meal. Or carrier. Or whatever the fuck. He was dead and the only thing Catfish could vent his anger and loss on was the creature below the ocean floor. And goddammit, he was going to blow that shit up.

His laptop beeped and he turned to the screen. The timer was flashing. 55 seconds left. "Here we go," he said.

Shawna walked down a few steps to watch. He gave her a wink and turned back to the screen. The seconds ticked off. When the timer hit zero, the view on the screen zoomed in. A blocky AUV floated near a vertical line. Catfish switched to the console. "And now for the boom." He typed in a command, hit return, and switched back to the diagram.

The vertical line jumped downward. The floor below below it seemed to cave in. The AUV remained motionless. He gritted his teeth and checked the sensor logs. AUV 2 thought it had detected a massive seismic event. So why wasn't it—

"There we go," he said. The AUV icon moved toward the gash and slipped under it. "And..." A metallic click echoed off the steel walls and a sizzling sound followed.

The front scoop of AUV 2 burned with intense white light. Catfish exhaled a long breath and then started to giggle. "Oh, Mr. Monster. I am going to fuck you up."

#

The medical bay was pitch black and had been for hours. Sobkowiak had fallen asleep in one of the beds, but only until the fire alarms went off. After that, he was wide awake, and waiting to die.

He had already decided to take care of himself before smoke or flame could. Just a nice overdose of morphine. Enough to stop his heart before he had a chance to suffocate or burn to death. *It'll be like going to sleep,* he told himself. *Only you'll never wake up in this nightmare again.*

So he'd put the syringe on the instrument table and kept it close to the bed. And if he didn't get a chance to use it? Well, then it would be over anyway.

His phone was charged and sitting on his chest. As soon as the lights had gone out, he'd plugged into the computer's battery backup. It still had quite a bit of juice left.

He'd traded multiple emails with the CDC via PPE's email address. They confirmed that the same organism was loose in Houston. They had so far managed to confine it to the lab's building, but they weren't certain they could contain it.

He'd told them about Harvey. He'd told them about the other three roughnecks that had been infected. He'd also told them what he saw in the stateroom. In a way, he wished he hadn't.

They had stopped replying to his emails when he admitted he had no idea how to kill it. They'd used him for the information they needed and after that, there was no reason to keep talking.

He could still try to communicate with Vraebel and the others, but didn't want to. If they were still alive, there was no reason for them to know that there wasn't going to be a rescue. Leaguer was quarantined.

Thousands of miles from civilization and parked in over five and a half miles of water, the world had nothing to fear from the infected rig. And Sobkowiak was sure the CDC wanted to keep it that way. He tried to imagine the press release PPE would put out on the wire about their newest, most expensive toy. Would they claim Leaguer had sunk? Would they blame equipment? A tsunami? Negligent crew?

Sobkowiak sighed in the dark. The fire alarms had silenced some time ago. The only sound was the air conditioner. The doctor wondered just how long it would be before one of those things decided to enter the room through one of the vents. At least the smoke hadn't been too terrible, although the bay still smelled like burned plastic and wood.

The surgical mask he'd worn while the smoke wafted through the vents had helped, but his lungs still felt like shredded cheese. The doc took a deep breath, nose wrinkling at the fetid air circulating through the room.

At some point, he'd have to make a decision. He'd either stay in the rig until the end, or try and find a way out of medical. The things were no longer scratching at the door and he hadn't heard any movement in the vents for over an hour.

What are you doing? he asked himself. *Preparing to die? Just staying in your little cage until what? The fucking world ends?*

He picked up the phone and turned on its flashlight. Sobkowiak glanced around the room. He had multiple bottles of alcohol, but no way to ignite them. For the first time in his life, he wished he was a smoker.

He rose from the hospital bed and walked two of the strong halogen lamps to within a few feet from the hatch. That done, he slid the UPS out from under the desk and put it between the lamps. In the dim light from the phone, he managed to plug the lamps' cords in. He turned them on. Bright white light shined off the hatch.

He adjusted the two lamp heads so their circles of light covered the bottom of the hatch. Although he had no way to create a flame, Sobkowiak grabbed a bottle of alcohol anyway. The full plastic bottle felt heavy in his hands, but he knew that was a joke.

Martin had told him the black burned like gasoline. Sobkowiak thought of that message and had to shake his head. Even though Vraebel knew the Doc was fucked, he was still trying to find a way to help his remaining crew. But the rig chief was kidding himself. There was no way out of this. At least he could try and make it to the deck with the others. If they were still alive.

He pocketed his phone and stood in front of the hatch. He put his ear to the metal. It was warm. Sobkowiak clucked his tongue.

Could be the residual heat from the fire. Or maybe that black shit was still trying to get in.

Doc put the plastic bottle of alcohol in his other pants pocket. It bit into his skin, but he hardly noticed. He put his pudgy hands on the metal wheel and took a deep breath. With a deep exhale, he spun it.

The wheel squeaked as it spun. His already thumping heart increased its beat at the sound. The wheel stopped spinning with a groan and a loud bang. He pulled open the door and peered into the hallway.

The warped floor had buckled. The black had destroyed all the sheetrock and most of the studs holding up the ceiling. The overhead lights were out. His halogen lamps were the only ones still working.

Sobkowiak stared at the floor. There was no way it would hold his weight. He was completely trapped. He started to close the door and then stopped. Something moved in the wall. He aimed one of the halogens directly in front of him.

The hallway filled with the sound of pork fat burning in a fryer. What he'd thought were shadows was the black. An entire river of it. It hung on the fractured uneven wall like paint. It bubbled and rippled as smoke rose off the illuminated spot. A gout of flame licked upward from the smoking swatch of black.

The creature split itself into three pieces. A large ribbon moved one way, a larger ribbon the other. Detached from the large portions, a foot wide sliver of darkness burned and crackled.

Sobkowiak shook his head and closed the hatch. He cycled the wheel until it stopped moving. He turned his back to the door and slumped to the floor. There was nothing left. No way out. Nothing.

He eyed the syringe of morphine sitting on the metal table by the medical bed. Sleep sounded like a good idea. With any luck, he'd be gone before the thing found a way to get to him. He turned off the halogens and walked to the bed to lie down. A little pinch from the syringe, and Doc took a flight into true darkness.

#

Lifejackets. Lifeboats. Safety tethers. Prayers.

That was the priority list Vraebel had given the remaining crew. Calhoun didn't know what the creature below the ocean floor would do when the shots went off. Hell, none of them did. But it was a fair bet it wouldn't be happy about it.

Once the shots were loaded, the team poured as much concrete casing down the pipes as they could. The casing would provide a backstop for the shots and hopefully increase the downward thrust of the explosion. If, that was, it didn't just blow the drill string apart.

Red emergency lights created paths to the lifeboats. Everyone, including Catfish, wore a lifejacket. As for the safety tethers, Bill and another roughneck were still setting them up.

Catfish and Shawna had taken one of the Zodiacs out to drop the AUVs. They were towing AUV 5 and AUV 1 out of the rig's shadow. They were the first two robots to fully charge. Catfish had performed his surgery on them and hooked up the strips of magnesium to the scoops.

Calhoun had only planned to dissect five flares, but after Catfish had told him how the flame burned and that there was no guarantee the lighting mechanism would work on both AUVs, he'd decided to pillage the rest of the flares from the lifeboats.

He and Vraebel had torn through over thirty of them and extracted the magnesium from the red flares' casing. When that was done, Calhoun felt like his fingers were going to fall off. But if it worked, it would be well worth the pain.

When Shawna and Catfish returned, they'd begin the countdown. Catfish had programmed the AUVs for a swift descent. It would still take them at least half an hour to reach the ocean floor. Before they passed into lower midnight, they'd squirt status data to the string. Based on their velocity, the robots would forecast their arrival at the planned coordinates. Calhoun wished he had a cigar. Just one last cigar and maybe a nice snifter of Highland Park 18. His mouth watered at the thought.

He glanced at the drill table. The drill crew was taking a break beneath the derrick. The falling rain barely touched them, but the wind gusts tore at their clothing and hardhats.

OCD to the last, Vraebel had insisted everyone wear hardhats and their safety gear. Calhoun thought the rig chief was making one last effort to protect his men. Laudable, but unnecessary. If Thomas was right about the thing living beneath the ocean floor, he had little doubt it was going to rock the rig into the water. They'd all be lucky to live another two hours.

#

The Zodiac skipped across the waves. Shawna had strapped herself into a safety harness. For the first time in his life, Catfish had too. He'd never run a boat in this kind of weather. JP usually did the honors regardless of the size of the waves.

Shawna had tended the boat while he'd dropped into the cold water to perform a last spot check on the AUVs. He'd untethered each of them from the tow-lines and then lingered. AUV 5, the bitch, and its well-behaved brother, were going to their doom. The robots didn't know it, but they were hopefully going to save everyone on the rig. Well, the nine that were left anyway. Catfish had chuckled to himself behind his mask as he opened 5's status panel and made sure all the lights were green. *Maybe you'll save the whole fucking world.*

Satisfied his babies were ready for their mission, he closed the panels and patted their hulls. *Swim well. And go kill that fucking thing,* he thought. He swam to the side of the boat and waved a hand. Shawna must have seen him and hit the remote, because a second later, AUV 5's screws began turning. The sound of its engine was a quiet hum. The ballast pumps took on water and a few seconds later, it disappeared from sight. AUV 1 followed close behind.

A wave crashed over him, but Catfish didn't care. The cold, the fear, he'd left it all behind. All that mattered now was seeing this through. And at least now, they had a chance.

Driving the Zodiac back to Leaguer took far too much patience. He wanted to be on his laptop to monitor his robots' progress as they reached lower midnight. Not for the first time, he wished he could ride with them to the ocean floor, see the fish up close, and watch as the world turned into darkness that not even deep space could match.

Catfish slowed the boat. The rig was lit up like a Christmas tree. Atop the bridge, red LEDs glowed and blinked. The oil derrick had green lights near its bottom, yellow lights up its middle, and the upper section was all red. From out in the ocean, he'd even been able to see the work lights on the deck.

Shawna turned her head. Her hair was a mess of salty moisture. "We there, yet?" she asked with a smile.

He grunted as he motored to the mooring. The bright bay halogens dissipated the shadows and he let out a sigh of relief. Returning to the rig was both terrifying and comforting. At least he knew what was on the rig. In the water? Impossible to know if one of those things was waiting for someone to fall in.

The white nylon line hung from the wall. Catfish wrapped it tight around the boat's cleat. "Okay, Shawna, let's—"

She hissed at him. Catfish turned and looked at her. Her jaw was stiff, cheeks hollowed, and her eyes were fixed on something above his shoulders.

He raised his eyebrows at her, but he already had a damned good idea of what she was looking at. Slowly, he moved a hand to the flashlight clipped to his wetsuit. She nodded to him and did the same. Light in hand, he flicked its switch and turned as fast as he could.

The light jumped up the superstructure wall. It sat perched on a piece of gleaming steel. Its eyestalk shuddered as he pointed his light at it. Even with the sound of the waves and the howling wind, he heard the sizzling. The thing flowed to the other side of the steel beam.

"Go, go!" he yelled at Shawna.

She dropped her harness and climbed up the boat launch. Catfish kept his eyes focused on the beam and played his light over its surface. The entire beam was clean and shined as though polished.

Another light joined his. "Get up here, dammit," she said.

He didn't wait to be told twice. He backed away and climbed up to join Shawna. Her light searched the beam as his had.

"If you need anything from the AUV bay," she said, "you better get it right fucking now."

Catfish shook his head. "Let's get to the deck and shut this thing in here."

"What if it gets in the water?" she asked. "What will it do?"

He shrugged. "No idea. But we can't kill it if we can't find it. And I'd rather it not find us first."

She nodded. "Okay. Let's move."

As they headed up the stairs to the rig deck, he was reminded of the trip into the superstructure. Cluster fuck. Everything was turning into one today. He reached the top of the deck and his light fluttered as he found his footing.

Something down in the bay moved. He turned his light. The thing crouched on AUV 3 just behind its yellow fin. "Yeah, you stay right fucking there," he said to it. He gave it one last blast of light before closing the bay doors behind him.

Up on the deck, the roughnecks stood beneath the derrick. The portable halogen work lamps bathed them with white light. Off to the side near the tool areas, Vraebel, Bill, and Calhoun stood talking. Calhoun noticed them and cast a glance their way.

Catfish nodded to him as he slid the bolt through the bay lock. If that thing wanted to get up on deck, it'd find a way. But for now, at least, it was in the bay and trapped by all those halogen lights. At least he hoped.

#

He stifled another yawn. The urge to open his mouth and roar a long one was becoming impossible to rein in. The rig rocked slightly beneath the punishing waves. Sheets of rain fell from the sky. This far from the halogen deck lights, it was darker than he'd ever seen.

Bill stood ten meters away from the superstructure. Some lights still worked on the first floor, but the second and third floors were dead. He wasn't even sure electricity was still working up there.

Once they had finished loading the shots and casing the drill string, he'd taken up sentry duty. That was more than an hour ago. Keeping himself occupied and awake was becoming difficult. But every time he felt as though he'd fall asleep standing up, he thought of those things filling the hallways of the superstructure and being trapped in there with them.

Just to be safe, he'd dumped the flashlight's batteries for fresh ones and taken another flashlight with him. The spare was clipped to his belt and waggled in the wind. The tight beam of light played over the steel door that led into the rig's superstructure.

They'd already closed the other hatches. The creatures had no way to get out onto the deck. Unless, of course, there was something they'd forgotten.

Bill had been thinking about that for several minutes. Well, they felt more like hours. His mind raced over Leaguer's blueprints trying to find a way for the things to get to the deck. And really, he couldn't think of any.

He continued flashing the lights around the lower deck trying to find any point of ingress. He was so tired and so focused on doing just that, he never thought to look up. From the bridge windows, a continuous stream of black oozed down the metal and to the lip which he, Sigler, and Vraebel had used to escape. The viscous fluid pooled and waited. Eye stalks popped up out of the sludge and began watched the deck crew. It took several moments for it to notice Bill. When it did, it began to move.

#

On the ocean surface, the waves continued to grow. Wind whipped across them spraying white froth. Jellyfish and Man O'War were caught in the continual advance of the storm surge. A pod of whales rose to the waves, took deep breaths, and headed back under for protection from the howling wind and rain.

AUV 5 filmed every movement as it plummeted toward the ocean floor. AUV 1 was a few meters behind it doing the same. This depth of the ocean didn't notice the sun slipping below the horizon. Thanks to the storm, its rays hadn't penetrated far into the water all day. Darkness was all AUV 5's camera's picked up until it ran across a school of lantern fish.

The ugly, alien looking creatures had risen from lower midnight in a frenzy of self-protection. Something was wrong with their ocean floor home. Very wrong.

As the robots swam deeper, the school broke apart in terror. They had seen the robots before and on some level, knew they weren't a threat. But now everything was a predator. An ancient instinct borne of millions of years of evolution told them to swim for their lives. AUV 5 caught pictures of them as they passed.

Other creatures, more ancient than even the lantern fish, were leaving the ocean floor as well. Some would survive the journey to the upper depths. Others would explode when the pressure they'd lived with all their lives began to subside. But all of them were obeying the same basic instinct: flee.

AUV 5 circled the drill string as it descended in a lazy spiral. It approached the 18k foot mark. The subroutine monitoring depth and pressure broke out of its sleep. AUV 5 sent a burst of data to the drill string. AUV 1 followed suit. The subroutine reset itself and waited for the depth to reach 27,320 feet. At 26,000 feet, it would begin monitoring for seismic disturbances.

The robots continued their swim to the bottom in complete darkness. Their creator would have been proud of the spiral course in which they moved. As they made their way into lower midnight, there were no fish to be seen, no life at all. The only life left in the trench waited for them.

#

The laptop beeped. Catfish had been staring at it for over half an hour as he tried to keep his stomach from rebelling. Vraebel filled the ballasts beyond the safety line to keep the rig stable, but the waves didn't seem to care. They kept coming and each one battered the rig's aft section.

He'd never even considered the damned rig could just plain sink before they had a chance to take care of business. That would be the final "fuck you" from the universe.

He grinned as the display lit up with information. Pressure. Depth. Speed. Coordinates. All the numbers seemed to dance before his eyes. He hit a button on the keyboard and the program started calculating averages. They appeared on the screen in neat rows.

His children had done what they were told and were heading straight down. Catfish closed the laptop and shoved it into the waterproof satchel. Before he left his station, he dragged three fingers lovingly across its surface. That little computer had been his constant companion for the last year or so. But the satchel? Hell, he'd had that since he left school. It had been through a dozen laptops and other gadgets. And now, he would probably never use it again.

Catfish blew out a sigh and ran out into the rain. A gust of wind hit him and he nearly slipped to the deck. Remembering how Aaron had broken his skull, he slowed his pace. Vraebel and Calhoun were hunkered down below the tool storage roof.

He looked at his watch. "22 minutes until they hit bottom!" he yelled at Calhoun. Catfish pressed a few buttons on his diver's watch and it started a 25 minute countdown. "That gives us three minutes of lull before we blow it."

Calhoun looked up at him and grinned. He turned to Vraebel. "We don't have much time."

Vraebel rolled his eyes and pointed to the superstructure. "Are you kidding? That's a fucking eternity for those things!"

"Got that right," Shawna frowned. She glanced at the superstructure. "We don't have enough lights up there."

The rig chief stood and held a hand above his eyes to knock out the glare from the work lamps. "Bill's on duty, Shawna. We have nothing—" Vraebel paused.

"What's wrong?" Catfish asked.

"I don't see Bill. Or his light," Vraebel said.

Shawna pulled the flare gun from her pocket. She had two spare rounds and one in the chamber. Calhoun turned on his light. Catfish pulled his from the wet suit. With the rain pattering down atop them, he hadn't seen any reason to change out of it.

Vraebel expertly kept his footing as he walked from the tool area and to the derrick. The roughnecks were still sitting beneath it, a circle of work lamps around them. They looked spent and on the verge of collapse.

Catfish watched as the rig chief said something to the crew. The men stood and pulled their lights. They had moved a few of the work lamps away from the drill table. Now it seemed it was time to put them back.

He thought about running over there and helping, but something in his back told him that was a bad idea. Struggling to get the AUVs into the water and all the running around hadn't exactly done his spine any good. Besides, the way he was tilting with the rig, he was afraid he'd drop one of the last halogens to the deck. And right now, they couldn't afford that.

Catfish watched as the men moved the generator and the four remaining lights to cover the drill table and the controls. The group stood on alert now. Vraebel waved to Calhoun.

Thomas, head down against the wind and rain, carefully walked toward the derrick. Shawna and Catfish followed. The rig rocked as another huge wave hit. Thomas stumbled, but Catfish managed to steady him.

"No falling down, old man!" he shouted above the din of the storm and machinery.

The rig crew spread out to different positions, each manning a control station. Vraebel stood behind a steel podium behind the drill table. Calhoun's remaining team met him there.

"The men already know how to do this," he shouted. "But just in case, here's how you drop the drill." The three of them watched as he showed them how to work the controls.

Piece of cake, Catfish thought. *Unless the black has hold of you.* He turned back to the superstructure. Something glowed near the front hatch. As he watched, the glow moved and then went out. "Guys?" They ignored him. He rapped a hand on the control box and their voices went silent. "Think I know what happened to Bill!"

In the dim glow spilling from the rig lights, they watched as the metal superstructure went from a gray to a gleaming silver. The black was coming down. All of it was coming down.

Vraebel screamed at the men around the drill table. They raised their lights and pointed at the superstructure with shaking hands and knees. The distance was too great to do more than illuminate the wave of black that flowed to the deck. Tentacles and eyestalks waved at them as it slowly covered the distance from the edge of the superstructure and toward the pipe fittings.

Catfish looked down at his watch. Fifteen minutes. They had to make it for another fifteen fucking minutes. "Shawna?" She stepped forward and stood next to him. "Light it up!"

"Not yet," she said. "Not yet."

#

He felt the warm trickle of urine as it jetted into his underwear and streamed down his leg. He would have been ashamed had he not been so terrified of what he saw. The thing wasn't just sliding toward them now. It was bubbling and popping and lifting itself upward. The creature contracted into itself, consolidating its mass, and finally, transformed into a shape.

Short, squat legs sprouted from its base. The liquid continued to climb up the makeshift limbs as it grew a wide torso. The eyestalks and tentacles slid across its surface as they met in its center. Five legs. Seven arms. Nine eyes. And the goddamned thing was growing taller by the second. He heard none of the cracking and popping as it rearranged its internal structure to provide support.

The ocean roared and another wave hit the rig's aft. Even with the ballast keeping the rig as close to the ocean as it could safely get, the rig bobbed up and down like a bath toy.

He grabbed the control panel's edge to support himself as the rig took another shock. The thing trying to stand didn't waver.

Vraebel opened his mouth to yell something and then closed it. What was there to say? What orders could you give when you were trapped on a football-field sized metal platform in the middle of the goddamned ocean?

He finally managed to pluck a thought out of the chaos in his mind. "Get to the fucking lifeboats! Now!" he shouted at the remaining crew. The roughnecks didn't move. They were just as frozen as he had been. "Goddammit! I said move!"

Finally, one of them did. He broke rank from the drill table and ran toward the lifeboats. He made it halfway across the deck before a long tentacle of black swished out from the thing's solid form and took his feet out from under him. Jason Jones flipped in the air and then landed on his back. He had time to start a scream before the tentacle wrapped around his head and dragged him into the creature's center. Jones' body disappeared inside it.

"Fuck!" Vraebel screamed.

#

Calhoun's heart stopped. Just for a second or two, but he felt it seize. The sight of the thing forming on the deck had been enough to freeze his brain and everything else along with it. Vraebel was screaming at it in obscenities.

Thomas shuffled behind Vraebel and searched the deck. There had to be something, anything they could use to slow it down and buy time. At this rate, it was going to be on them long before the AUVs could reach their target.

Then he saw what he was looking for. "Martin!" The rig chief turned to him with wild eyes and shaking legs. "The gas for the generator! We need to light up the deck!"

Vraebel blinked at him. Thomas slapped him hard across the cheek. Vraebel recoiled and then his eyes bore into Thomas'. "The gas!"

"Right," Vraebel said. "Right." He turned to the crew. "Get that barrel of diesel. We need to pour it across the deck. Make it come through the fire. Come on. Move!"

Vraebel and the three remaining crew ran to the orange and red barrels sitting by the tool area. Vraebel and one of the roughnecks walked a barrel toward the middle of the deck. The other pair of men did the same with the second barrel.

The thing moved toward them. "Hurry!" Calhoun shouted.

Vraebel tipped his barrel over. Diesel fuel poured out onto the deck in a thick stream. The other barrel tipped further down. Black tentacles surged toward them. For a moment, Calhoun thought the thing would drag them back, just as it had with Jones. But the tentacles ignored them and moved for the men.

"Shoot it!" Calhoun yelled.

Shawna took aim at one of the barrels and pulled the flare gun's trigger. The flare shot out of the gun with a bang and a puff of smoke. The deck turned red for an instant before the burning magnesium round struck the deck near the barrel of fuel.

A line of fire of rose from the deck's metal surface. The diesel fuel that hadn't slipped through the steel grates formed a flickering zigzag of flame. One of the creature's tentacles burst into bright licks of fire. The tentacle flopped and splashed into burning liquid.

Calhoun looked up at the creature. The burning remains of the tentacle were no longer attached to it. The thing had simply severed it.

"Fuck me," Calhoun said. The diesel fuel would buy them a few minutes, but when it was done burning, they had nothing left to stop it but flares.

\#

There was nothing to see unless it was through AUV 5's blue-light cameras. It had reached its target coordinates and now it was holding its position. From the imagery AUV 5 had taken of the tube worm beds around the spud site, Catfish had worked out a safe area for the AUVs to hover. While he'd been dead on with AUV 5, he'd been a little off on AUV 1's position.

The AUV descended right on top of a tube worm bed. The tentacles wrapped around it like an octopus clutching a shell. Its metal skin slowly crumpled. A giant maw opened and then swallowed its metallic prey.

AUV 5 noticed its brother's signal had disappeared and took note of when the signal ceased. The tentacles tried to reach it, but it was just a few feet out of their reach. AUV 5 was oblivious to their movements.

The spud site was caked with a brownish sludge. Had Catfish been able to see through the cameras, he would have thought it was a scab. The trench topography had changed yet again. The valley walls were closer together and a great hump had risen around the drill string.

As AUV 5 sat in its position and waited, its seismic sensor registered a small tremor. It wasn't the signal it had been programmed to look for, but it took the sensor readings and filed them away. The ground beneath it moved. A cloud of rock and sand puffed out.

The tube worms stopped waving their tentacles and instead stood still. The ground rumbled as something started to dig its way out of the rock. AUV 5's cameras finally noticed the movement and adjusted. If Catfish could have seen the monstrous eye that blinked below AUV 5, he would have screamed.

#

Vraebel slid toward the control box. The rig rocked again as another wave crashed into it. Saltwater sprayed over the crew and the fiery deck. The diesel fuel fire was fading fast. The thing knew it too.

"Standlee!" Vraebel screamed. "It has to be now!"

Catfish looked at his watch. He hoped like hell his babies were ready. "Hit it!"